TRIAL
BY FIRE

TRIAL BY FIRE

P. T. Deutermann

ST. MARTIN'S PRESS
NEW YORK

First published in the United States by St. Martin's Press,
an imprint of St. Martin's Publishing Group

TRIAL BY FIRE. Copyright © 2021 by P. T. Deutermann.
All rights reserved. Printed in the United States of America.
For information, address St. Martin's Publishing Group,
120 Broadway, New York, NY 10271.

www.stmartins.com

Book design by Jonathan Bennett.

Library of Congress Cataloging-in-Publication Data

Names: Deutermann, P. T. (Peter T.), 1941– author.
Title: Trial by fire / P. T. Deutermann.
Description: First edition. | New York : St. Martin's Press, 2021.
    | Series: P. T. Deutermann WWII novels
Identifiers: LCCN 2021006883 | ISBN 9781250273048
    (hardcover) | ISBN 9781250273055 (ebook)
Subjects: LCSH: Franklin (Aircraft carrier)—Fiction. | World War,
    1939–1945—Naval operations, American—Fiction. | World
    War, 1939–1945—Campaigns—Pacific Ocean—Fiction.
    | GSAFD: War stories. | Sea stories.
Classification: LCC PS3554.E887 T75 2021
    | DDC 813/.54—dc23
LC record available at https://lccn.loc.gov/2021006883

Our books may be purchased in bulk for promotional,
educational, or business use. Please contact your local bookseller
or the Macmillan Corporate and Premium Sales Department
at 1-800-221-7945, extension 5442, or by email at
MacmillanSpecialMarkets@macmillan.com.

First Edition: 2021

10 9 8 7 6 5 4 3 2 1

This book is dedicated to the memory of the officers, chiefs, and enlisted men of USS *Franklin* (CV-13) who were *not* members of the 704 Club, in recognition of their unsung bravery, suffering, and ultimate exclusion from the amazing story of what happened to their ship in March 1945, off the shores of Japan.

TRIAL BY FIRE

PROLOGUE

KYUSHU, JAPAN
MARCH 1945

It was pleasantly cold at a makeshift airstrip ten miles out of the port city of Kagoshima on the island of Kyushu, Japan. There was a high overcast and the nearby mountains had a dusting of Spring snow on their flanks. Six *Yokosuka* D4Y carrier dive bombers were lined up in front of the hangars, which had been disguised to look like a row of farm storage sheds. Their engines were turning over, almost reluctantly, with individual cylinders popping and banging in the clear morning air. A small team of maintenance men clustered around one of the bombers, trying to fix some problem with its engine, while the pilots stood around, smoking cigarettes and trying to look bored.

Arakatsu Kitigama, a commander in the Imperial Japanese Navy, stood waiting outside of his plane's rustic "hangar." He hoped that whatever was wrong with that plane could be fixed with a work-around that would not require parts. There were no repair parts here; there weren't many at the regular airfields, either. Arakatsu stood alone and aloof from the cluster of waiting pilots, who were clearly wary of him. By naval aviation standards he was an old man at thirty-three. Old and grizzled, in the eyes of the absurdly young pilots waiting to clamber up into their planes. He'd apprenticed as an aviation gunner in China and Manchuria in the late thirties, gone to flight school, then flown in the battles of Midway, the Coral Sea, the Solomons, and the Philippine Sea. And now he was here, suited up to launch one more time, not from a mighty aircraft carrier of the Kido Butai, but from a dirt road that lay between two fields stinking of night-soil, fetid paddy water, and buffalo dung. For one weak moment he could visualize the faces of his many fellow naval aviators, now asleep in the icy caverns of the deep Pacific. After *years* of war. And for what, he asked himself.

He knew that he was now destined to witness the utterly dishonorable end to the Army's Great Folly—starting a war with America. Sheepishly, he remembered celebrating Admiral Isoruko Yamamoto's brilliant and supposedly decisive strike against the sleeping American battle fleet in Hawaii, right along with the rest of the nation. Little did any of them know what kind of sleeping dragon that attack had awakened. His last fleet assignment had been as a carrier dive-bomber squadron commander flying from the carrier *Shokaku,* which now lay four *miles* down in the Philippine Sea, along with 1,200 of his shipmates, the victim of an American submarine.

Like all too many of Japan's surviving naval air warriors, Arakatsu had nothing left to go home to. He still hadn't totally recovered from the news that his wife and three teenaged children had been incinerated in the firestorm that followed a massive B-29 air raid on Tokio days ago. He'd also lost all of his venerable relatives as well as the family compound. An officer who'd seen the aftermath said there was nothing left but block af-ter block of ashes. The hundreds of small drainage canals, which threaded through many of the city's neighborhoods, were now filled with so many black lumps—people who'd fled to the nearest water and then died once the firestorm had consumed the houses and then boiled the water in the canals—that one could no longer see the water.

His heart was filled with a leaden sadness. The rumors were that 83,000 Tokio residents had perished, although the official news outlets were glossing over the scale of the attack. As usual. The ashes of his en-tire family were now dust particles in the wind over Tokio Bay. Soon he, too, would be just a memory. Death in battle was inevitable as it was acceptable. His only regret was that there would be no one to remember him now. Otherwise his mind was devoid of emotion. Dai Nippon was doomed. When it was finally over, *how*ever and *when*ever that came to pass, life in Japan would not be worth living. The shame alone would demand the self-immolation of any man with even an ounce of pride. So: if ever there had been a day to die, today was the day. If nothing else, he might soon be reunited with his family, whom he hadn't seen for over a year. For one sad moment he wondered what they would all look like, drifting in the afterlife. If there even was one.

"Arakatsu *san*," a young voice called. "It is time."

"Assemble the flight," he ordered.

The young sailor bowed and ran to get the other pilots, who trotted over, lined up, and bowed simultaneously. Arakatsu nodded imperiously at them, noting that it was going to be a five-plane flight, not six, after all. Not a one of them appeared to be over sixteen years old.

"Pay attention," he barked. "The mission today is to bomb carriers. Not battleships, not cruisers, not destroyers, or anything else. Carriers. You have each been armed with a single two-hundred-and-fifty-kilo semi-armor-piercing bomb. If the carrier is moving, you must aim for where she *will* be when the bomb arrives, not where she *is* when you begin your dive.

"The American fleet is huge. There are many carriers. There are dozens of escorts. They are all only about one hundred sixty kilometers away. They have established a circular air defense, a series of concentric rings around their fleet, with fighters stationed in the rings at all times. All their ships have radar; even some of their fighters have radar, so they can see us, even at night. Therefore we must approach them at just above sea level, not from the usual attack altitude. If there are low clouds, we must stay in them until the last moment.

"This is not a kamikaze mission. This is a bombing mission. Once you drop your bomb, flee. Your airplane is the fastest warplane in the Pacific. Get back up into the low clouds, head west, and go fast. And stay low. We need you to get back. Do you know why?"

There were polite if nervous looks from the four remaining pilots.

"Because," he said with a frosty smile. "*If* you get back, you will have the great honor to go out again tomorrow."

He let that grim news sink in, then continued. "Once we take off, follow me to the enemy. I will tell you when to break the formation, and then you will be on your own. Drop from the cloud, see an aircraft carrier, and bomb it. It could not be simpler. Do you understand?"

Four emphatic nods.

"Man your planes. Good hunting."

Forty-five minutes after launching, the five planes, tucked into a tight line formation at 1,200 feet, crossed beneath the American fleet's outer defensive combat air patrol ring. It was early morning and the low gray clouds offshore offered perfect cover for what they were trying to do. There were occasional breaks through which they could see the cold Pacific below, where a formation of perfectly parallel white wavetops marched soundlessly across the sea. They'd flown southeast on a dead-reckoning magnetic course and now should be within ten or twenty miles of the enemy's carriers.

Arakatsu had decided to disperse the formation and break out of the clouds when the first American anti-aircraft shells began to pop up around them. Even at their low altitude, that many ships with radars meant that at least one if not more of the escorts would soon detect the raid and start shooting. It also would mean that they were very near their as yet invisible targets. Normally he would have had a gunner in the backseat to keep lookout, but there were no longer enough backseat gunners to go around. Just as well; he knew he wasn't coming back today.

A loud clanging noise compressed his ears as a five-inch round exploded nearby, followed closely by three more. Fragments from the shells pinged off his fuselage. He never saw the airbursts, just like the ships shooting at him never saw him—so this had to be radar-directed fire. It was time.

"Get in on them," he yelled over the radio. "Get *in*, get *in*, get *in!*"

Then he pulled back on his stick to clear their little formation, not wanting to collide with his inexperienced little division as they scattered and went down, seeking glory. He banked hard right and then dove down to get clear of the cloud bank, bursting into a slate-gray sky—which was filled with an astonishing number of airplanes. They were everywhere, swirling in seeming chaos above at least *five* carriers.

"*Hai!*" he shouted with joy. The carriers were launching. He'd caught them in the middle of a launch cycle! Confined to a straight course directly into the wind as they cast their venomous progeny into the cold air, they were sitting ducks. He picked one out, an Essex-class by the look of her, ploughing ahead at full speed, spitting bombers and fighters, one after another. More bangs erupted as he swooped lower and made his turn. Bow on. Something hot bit through his canopy windscreen and grazed his right ear. He grinned. You see me now, but I also see you. Prepare to die.

Wait, he thought. I'm not aligned. He shoved his descending bomber into a ninety-degree bank to the left, pulled back on the stick just a bit, and then swiftly leveled back off. His target was now coming straight on, her white centerline perfectly aligned with his bombsight. He reached down and armed his bomb. He heard his bomb-bay doors grinding open.

Lower, but not too low, he told himself as he came in on the carrier, whose image was growing bigger and bigger in his canopy screen. He climbed a few hundred feet to make sure the bomb would hit at a more acute angle and *penetrate,* not skip across her flight deck. He'd been out on IJN *Kaga*'s flight deck that terrible day near Midway Island back in 1942, watching their fighters make fish food out of an entire American torpedo bomber squadron when he'd heard the lookouts scream. He'd whirled around, saw the terrified sailors looking *up,* and raised his gaze just in time to see a 1,000-pound armor-piercing bomb coming down on them. He'd only had time to begin his own scream when that black bomb crunched right through *Kaga*'s flight deck and exploded down in the hangar deck, tearing her guts out and throwing him into a nearby catwalk.

But now? Now it was time for some imperial revenge, and better yet, an honorable death in battle while killing an entire carrier. There was no better way to go. There was no honor more supreme. He closed his gloved fist around the drop switch and began chanting his funeral dirge, even as he saw the first Corsairs turning his way, their wings ablaze with machine-gun fire. Too late, *gaijin* bastards, he thought, with an icy grin. This one's all mine.

1

THREE MONTHS EARLIER, ABOARD USS *FRANKLIN* (CV-13),
PUGET SOUND NAVAL SHIPYARD
JANUARY 1945

C'mon, Billy," George said. "We're sailing in two weeks. There's a big difference between guys going over the hill for a honey or a ten-day toot and actually jumping ship. They'll be back."

Billy shook his head. "I don't think so, XO," he said, getting up and starting to pace around the cabin. "My chiefs don't think so, either."

George Lowry Merritt, Commander, USN, and executive officer in *Franklin,* didn't want to pursue this conversation. There was every chance that Billy-B Perkins, also a three-stripe commander and the air boss in *Franklin,* might be right. Billy was a fidgeter. He simply had to be moving, all the time. He had skippered a squadron of fighters on the Big E before becoming the air boss in *Franklin.* He'd been aboard only three weeks back in October when that kamikaze had torn the ship up, sending her all the way back to the Ulithi anchorage. Once the Ulithi repair people had seen the extent of her damage, the decision had been made to send her to a shipyard on the West Coast for repairs. "Bad enough that we've got practically a brand-new crew," Billy continued. "But this new captain—"

George raised a hand. "That's enough," he said. Whatever his own thoughts about the ship's new commanding officer might be, he wasn't going to allow any of that kind of talk, especially from the third most senior officer in the ship. Besides, as a three-striper and academy graduate, Billy-B knew better than to indulge in talk like that.

"Yes, sir," Billy said. "Sorry about that. But just 'cause we can't say it, everybody knows what the problem is." He sat back down; the exec's cabin wasn't big enough for serious pacing.

George fell back on a tried-and-true excuse. "We've had almost a fifty percent crew turnover since November, Billy," he said. "The Navy's putting a new carrier into the water just about one every month. They need experienced hands at all levels, so when one comes into the yards, they rape and pillage to seed the new construction with some experienced people. The captain knows he's got a boatload of greenies on his hands. They're all new to a big-deck and they're all new to him—and him to them. He's taking a hard line because you only get one chance to do that, and that's right at the beginning. You start easy and then try to tighten up later? Doesn't work. Not in a ship of this size. You start with an iron fist; you can always relax a bit later. And keep in mind: once the air group joins, there'll be thirty-six *hundred* men aboard. This isn't *anything* like running a fighter squadron."

"Yes, sir," Billy grumped.

George waited. He knew Billy still had something to get off his chest.

"It's just what he said at the change of command," Billy said, finally. "I can*not* believe he said that. That wasn't taking a hard line on discipline. That was just plain rude."

George wished his cabin had a porthole. He'd have loved to be able to look outside, even if the view was mostly a forest of steel masts, pier-side cranes, and the ever-present Puget Sound rain. Better let him have his say, he thought. It's not like he's entirely wrong.

"I've always been told that there's a traditional format for a change of command," Billy continued. "The outgoing skipper makes a speech, praising the ship and thanking his officers and crew. The new guy then gets up, says he's glad to be here, congratulates the outgoing CO for doing a fine job, and then he reads his orders. He doesn't go criticizing the ship and the crew and making the departing skipper look bad. That was totally un-*sat*!"

George nodded. The change of command had happened at the Ulithi fleet anchorage in the Caroline Islands, thousands of miles from here, following a kamikaze strike, which had caused great damage to the carrier. The change of command had been scheduled for months, and Captain Shoemaker had been widely praised for his actions after the kamikaze hit, so it hadn't been as if he was leaving under a cloud. George had been as shocked as the rest of the carrier's 3,600-man complement at what the incoming captain said when he finally stood up prior to formally announcing that he was now the skipper. Instead of the customary polite words, the new captain had glared out at the assembled multitudes arrayed by department and division on the still-blackened flight deck. "*Franklin* is here," he'd said, "because *you,* the ship's company, failed to defend her from Japanese attack. I intend to address that failure and your obvious lack of training until *I'm* satisfied that you are fully prepared to resume wartime operations in the Western Pacific theater of operations. I will now read my orders."

None of the ship's company could believe it. The new skipper was openly naming the entire crew and the air group, officers, chiefs, and enlisted men as the reason why *Franklin* was headed to the yards in the first place, right in front of the outgoing CO, Captain Shoemaker, who'd been their skipper for over a year and a damned good one, in George's opinion. Truth be told, the entire fleet was reeling from the appearance of the Jap suicide-aircraft corps, whose depredations had been going on since October of last year, at Leyte Gulf. Either way, the new captain's statement had been nothing short of outrageous and a huge breach of naval protocol. George had had to force himself not to react visibly, even as he and everyone around him had wanted to yell: Hey! That's not true!

Thus, it had been a resentful crew that had taken *Franklin* back to the West Coast. During the first weeks in the yard, almost half of them had received orders to pack their seabags and head off to form the precommissioning crews on new construction. And now, before the ship had even completed her repairs, guys were jumping ship and deserting? George let out an audible sigh and looked at his watch. It was just after four in the afternoon. He needed to stretch his legs.

"Let's go take a tour, Mister Air Department Head," he announced. "I want to see all the new stuff."

The air boss snorted. "If you can find it in all that damned smoke and staging, XO."

George saw what Billy meant once they got up to the hangar deck, that steel cavern that stretched almost the entire length of the ship, two decks below the actual flight deck. They stopped at the top of the ladder that went from the second deck to the hangar deck, overwhelmed by a scene of what looked and sounded like industrial chaos: the roar of yellow-gear tractor engines, the hammering of a hundred needle guns on steel, grinders and pneumatic drills showering sparks through the lattice of staging, all lit up by the continuous spat of eye-watering welding arcs, which had created a thin cloud of vaporized metal smoke across the space's overhead.

Two weeks to go, the yard's ship superintendent had told this morning's meeting, George remembered. We'll have you out of the drydock and starting your onload in two weeks, guaranteed. No way in hell, George remembered thinking. He could see that Billy was thinking the same thing. The hangar deck was almost 700 feet long, and there wasn't anywhere that was not covered in metal pipe-staging and crawling with shipyard workers. The only good news was that there was no longer much evidence of what that suicide plane had done to *Franklin*. Nor were there any signs of the fifty-eight men who'd died during that attack. George could still visualize all those blackened lumps scattered everywhere in the hangar once they'd put the fires out.

"Isn't that the captain?" Billy asked, pointing with his chin.

George looked. Had to be, he thought. The captain was a big boy, so big everyone wondered how he'd ever squeezed into a fighter plane's cockpit. He was a burly six-five, with a round face, permanently wavy hair, and a cleft, double chin. He was big enough that anyone he encountered when going through one of the ship's passageways had to flatten himself against a bulkhead *and* inhale so the captain could squeeze by.

He was also one of those big guys who gave off the aura of "move aside or I'll walk right over you." He'd taken a reduction in rank, from commodore back to captain, in order to get command of *Franklin*. Given his obvious disdain for the ship's company, everyone kind of wondered why. One of the chiefs had summed it up neatly: this new skipper has a perpetual red-ass.

George, the one officer who spent the most time with the captain, couldn't argue with that, but he also could not permit that sentiment to be voiced out loud. If the captain sensed that the crew didn't like him, he gave no sign of it. George suspected that he had become accustomed to being someone whom nobody liked very much, but right now, there he was, standing conspicuously amid the frantic repair efforts surrounding him, his two Marine orderlies at parade rest close by, and radiating his displeasure. Interestingly, George observed: there wasn't a single crew-member within fifty feet of him. When the captain saw George and Billy-B, he beckoned imperiously.

"Oh, great," Billy muttered, through clenched teeth.

George almost laughed. Almost—the captain was still looking right at the two of them. "C'mon, there, Air Boss," he said, finally. "This is your fault, after all."

Billy strangled a laugh, and over they went. The first thing the captain said was: "About time, XO."

"Sir?" George replied in as neutral a tone as he could manage.

"*Look* at this mess," the captain said, having to shout to make himself heard above the clamor of the repair efforts. "They're getting nowhere. What are you doing about that?"

"The ship's supe says they'll be done in two weeks, Captain," George pointed out.

"Bull*shit*!" the captain said. "Nothing's finished. They're falling all over each other and they're getting nowhere. And where the hell are our people? They just sitting back, watching this circus?"

"Our people aren't allowed to interfere with the shipyard's workers, Captain," George said. "They can help, but only if they're asked to. So far, none of the shops're asking, and because of that, I've got them in training in other parts of the ship. We've got a lot of boots on board now."

The captain peered down at his exec in total frustration. His hands, which were disproportionately small compared to the rest of him, were clenched into sweaty fists. He'd been furious when he'd learned of the scale of the transfers when *Franklin* had first arrived at the Puget Sound Naval Shipyard in Bremerton. That had been the exec's fault, of course: "God*dammit*, XO, why didn't you protest? They're taking all the experienced hands." It had become a familiar theme: *Do* something, XO. Don't just sit there. George, of course, had had to swallow the obvious retort: You're the captain—why don't *you* do something? You draw a whole lot more water than I do as exec.

"What kind of training?" the captain asked, still shouting. George was tiring of being yelled at, but then remembered it was because of all the noise, and, like many aviators, the captain probably was more than a little bit deaf. He noted that Billy-B had somehow managed to move away, taking a sudden interest in the newly installed hangar deck firefighting stations. George could just hear Billy's thinking: *You're* the lofty executive officer. Second in command, and all that. *You* deal with him, while Boss, here, makes his creep.

"Well, sir," George said, "for starters, how to find their way around the ship. Basic stuff—where's the messdecks, where are their berthing compartments. Where are their watch-stations and their GQ stations. How to get from one to the other. A whole lot of them're either boots or rated men who've never been on a carrier. I thank God we've got two weeks. I'd take two months if I could."

"Well, you can't," the captain said. "And *I* won't, got it? We're coming out of dock in two weeks? Okay, I'll take your word for that. But then we're going to sea. And if people need training, I'm just the sonofabitch to provide it. Meantime, I want you to stay on these yardbirds, XO. Stay on 'em like stink on shit. There's a big war on, and *Franklin*'s gonna be there when we win it, not back here in this shithole called Bremerton. Got it?"

"Absolutely, Captain," George said.

The captain gave George an encouraging glare and then stalked off, headed forward, probably to see just how far this ineffectual "circus" extended. George saw crewmen dematerializing into the industrial haze when they saw him coming. God, he thought. This is gonna be a long cruise.

The captain had risen from the enlisted ranks to a commission and was now the first mustang, as formerly enlisted officers were sometimes called, to command a carrier. George thought he was nothing if not full of himself. He'd been a fighter pilot, squadron XO and CO, and had been promoted to the temporary rank of commodore when he took command of the Aleutians defense forces. He'd had to take a step back in rank to captain in order to gain command of *Franklin*. George could understand the new CO's dismay at being handed a seriously damaged ship, but the conventional reaction to that situation in the fleet was things could only get better, so get on with it and quit your complaining.

The kamikaze had hurt *Franklin* badly. He'd brought a 500-pound bomb with him and, between his plane hitting the ship's wooden, un-armored flight deck at 400 miles per hour and that bomb going off just below the gallery deck, fifty-eight men died and more than thirty were wounded, most with horrible burns. The hangar bay deck, made of steel and reinforced with two and a half inches of armor, had held, but flaming aviation gasoline got into an ammunition trunk and spread fire every-where. The ship's own firefighting efforts had put enough water below-decks to give her a three-degree list. George thought the shipyard had worked wonders, given the scope of the damage, although, even if they were working three shifts around the clock, he did wonder about that two-weeks' prognostication.

Adding to the workload were all the modifications ordered by the Bureau of Ships back in Washington. Improved radars, a significant increase in the number of AA guns along the flight deck, a second catapult forward, a change in the incoming air group's fighter-bomber mix, which meant heavier and more powerful airplanes, beefed-up fire-suppression systems controlled by a new conflagration control station above the hangar deck, and a division of the hangar bay into three sectors, with fire curtains to make sure a big fire didn't turn into a ship-sinking fire. Firefighting systems along the flight deck were also being expanded, and fifty-foot-long hoses were being replaced with one-hundred-foot hoses. *Franklin* was nearly 900 feet long and displaced close to 36,000 tons when fully loaded. Even so, when all the additional modifications were made, the Bureau had expressed concern about her stability due to all the additional topside weight. As large as she was, *Franklin* would probably capsize if hit by two or more Jap Type-93 torpedoes with their enormous warheads. The truth was they didn't have a choice. The Divine Wind was upon them and *Franklin* would need every single AA gun she had to deal with that grotesque threat.

George looked around for Billy and saw that he'd succeeded in disappearing into the industrial swirl, whose noise was beginning to hurt his own ears. He decided to go back to his office, where there were three in-baskets' worth of paperwork waiting for his "immediate and urgent" attention. Conversation was difficult in the ship's office, as his lair was called, because of the noisy repairs going on throughout the gallery deck. It was 1630, and George longed to get off the ship and back to his BOQ room ashore, where a bottle of good Scotch was calling to him. But—he had to at least shuffle through the baskets of paperwork to make sure there were no painful surprises lurking. It was better that he found out about problems before the captain did. Between incoming naval action messages and the official mail, all of which theoretically went through the XO before going to the captain, George spent at least four hours out of every working day on paperwork. Like most aviators, he absolutely hated it. Having been both XO and CO of a torpedo bomber squadron, he'd learned how to prioritize it, but the endless paperwork was the bane of his existence.

The ship's paperwork had a bastard child, the new captain's buzzer. Captain Shoemaker had used the ship-wide sound-powered phone system when he wanted to talk to someone. The phone would squeak and there he'd be, calling you by your first name or title, in George's case, XO, with a question or some news. The new captain had had a one-way buzzer system installed that connected to George and the department heads. When that thing went off, one was expected to drop what he was doing and immediately pick up the separate handset, painted red to denote its importance. George had accidentally discovered that the department heads were beginning to experiment with a selective response to the detested buzzer. They'd simply get up and go somewhere else when it went off in their cabins or offices. Sorry, Captain, I must not have been there when you called. It wasn't a surprising development, given the captain's abrasive if not downright abusive demeanor, but George had been struggling to decide what to do about it, because if the captain couldn't raise one of the department heads, he'd of course buzz George.

He looked over at the framed picture on his desk of Karen Brooke, the lady doctor he'd met after completing his command tour and reporting aboard *Franklin* as the commissioning XO. She was a plastic surgeon at the naval hospital in Portsmouth, Virginia, close by the shipyard where the brand-new *Franklin* had been fitting out. He'd met her at a reception given by the naval district's commandant for the *Franklin*'s wardroom at the Portsmouth officers' club. She'd been with an older-looking three-striper who was wearing medical corps sleeve insignia and pontificating about something very important when their eyes met and George convinced himself she was sending an SOS signal, so he'd moved right in. Minutes later they were at the bar.

"Gonna call you Swoop," she'd said, with a smile. "And thank you very much, kind sir."

That smile tickled George's backbone, and for once he was at a loss for words. Karen was petite, very pretty with dark hair, bright blue eyes, and filling out her uniform in all the right places. As George remembered, he'd managed to mumble something. They'd seen each other several times after that, but it had been difficult. She was a junior surgeon at a major naval hospital and he was the second-in-command of an aircraft carrier coming to life for the first time in the early spring of 1944. By late May they'd become close friends, but when *Franklin* left for the West Coast and the final drive on Japan, they'd made no promises. George had been a dedicated bachelor up to that point, but he'd found himself thinking the unthinkable every time he was around Karen.

Now, in January of 1945, they'd been corresponding by wartime mail much like many husbands and wives were doing. George was the chief censor for all outgoing mail in the ship, with a little help from the three chaplains embarked, so he couldn't tell her anything about what they were doing or where, which meant that letters tended to focus on personal feelings. It proved to be a surprisingly good way to establish a relationship.

Once the ship came back for repairs, they'd talked about her coming out to the West Coast while *Franklin* was in the shipyard, but reality had intervened. George was busier than the fabled one-armed paper-hanger, overseeing the repairs and modernization projects, while Karen, being a relatively new surgeon, was buried under her hospital workload with burns cases courtesy of the casualty load from Europe. It was generally assumed that Germany was on the ropes, but apparently no one had informed the Germans, so the fighting was fierce. Besides, the cross-country train ride alone would have taken ten days, round trip. George had been given a room at the shipyard BOQ when *Franklin* first arrived, so now they made do with a weekly phone call over a hallway pay phone. He found himself living for those quiet phone calls and the sound of her voice.

George had grown up in Boston, the son of a prominent dentist. He'd graduated from the Naval Academy in 1928, done his mandatory two years of sea duty on a battleship, and then volunteered for flight school and the newly developing naval air arm. By 1939 he was a flight instructor at Pensacola, where the Navy was transitioning to a new generation of fighters, dive bombers, and torpedo bombers. He was tall for an aviator, nearly six feet, with a shock of black hair and heavy eyebrows, and a genial smile on his face. He'd stayed single mostly because he enjoyed his Navy career and saw little point in pursuing a family, given what he did for a living. Karen had complicated that notion, but the war made it easy for both of them to put off any big plans or decisions.

The captain's buzzer flattened his memories.

"Yes, sir?" he answered.

"I want to see you and the chief engineer in my cabin," the captain said. "Now would be nice."

"Aye, aye, sir," George said, and hung up the handset. Now would be nice—why did he have to say crap like that? He told one of the yeomen in his office to find Lieutenant Commander Walt Forrest, the chief engineer, and give him the good news. So much for a Scotch at the BOQ, he thought.

2

Lieutenant John Ryan McCauley, USN, the *Franklin*'s fire marshal and assistant damage control officer, stood in the almost-finished hangar-deck conflagration control station with Marty Hanlon, the lead electrician from the yard's Shop 51 (Electrical). He was known to his shipmates in the engineering department as J.R. He was an Academy graduate, twenty-eight years old, and born in Havana, Illinois, into a family of six kids. He had reddish hair, blue eyes, and an unmistakably Irish face. He was a surface ship officer who'd served six years in destroyers before being assigned to the engineering department of the brand-new USS *Franklin* commissioning crew. The Navy had offered him a career designator change to become an engineering-duty-only officer, but he hadn't made up his mind about that. If he stayed in the surface line, he could one day rise to command at sea; EDOs couldn't do that.

"This is quite something," he said, looking around at all the control panels. The station was built like an airport control tower. It had slanting square reinforced glass windows and was mounted high up on the underside of the gallery deck. "We'll be actually able to see the problem now."

Hanlon nodded. "As long as the problem ain't right underneath, you will," he replied. "Then this'll become an oven."

"Yeah," J.R. acknowledged. "Except, before this, I had to wait down in DC Central for reports from people actually on the hangar deck to even know what was going on. Now we can act a whole lot faster. Is there an operating manual for all these controls?"

Hanlon shook his head. "I can get you the wiring diagrams for the installation, but you guys are gonna have to write your own manual."

J.R. groaned. That meant *he* was going to have to write a manual, which meant that he would have to learn the controls himself first. He asked Hanlon for a quick tour.

"This one here is the water curtain panel," Hanlon began. "As long as there's pressure in the fire-main system, these four handles will activate all four water curtains, or whichever ones you want individually. They send an electrical signal to hydraulically operated gate valves in the overhead, which then pressurize the manifold. The deluge sprinkler heads don't have valves, so: you pressurize that manifold, you get Niagara Falls on demand."

The 700-foot-long hangar deck was theoretically separated into three bays for damage control purposes. It wasn't a physical, steel separation, but three sectors in the overhead, or ceiling, that contained deluge sprinkler systems to isolate really big fires.

"And if that system doesn't work, can those gate valves be opened manually?"

"Three men and a boy might could do it," Hanlon said, lighting up a cigarette. "But those are six-inch gate valves with a hundred twenty-five psi on one side of the gate. That's a force of some three thousand pounds they gotta overcome. You'd prolly want to mount some six-foot-long crow's feet nearby."

McCauley pulled out his little green pocket notebook and wrote the word "crow's feet" in it. He knew that a crow's foot was a homemade, three-pronged, long-handled wrench that could fit horizontally through the spokes of a gate valve's operating wheel to give additional leverage when trying to open or close it. They were technically unauthorized, but every engineering department afloat had a stash of them for valves that were known to be balky.

Hanlon continued the tour, moving to a small panel to the right of the water curtain controls. "This right here can air-start the two emergency fire pumps in case fire-main pressure starts coming down, but somebody would still have to physically open their discharge valves to put 'em on the line."

"Those spaces are manned at GQ," J.R. said. "But I'd'a thought the discharge valves would have remote controls, like the water curtains."

Hanlon shrugged. "Well, they don't," he said. "Somebody at BuShips saving a buck or two, I guess. Now: over here are the foam system controls."

"Foam?" J.R. said. "That's manual. We want foam, we gotta plug a foam nozzle into a can of concentrate first and then connect that to a fire hose."

"Up on the flight deck, yeah, that's the way it is. But this baby's got two high-pressure foam heads mounted in each bay. They're mounted down on the actual hangar deck; one points forward, one points aft. You'd only use 'em as a last resort. Each nozzle has a two-hundred-gallon concentrate tank built into a bulkhead. These controls right here open the valve between the nozzles and the tank; these right here open gate valves to the fire main, which then pressurizes the tank and makes foam."

"Wow," J.R. said. "This is pretty amazing stuff."

"It is," Hanlon acknowledged. "But you gotta understand, Lieutenant, all this new shit right here? It involved a lot of new cabling and piping. Like I said, we can give you the plans for the various installations, but some poor sumbitch's gonna have to go hand over hand to make sure the actual installation matches the plans. You know how that goes."

"Yes, I surely do," J.R. said. He knew that, although highly trained naval architects designed the routes for the miles and miles of electrical wiring and piping in a ship of this size, the actual shipfitters—the yard workers who manhandled piping and heavy cables into position—would often encounter obstacles not shown on the ship's plans. They would then re-route whatever system they were installing to make it all work. He was beginning to appreciate the sheer magnitude of recording all this. All the damage control plans and blueprints down in the Engineering Log Room were original-configuration, pre-kamikaze vintage. Dismayed, he realized he was going to need help, *and* that he'd need officers to do it.

"We're not done yet, there, Lieutenant," Hanlon said with a sympathetic smile. "There's more. Lots more."

"Great," J.R. said, shaking his head. "Just great."

An hour later, he made his way down to the engineering department's main office, called the Engineering Log Room. J.R. was a relatively junior member of the engineering department, which was headed up by Lieutenant Commander Forrest. His title was chief engineer, sometimes spoken as "cheng." Following the Navy's tradition of abbreviating absolutely everything, the rest of the department consisted of the main propulsion assistant, or MPA, the damage control assistant, or DCA, the repair officer, and the auxiliaries and electrical officer, or A & E, who were all senior lieutenants. J.R. was on the third tier of the chart, as assistant DCA and fire marshal. It was a long way from Havana, Illinois, where the most complex machine was one of the newfangled combine harvesters. His father, having watched the boom-and-bust cycle of agriculture beat down the actual farmers, had built a grain elevator at the edge of town. However the harvest came out, the farmers always needed a place to put it. By the time J.R. had gone off to a year at college and then the Academy, that single elevator had grown into six, making his father one of the wealthiest men in the county.

Franklin had six main engineering spaces: four boiler rooms, called firerooms, and two main engine rooms, which combined to drive four propellers. There was additionally an auxiliary machinery space at either end of the main spaces. The main propulsion plant produced 150,000 shaft horsepower, which could drive the huge ship at a speed of thirty-three knots, or almost forty miles per hour. Additionally there were four turbogenerators and two emergency diesel generators, two distilling plants that made desalinated fresh water out of seawater, fuel tanks that could hold 240,000 gallons of boiler fuel oil, gasoline tanks that held 230,000 gallons of super high-octane aviation gasoline, machine shops, welding shops, shipfitter shops, damage control equipment, and electrical shops, and a crew of almost 600 men to actually run the entire engineering department.

The Log Room, located beneath the hangar deck on the second deck, was the central office for the entire department. It contained several rooms, actually, with spaces for general admin, machinery logs, boiler and drinking water testing records, maintenance logs for every machine aboard the ship, blueprints and schematics for every system aboard the ship, and a large space called Damage Control Central, or DC Central in Navy parlance. That space had diagrams of the entire ship mounted on the bulkheads, deck by deck, bow to stern, and there were seven decks. There were also duplicate, wall-mounted plates, as they were called, which overlaid various systems—hydraulic, steam, fresh water, electrical, compressed air, fire main, and ammunition handling—on the basic overall diagrams. This was the kingdom of the DCA and his assistant, Lieutenant J. R. McCauley, who manned this space during general quarters, where they communicated with several so-called repair lockers located throughout the ship.

J.R. plopped down at his desk in DC Central and tried to figure out how he was going to deal with all the modernization modifications that had followed the October kamikaze strike. The forty-four wall-mounted damage control plates would eventually be replaced with new versions, but with the ship scheduled to go back to the Western Pacific in two weeks, he was going to have to draw in the new systems using a grease pencil right on the existing diagrams. He was assuming that the yard would provide actual blueprints and schematics before they left, but he couldn't construct the new diagrams accurately until the hand-over-hand inspections had been done. He was startled when the chief engineer stuck his head into Central and called his name.

"Yessir?" J.R. responded, turning in his desk chair.

Lieutenant Commander Forrest stepped into the space and looked around. He was not an aviator, but rather a destroyer officer who'd come to *Franklin* from command of his own ship. This was standard practice for carriers: aviators knew next to nothing about ship's systems, so they had to get fleet officers from battleships, cruisers, or destroyers to man up the engineering billets aboard a carrier. Walt Forrest was a lanky Texan who ran a taut department but without any of the chickenshit of an officer who was all orders and no experience. He'd been a steam engineer as a junior officer, an engineering department head on a cruiser, and then an executive officer on a destroyer. He was unflappable, polite, and demanding in his own quiet way, knowing as he did more about steam propulsion plants than everyone aboard except perhaps for the engineering chiefs, and since he and the chiefs were about the same age, he managed a thoroughly professional, while friendly, relationship with the chiefs. Engineers in Navy ships were called "snipes," and everyone in *Franklin's* engineering department recognized Forrest as a snipe's snipe. The engineers had a saying: if you're not a snipe, you're just along for the ride.

"What'cha y'all crankin' on, there, J.R.?" Forrest asked.

J.R. told him about the problem of bringing the DC plates up to date, including the hand-over-hand inspections required. He also described the matter of the conflagration station controls, piping, and wiring.

The cheng sat down next to him in another desk chair. "I'll tell y'all how to do that," he said. "But it's gonna take a while."

J.R. could only shake his head. "It's gonna take forever, Boss," he said.

"Not quite," Forrest said. "Here's how you do it. We'll find two en-signs who are *not* engineers. That's important. They've got to be com-pletely 'igorrant' of engineering systems. I'll task them with doing the system traces. You pick a system, like hangar deck fire main, and then you show them how to do a hand-over-hand trace, *and* how to record it. Once they've got the picture, turn them loose to do every system. *Every* system. Make sure they understand there's urgency, but that *accuracy* is more im-portant than urgency. *You* will have to amend the DC plates, but we'll let them do the legwork."

J.R. thought about it for a moment. That still was going to take a lot of time. And an ensign loose with a pencil? *That* was a prescription for disaster.

As if reading J.R.'s mind, the cheng smiled. "Yeah, that'll be a slow process. In a perfect world, BuShips would've provided us new DC plates before we left. It ain't a perfect world, young man. We're headed back to the final push. The Japs are at their rope's end, but American Navy carrier bombers hitting the home islands is gonna bring fire from the sky, you'd best by God believe it. So do the best you can."

"Aye, aye, sir," J.R. said, glad that the boss understood the magnitude of the problem he was facing.

"There you go, Lieutenant," Forrest said. "What could go wrong, eh?"

They both laughed, but not very hard. The cheng's allusion to fire from the sky was enough to remind anyone who heard it of the sheer terror caused by those fanatical pilots who were willing, even eager, to drive their planes and themselves right through the decks of American ships.

3

Lieutenant Gary Peck, USN, lay on his back, fighting off the beginnings of drowsiness. He was inside the steam drum of number two boiler doing a waterside inspection. The steam drum was twenty-two feet long but only forty inches in diameter. The drum was made of thick steel, the bottom half featuring dozens of holes in neat rows, each of which was connected to a generating tube. It smelled of warm, fresh rust, boiler compound, and his own nervous sweat. He'd learned not to think about where he was: inside the steam drum of a marine boiler, at the top of said boiler, in a compartment that was down on the fourth deck, below the waterline, with the mountain of steel that was the USS *Franklin* pressing down on his imagination from above. He shook it off and began counting the number of plugged tubes and then examining the interior surface of the drum with his flashlight for evidence of pitting or incipient leaks around the tube heads. The drum sat directly above the fifteen-foot-high generating bank of 650 tubes, around which passed the fire and furious heat from the firebox down below.

He always went in feetfirst through the twenty-six-inch end plate access hole. He'd gone in the other way the first time and had not liked the view from the far end of the drum, especially after some of his mischievous snipes had crawled up the boiler-front and noisily replaced the hatch. He'd known in advance about this particular rite of passage but he'd still had to do some slow, heavy breathing. They opened it ten minutes later and he'd pretended to be asleep, lying on his side like a kid in his bed, trying to ignore the sharp rims of the tubes stabbing him along his full length. There'd been general laughter, but his initiation was complete. His predecessor as the ship's boilers officer, one Lieutenant Sandringham, had been somewhat overweight and had had quite a time trying to squeeze through the access hole. He'd actually gotten stuck trying to get out and he'd never done another boiler inspection, so the crew of Number One Firehouse, as snipes fondly called the number one fireroom, were anxious to see what Lieutenant Peck was made of. You couldn't be a real fireroom engineering officer if you were afraid, or physically unable, to crawl into the steam drum. Fat boys in B-division were conspicuously absent. Just standing a watch in a fireroom under way at full power could take five pounds off you in four hours.

As boilers officer, Gary was responsible for the care and feeding of the ship's eight enormous Babcock & Wilcox marine boilers. They were mounted in four separate compartments way down in the bowels of the ship, each fireroom hosting two of them. At full power, with 'eight-on-the-floor,' they generated enough 600-psi steam, superheated to 850 degrees, to drive four geared main-engine turbines, all four turbo-generators, and a host of steam-driven pumps. Gary had served as a main propulsion assistant on a destroyer and then as chief engineer on a second tin can. He knew his stuff as a steam engineer, but nothing had prepared him for the sheer size of *Franklin*'s main spaces. Everything was oversized: the fresh water evaporators, the ship's electrical generators, the three-story-high boilers themselves, and the massive main-engine turbines. The drive shafts, running from the main engines to the propellers, had been eighteen inches in diameter on his destroyers. *Franklin*'s were twice that.

Gary loved the world of naval engineering. He'd grown up on the outskirts of Omaha, Nebraska, the son of an engineering professor at Creighton University. His father taught the hands-on part of engineering, and Gary had spent many an hour in his father's labs, where the students got to take big machines apart and learned firsthand the greasy side of a mechanical engineering degree. He'd been the third alternate for an appointment to Annapolis and was already starting freshman year when the Navy called and asked if he was still interested. He'd done two tours in engineering departments before coming to *Franklin*.

He knew there was a whole world of totally different activity going on literally four decks above him, including a floating airfield, a forest of guns, radars, communications centers, the Combat Information Center, the captain and the exec, and even an admiral and his staff. But down here, on the deckplates, was the world of high-pressure steam, roaring turbines, keening steam pumps, what seemed like a thousand valves, hot black oil fuel, oppressive heat, constant noise and vibration, all running to strict naval engineering specifications. He loved machinery because, with a machine, it was all pretty much black-and-white. Find the tech manual, read the performance specs, and then measure the machine's output. It was either in-spec or it was not. No gray areas or room for opinions. If it wasn't, there was a specified way to fix it. If it was running properly, a snipe would happily pat it on its hot metal ass, but always with his gloves on.

He was also most at home with his fellow snipes. The engineers were often the forgotten brigades, working as they did down in the nether regions of the ship. The only time the rest of the ship's company even thought about the engineers was when stuff broke, the lights went out, the fresh water quit, or the ventilation stopped. Then *every*one became an engineer, calling down to Main Control or DC Central to complain about this or that and also to offer advice on what to do about it.

There were two kinds of snipes: main-hole snipes and auxiliaries snipes. The main-hole guys owned the really big machines: the boilers, main engines, and the turbo-generators, plus all of their supporting equipment. The auxiliaries engineers owned everything else—electrical lighting throughout the ship, air compressors, ship-wide ventilation, the fire main, as well as the sewage, potable water, and damage control systems. Both varieties referred to the rest of the carrier's crew as the Heroes, the guys who operated on the hangar deck and above; the men who saw sunlight, exciting battle stations, fresh air, and the sea on a daily basis. These were the pilots, the flight deck crews, the air-defense gunners, the navigation team, the aviation maintenance brigades, the weaponeers, the air boss and his assistant, the mini boss, the aviation squadron commanders, the carrier air group commander, or CAG, the captain and his exec, and the admiral and his staff.

The Heroes rarely interacted directly with snipes. It wasn't an antagonistic thing—the Heroes dealt with the daily (and nightly) drama of carrier warfare: launching and recovering airplanes, the routine handling of bombs, torpedoes, rockets, and super high-octane aviation gasoline. The gunners in their hundreds were charged with shooting down Jap attackers. The deck divisions tended to seamanship, boats, anchors, rigging, hull preservation and painting, and the dangerous ship-to-ship evolutions such as refueling destroyers and conducting ship-to-ship personnel transfers using rope highlines strung between two ships.

The snipes, crouching down under the ventilation blowers in their below-the-waterline compartments, were confident that they were the ones who made it all possible and were thus content to tend to their fiery charges in relative obscurity. There was a minimum of brass-driven chickenshit once you went below the third deck. Salutes, sudden calls for attention-on-deck, proper uniforms, formal address, strict chain-of-command rules—those things were for the Heroes. The engineers were a proud bunch because they were the guys who made everything on the ship work. Anyone who wanted to challenge that notion would be invited down to a fireroom and introduced to a boiler-front, handed, literally, a flaming torch, and told to go ahead, see if you can light Baby off.

Gary Peck was a respected member of this steam, fire, oil, and water fraternity. As he crawled headfirst out of the boiler's steam drum and dropped down to the steel deckplates of the upper level, he grinned. He loved his job. Then his senior boilertender chief petty officer reminded him he had six more inspections to do. Gary groaned, but then declared in a loud voice: "Hell, yes, Chief. WETSU," which was short for: "We eat this shit up."

The chief laughed and nodded approvingly until Gary told him that *he* was going to come with him for the rest of the inspections. Then it was time for the snuffies to laugh.

4

George and the chief engineer were cooling their heels in the captain's office when one of the Marine orderlies poked his head in and announced that the captain would see them now. George got up and gave the cheng a meaningful look which said: Follow my lead, Walt. The cheng rolled his eyes, but nodded. They went through the short passageway between the office and the captain's cabin, where a second Marine opened the door to let them through.

The captain was at his desk. He looked angry. Par for the course, George thought. He tried to remember when he'd last, if ever, seen the captain looking pleased about something. Anything. He apparently just couldn't manage it. The clock on the bulkhead read 18:15.

"Okay, XO," the captain said. "The yard is still claiming they'll have us out of here in two weeks. Do you really believe that?"

"Well, Captain," George said. "There's no way I can challenge that. I've got my doubts as I look around, especially in the hangar bays, but this yard has a pretty good reputation for coming through on delivery dates."

"I don't care about their Goddamned reputation," the captain said. "From what *I've* seen of their progress, *I* don't believe it. What I need now are concrete facts—degrees of progress on both the repair jobs and the new stuff. I don't put much stock in promises. Cheng: what's your take?"

The chief engineer shrugged. "Our upgrades are all finished," he said. "The main holes're in the op-testing phase, especially for the new fire-main additions. I can't speak to the topside modernizations—guns, radars, flight deck. The structural repairs are complete where the kamikaze hit us, but, like I said, I'm kinda out of the loop as to the upgrades. I have heard about one potential problem, though: the electrical cabling to hook everything together."

"Cabling? Why?"

"Because of the stuffing tubes."

The captain gave a pained expression. "What the hell is a stuffing tube?"

"The ship is divided into hundreds of watertight and airtight compartments, sir. When a cable run has to penetrate a watertight bulkhead or deck, it goes through a stuffing tube, which lets the cable through but not water or smoke. The tubes are sized to the diameter of the cable or the bundle of cables going through it, then welded into the bulkhead."

"So?" the captain asked, impatiently.

"I'm hearing rumors that there's not enough room in the existing stuffing tubes to pass all the new cabling through," Walt said.

"And so, the yard is putting in additional tubes, right?"

"Apparently, nobody at BuShips thought about that. There aren't any tubes available."

"Oh, for *God's* sake," said the captain. "XO, did you know about this?"

George shook his head. "The ship's supe hasn't mentioned it to me, Captain. I'll run this down."

"Goddamn right you will, XO," the captain growled. "Look, you're supposed to be on top of this entire yard availability. Corral the department heads and get me a reading, especially on shit like this. I do *not* want any more surprises, got it?"

"Yes, sir," George said, even as he wondered if the captain knew just how many repair and modernization projects were under way in *Franklin*. For that matter, he doubted that even the department heads knew.

"And you, Cheng," the captain continued. "You can stop hiding behind your boilers and turbines. We're not running a union shop here. If your main-hole work is done, get involved in tracking the combat system stuff. You're a ship driver. The XO, air boss, and the navigator are aviators, like me. We depend on you black-shoes to keep track of what's being done to the ship. All of it. Got it?"

"Yes, sir," Walt said.

"I want a report in forty-eight hours," the captain said. "That's all."

They left Captain's Country, trying to ignore the sympathetic looks from the Marine sentries and office yeomen. The captain had a voice to match his oversized frame and they'd undoubtedly heard every word. George headed for his office down below; the chief engineer fled to the Engineering Log Room.

George called a quick department head meeting in his office thirty minutes later. The navigator, Commander Alvin "Big Al" Frost; the air boss, Commander William "Billy-B" Perkins; the chief engineer; and the supply officer, Lieutenant Commander Benton "Chop" Crockett, Supply Corps, arrived fifteen minutes later. George cleared the office of yeomen, told the department heads what the captain wanted, and then waited for the bitching to start. He gave them a minute to squawk and then held up his hand.

"Easy way or hard way, gentlemen," he declared. "Easy way is for all of you to get around the table and go over *all* the jobs. I'll chair it, and we'll comb every one of the projects for surprises. The alternative is that I'll send you each individually to see the captain, so he can, *ahem,* share his thinking with you, and you with him."

That stopped the noise, and then George explained exactly how he wanted to do this. Two hours later they were all pretty much on the same page, so George ended the meeting. He told the duty yeomen that he was going ashore and, if anybody asked where he was, to tell them he'd taken the ferry over to Seattle in search of whiskey, wild women, and maybe even an opium den. The guys pretended to take all of that seriously. One of them even asked him how to spell opium.

It took five minutes to get from his office, up to the hangar bay, out onto one of the sponson decks, down the hundred-foot-long brow, and out onto the actual pier. It was, of course, raining, but his thoughts were on a much-needed Scotch. And maybe even a phone call to Karen, he thought, although it would be pretty late back East. God *damn* this war and everything Japanese, he muttered, as he slouched through the eternal Pacific Northwest rain, taking care not to step in crane tracks on his way to the BOQ. He could see the flash of welding arcs through *Franklin*'s open hangar bay doors as he made his way down her port side to the head of the drydock. The carrier was afloat in the drydock, her underwater hull having already been sandblasted and recoated with anti-fouling paint. The 100-foot-high pier cranes rose into the rainy mist, their white lights casting cones of jittering lights and shadows against the carrier's sides.

Karen had once brought a nephew down to the Portsmouth piers. The little boy had been five and he'd looked up at the towering mass of gray-painted steel and declared: that's a *really* big boat. It had become an inside, personal joke between them. Karen would never refer to *Franklin* by name, only by the term: *really* big boat. It was one of her endearing features, he thought, and then jumped sideways when a crane right next to him got under way with a clamor of warning bells.

He chided himself. I should have just stayed aboard and gone to bed, he thought. On the other hand, there were no buzzers in the BOQ. And there was his increasingly good friend, a jug of twelve-year-old Macallan. He hoped Karen would still be awake and not elbow deep in some gory procedure or another. He'd often speculated as to whether they were "in love" or just a man and a woman who were very comfortable with each other. Their few experiences in the bedroom had been entirely satisfactory but hardly scenes of great passion.

The problem was this Goddamned war. When they could manage to get together after work, they'd both been exhausted, she by the demands of wartime surgery as the fighting climaxed in Europe, and he by the avalanche of admin and personnel problems attendant to bringing a huge ship to life. Captain Shoemaker was hardly a slave driver, but the sheer scale of activating such a large ship and crew wore them both down. As often as not an evening together consisted of dinner in the Portsmouth Naval Hospital BOQ dining room, followed by a hot shower, a quick cuddle, some preliminary moves, and then instant sleep. Everyone in the Navy was tired, with no end in sight for the foreseeable future. Hanging over all that had been the certain knowledge that he was going to sail away to the far Western Pacific in a few weeks, coming back, if he came back, God only knew when. They'd both wondered aloud how all those gorgeous characters in those wartime romances portrayed by Hollywood had found the Goddamned time.

5

Three weeks later, not two, George stood on the starboard bridgewing as ten tugboats extracted *Franklin* out of the drydock. It was raining, of course, but George was wearing his regulation black Navy trench coat and his "brass" hat, so he was relatively dry. The sailors manning their sea-detail stations wore peacoats, but their white "Dixie Cup" hats did little to keep their faces dry. The captain sat in his chair behind him, staring straight ahead. George thought he looked hungover. He hadn't said two words to the yard's harbor pilot who was wrangling the tugs on an FM radio. Every time the pilot gave an order the tugs would acknowledge with a hoot of their horns. The ship was on her own power now, but the main engines wouldn't be used to execute the delicate maneuver of sliding a 36,000-ton aircraft carrier out of a drydock that allowed only eighteen feet of room between her steel sides and the waiting granite edges of the dock.

George was just as happy with that arrangement. The captain had insisted that he would conn the ship alongside the pier in Bremerton when they'd arrived from Pearl. He'd made a hash of it, damaging the pier and parting several mooring lines, much to the embarrassment of the crew lining the flight deck. The shipyard pilot, whose services the captain had imperiously rejected, remained standing on the bridge with one of the best stone faces George had ever seen, appearing to enjoy the scenery. It had been a clear day for once and the Olympic mountain range had been in full view. Today George was quietly grateful for the rule that required a yard pilot for any evolution involving a drydock.

The one-week delay had been caused by a laundry list of relatively small projects, and of course, it had been George's fault for not having employed the lash to make the shipyard workers go faster. The captain's daily tantrums had actually had the opposite effect among the civilian shipyard workers, who'd begun to bait him as he stood there criticizing. Their favorite trick was to see him coming, wink and nod, and then all of them stop working. When he'd approach and demand to know why, the foreman would tell him that they were waiting for a particular tool that, unfortunately, was being used in another ship. The foreman would declare, with a perfectly straight face, that they couldn't proceed until they got their hands on the frammus or whatever, and, unfortunately, the yard owned only one frammus. The captain would then stomp off to call the shipyard's commanding officer, and then everyone would get back to what they'd been doing. Walt Forrest had been the one who told George that this was going on. By then George, seasoned aviator that he was, knew that there was absolutely zero point in his raising hell with the much-maligned ship's superintendent.

But now Big Ben was actually moving, although more like a glacier than a fast attack carrier. She was being moved to a regular pier, where she'd be fueled and provisioned, a two-day task. Then there'd be a sea trial to make sure everything worked, after which she'd sail back to Pearl with a four-destroyer escort. George knew that this would be no holiday cruise to Hawaii. The captain had written up a nonstop refresher training program that would introduce all the new crewmen to the business of operating such a big ship. Then, once they got to Pearl, the air group would embark, and then there'd be another two weeks at sea while the various squadrons were integrated into the ship's operations.

The captain's training program proposed a punishing pace, which George actually thought was entirely appropriate. Once they left Pearl for the Western Pacific, all the drills and exercises would become real all too soon and this would no longer be a training cruise. Besides, the admirals would expect Big Ben to arrive on station off Japan ready to fight and fight hard on the very first day. He knew that those expectations might be really hard to meet. *Franklin* had been there before, right from the beginning of her operational life, through several of the 1944 island campaigns, but George wondered if the big brass realized how many of the carrier's new crew had never even been to sea.

"XO?"

George turned around. "Yes, sir?"

"You see that man sitting on that ammo locker down there, starboard side, forward?"

George looked down at the 300 feet of flight deck stretching out in front of the island. The crew had been ordered to "man the rails," which meant they were supposed to line up on the edge of the flight deck, facing outward, and stand at parade rest. Way up toward the forward edge of the flight deck one sailor had decided to rest his feet.

"Put that man on report, XO," the captain said. "I won't tolerate lolly-gagging when they're supposed to be on Goddamn man-the-sides parade, got it?"

"Aye, aye, sir," George said mechanically, and reached for a phone to call the master-at-arms office. The harbor pilot was standing near the centerline conning console waiting for the carrier's bow to clear the sill of the drydock. George saw him give a slow-motion sympathetic shake of his head as he watched George make the call. They exchanged a quick look. Lucky you, the pilot's expression said.

6

Four days later, not the predicted two, Gary stood in one corner of the boiler-front area in number two fireroom, watching his snipes prepare to light off 3B boiler. It was a comfortable eighty-five degrees in the fireroom, courtesy of January temperatures outside and the fact that neither boiler was as yet on the line. He reviewed the preliminary steps to actually lighting fires: valve and piping lineups, filling the boiler with hot feedwater, circulating fuel oil through the steam heaters for one hour, water tests on the feedwater and the deareating (DA) feed tank, high-pressure and low-pressure drains lineups, and the main steam valves closed to build pressure. The list went on, but he knew every step of it, as did the chief boilertender and his senior petty officers. The new boots, so-called because many of them had come to the ship directly from boot camp, were nervously following orders without having the first idea of what they were doing or why.

The boilers were Babcock & Wilcox M-types. The front of the boiler supported the burners: four on the left side to make steam; three more on the right side to superheat that steam from 450 degrees to 850 degrees. It was a two-stage process, because some of the machinery needed saturated steam to run their turbines, while the turbo-generators, the main engines, and certain large turbine-driven pumps needed superheated steam. The burner's job was to mix hot oil and pressurized air to form a cone of vaporized fuel oil going into the firebox. To light off the boiler required four things: the boiler filled with purified feedwater and with all steam discharge valves shut, an electric motor-driven blower to force air into the firebox through the burner assemblies, and hot fuel oil available; the fourth thing was the torch, which, given the mechanical complexity of a steam plant, was something of a crude throwback. Until recently, the torch had been made up using a standard Navy mophead, soaked in diesel and gasoline, attached to a long wooden handle. Now it was a metal rod with a cotton head, but still soaked in a mixture of diesel oil and gasoline.

When everything was ready, one of the snipes would open the lightoff port while another lit the torch. Since the firebox was being pressurized by the incoming air, inserting the flaming torch would inevitably create a tongue of fire blasting back up the handle, thus making it a perfect job for a brand-new fireman. Once the torch was inside the firebox, and still burning, the chief would cut in the fuel oil, which resulted in a small and relatively controlled explosion within the firebox. The torch would be withdrawn once the chief heard the thump of ignition and the boot was dancing around on the deckplates, desperately trying to avoid the serious flame front that was coming out of the lightoff port, much to the delight of the experienced hands.

Then the boiler began the heat-up phase. Over the course of the next hour, the fires would be controlled to bring the boiler up to setpoint temperature and pressure by cutting in more burners, but slowly enough that the internal piping, firebox brickwork, and insulation had time to flex and expand. After that, steam would then be sent to the auxiliaries—feedwater pumps, the DA tank, fuel oil pumps, and to warm up the steam-driven forced-draft blowers.

Gary noted the time and then made the traditional log entry: fires lighted under number three Baker boiler. He stood there for a while, watching the color of the light emanating from the firebox peephole, the various gauges as pressure began to climb, the boiler water level sight glass to make sure it wasn't dropping, the smoke periscope to make sure he wasn't blanketing the shipyard in a cloud of black boiler smoke. Or worse:

a cloud of *white* smoke, which meant that a boiler explosion was immi-nent. He also listened carefully to the auxiliaries as they came on line, one by one, adding their noise to a familiar chorus of happy machines.

Experienced steam-plant engineers needed only their ears to detect a mechanical problem in the making. He remembered that the skippers of his two destroyers had been able to hear a problem in the main plant before he did just from a change in the machinery sound, and to do so while they were on the bridge, three decks away. He grinned as the boot tried to figure out how to extinguish the still-burning torch and then yelled at him when he moved to snuff it out in an oil can. He intervened only because the chief of this firehouse was perfectly capable of letting the boot do that to teach him an indelible lesson, but Gary didn't need a fire down here, if only because he didn't want to attract the captain's attention.

The new captain had been on the warpath ever since the promised two-day departure date for sea trials had not materialized. There was a whole lot of khaki between Gary and the captain and, from what he'd heard about the new CO, he was more than happy to keep it that way. The chief engineer had told all the officers in the department just to keep their heads down and do their jobs to the best of their ability. Everybody be smart, he'd said: Let the Heroes deal with the Hero-in-Chief. Once we get to WestPac, I guarantee you'll have other things to think about, and most of those things will be bent on killing you.

Gary saw that the boot, now looking very pleased with himself, was safely out of the way. He nodded to the chief. "Okay," he said. "Now: light off three–Able boiler."

7

J.R. McCauley saw his two sacrificial ensigns, both shanghaied from the weapons department, headed his way. He'd first met with them the day after the ship came out of the drydock, courtesy of an arrangement made between Lieutenant Commander Forrest and the weapons officer, Lieutenant Commander T.K. Hood. They'd been assigned to J.R.'s systems-trace project for two hours of every day; their divisional duties back in the weapons department awaited them when they were done. One had introduced himself as Chuck Sweet; the other as Bill Sauer. Both of them were ninety-day wonders, one from Iowa, the other from upstate New York, and fresh out of OCS. Even J.R. thought they looked like a couple of high school kids dressed for a costume party in their ill-fitting borrowed overalls. It had taken the Log Room yeomen about five minutes to start referring to them as the "sweet and sour" twins. The two ensigns were, for the moment, blissfully unaware of their nicknames. More importantly, they'd just completed their first hand-over-hand survey of one of the hangar bay fire-main systems. They had news.

"It's probably because we don't know exactly what we're doing," Chuck said. He was the taller of the two, with a somewhat cherubic face. "But the stuff we looked at doesn't match what's shown on this plan."

"At all?" J.R. asked with a sinking feeling.

"Well, sir," Chuck replied, pointing to the schematic. "We started at the fire-main control valve block in Bay One. It's right where it's supposed to be, starboard side, back end of the bay, deck-mounted. Six valve wheels, six twin connection pipes, and five hose lockers right next to them."

"Okay, and?"

"Plan says there's supposed to be *eight* connection pipes."

"Aw, shit," J.R. muttered. "What else?"

Bill Sauer took up the report. He was just over five-six and already showing signs of an incipient weight problem. He sported a razor-thin moustache on his upper lip, which made him look faintly ridiculous. "The five hose lockers are empty," he said. "No fire hoses, no nozzles, no applicators. There's also supposed to be something called a cage-stack for foam cans. Not there."

"Were you able to trace the actual lines that feed that control valve block?" J.R. asked, studying the plan again. "Should be a four-inch line coming up from the second deck that connects to the starboard-side fire main below the hangar deck."

"Um," Chuck said. "Line? At OCS they told us line was the Navy word for rope?"

J.R. took a deep breath. "Okay," he said. "You said: pipes. In the Navy, piping is referred to as 'lines.' Main steam line. Hydraulic fluid lines. Fresh water lines. Like that. Wires are referred to as cabling or cable-bundles. Those square metal structures mounted on the overhead—that's the ceiling—that supply ventilation air to a compartment? They're called vent ducts. Where they meet or originate—that's a plenum chamber. Those really big square ducts on the starboard side of the hangar bay, right under the island? They supply combustion air to the boilers. They're called *in*takes. The big round pipes next to them that take the products of combustion back out of the boiler fireboxes? Those are called the *up*takes."

The two ensigns nodded dutifully, with expressions on their faces that said: if you say so, sir.

"Once again," J.R. asked. "Was there a four-, maybe six-inch-diameter line coming up from the deck below connected to the bottom of that valve block?"

The two youngsters looked at each other. They simultaneously produced another embarrassed "um."

"Okay, guys," J.R. said. "You're new to this. I understand. Your assignment is to take the plan or schematic I give you and physically lay hands on every valve, valve block, and line—pipe—shown on the plan. I'll want you to do this one again."

"Yes, sir, sorry, sir," Chuck said.

"Don't be sorry," J.R. said. "You'll get the hang of it pretty quick. By the way, what info you did bring back was vitally important, okay? Good work. My only concern is that there are three hundred fifty schematics to go. Preferably before we go back into Injun Country."

J.R. made some notes after they left. The empty lockers weren't the yard's fault. The ship was responsible for hoses, nozzles, and applicators. The missing two fire-main risers were a more serious problem, and they wouldn't probably ever be fixed. One thing was clear: the sweet and sour twins' first foray into systems verification had already uncovered some problems. He couldn't imagine what they might find when they got into that conflagration station. He was reminded of something the ship's superintendent, the engineering duty officer who'd been responsible for all the shipyard jobs on the carrier, had said after a meeting with the captain.

He wants everything right now, doesn't he. Gets all excited. Yells at people. Wants it really bad.

Yes, we know, J.R. had said.

There's an old labor union rule, brother: if you want it bad, you're probably going to get it bad, know what I mean?

Now he did. He took a deep breath and went to find the cheng.

G eorge watched in awe as the first Marine Corps F4U–1D Corsair
came aboard. He'd heard the plane's engine was so long that the pilot
couldn't actually see the flight deck just before landing. He had to approach the ramp at an oblique angle and then turn sharply to line up with
the flight deck just before touching down. After that he had to depend
entirely on the landing signal officer (LSO) to tell him when to cut the
engine. The Marine Corsairs were configured as fighter-bombers these
days, capable of defending the carrier or joining in a strike with bombs,
rockets, and machine-gun fire. George was one of many watching the
Franklin's new air group come aboard twenty miles offshore of Pearl Harbor. He was standing inside the air boss's control station, called Primary
Flight Control and known as PriFly, which was mounted high up on the
port side of the island. Billy-B, the air boss, and his mini boss, Lieutenant
Commander Joe DeSantis, were wholly immersed in the complex business of landing an entire air group, 108 planes.

Just aft of PriFly was an open-air gallery which everyone called vultures' row, where various spectators lined a catwalk to watch the show.
There were also two movie cameramen posted at the very back, whose
job was to film each landing. Their film would be used to reconstruct

events whenever there was an accident or even a rough-enough landing that the aircraft was damaged. George got to watch from inside PriFly only because he was the XO. It had the advantage of being out of the relative gale whistling over the flight deck at almost forty miles an hour. Being in PriFly instead of on the bridge also meant he didn't have to listen to the captain criticize every landing with a string of nasty comments. Billy-B, knowing why George hung out there, had had a coffee mug with the letters XO painted on it hung on the bulkhead with the rest of the PriFly crew's mugs.

George was particularly interested in those Corsairs, because they'd had a rocky start in carrier aviation due to some technical problems with their landing gear and the pilot's inability to see the actual landing threshold when coming aboard. The Navy had taken them off carriers and sent them to the Marines in the Solomons as land-based fighters, where they'd become famous. Now, with the landing gear problems resolved, they were replacing the trusty F6F Hellcat, mostly because of their impressive speed, armor, bomb capacity, and rate of climb. Their new air group had one Navy Corsair squadron and one Marine Corps Corsair squadron. A Corsair was immediately identifiable by its extra-long nose, which contained a 2800 horsepower Double Wasp engine, and its distinctive gull wings. The Navy was determined to get them back aboard the carriers because of their dual capability, fighter or bomber, or both.

The next Corsair made its approach as the one which had just landed was hustled forward on the flight deck to the nearest available elevator. As soon as it was clear of the landing zone, the crash barrier netting rose up off the flight deck and locked back into position. The flight deck crews had to really hustle to get the barrier set back up in time for the next landing. Billy-B, standing at the window with a microphone in his hand, was focused on the approaching Corsair, evaluating the approach. Suddenly he was shaking his head. He keyed the mike: "No chance, Paddles; no chance."

His voice echoed over the entire flight deck through topside speakers. The LSO frantically began waving off the approaching pilot, who gunned his engine and, wings wobbling, clawed for altitude while banking left and away from the flight deck. George nodded. He'd thought the guy was too low, too. The wave-off flew away from the carrier and then began the process of rejoining the landing pattern. The next plane was already on short final and beginning his turn in toward the ramp. Then the hated buzzer went off. Billy rolled his eyes, then gestured for George to pick up; he had to stay focused on the approaching Corsair. The LSOs were in control, but the air boss had the final say as to whether or not an approach was good enough.

"PriFly, XO speaking, sir," George said.

"Was that one of those damned Marines?" the captain asked.

"I wasn't paying attention to his markings, Captain, and I can't see them now."

"I think it was," the captain said. "Those guys can't land for shit. If he gets waved off again, tell Boss to send him back to Pearl."

"Aye, aye, sir," George said.

The next plane got aboard. It wasn't pretty, but he made it without scaring anybody, at least not too much. And yes, George noted, it was one of the Marine aviators. He told Billy-B what the captain had said.

"Man's got a hard-on for those jungle bunnies," Billy said. "Don't know why."

Then he squinted at the next Corsair coming in and keyed his microphone again. "Power, power, *power*, Paddles!"

The approaching plane appeared to be making the same mistake as the waved-off fighter. The pilot firewalled his throttle, his hose-nosed beast responded, and then he landed hard enough to burst both his tires, although he did manage to catch a wire. The flight deck crew signaled the pilot to ignore his flattened tires and taxi forward; the next Corsair was already making his approach. George decided he'd had enough excitement for one morning. He had several hundred carrier landings under his belt and watching the new guys was stomach-churning sometimes.

He went into the island to the ladder well and then paused. He knew he really should go up to the bridge but he simply wasn't up to listening to more of the captain's constant carping and criticism. He decided to go down instead, all the way to the hangar deck. He wanted to observe how the hangar crews were handling the steady stream of fighters, torpedo planes, and bombers coming down from the flight deck. Not all of them would end up below; those that did had to be slotted carefully into parking positions with their wings folded. That required a noisy ballet of yellow-gear, as the plane-tugs were called. A plane would arrive at the threshold of the hangar bay, where a tug would hook it up and then pull it off the elevator and into the depths of the hangar bay according to a preassigned plan. The elevator would rise again amid a clamor of warning bells to grab the next customer.

The whole scene was a blur of what looked like motorized chaos: planes, roaring tractor-tugs, gesturing wing-walkers, crawling tie-down crews, all hustling through an atmosphere of yellow-gear exhaust, shouting chief petty officers, a flurry of hand signals interspersed with the crash-bang sound of the next plane touching down up above. Each landing sounded like an actual crash to the uninitiated down on the hangar deck, but George had long ago learned to differentiate the sounds from the flight deck. There were enough new guys doing this that there seemed to be an inordinate amount of shouting, but, as he observed from a gallery platform above the actual hangar deck, it appeared to be coming together. That said, they weren't ready for a visit from the captain. Fortunately, Himself was nailed to the bridge until flight operations ended. God willing.

He spied two very young-looking officers amid all the frenetic activity, clambering over a nest of firefighting piping over on one side of the middle bay. One of them had a clipboard, the other a flashlight. They seemed to be doing a hand-over-hand inspection of some kind. Two ensigns: one loose with a pencil. He grinned when he remembered the old Navy saying: the three most dangerous things in the Navy were a boatswain's mate with a brain, a yeoman with muscle, and an ensign with a pencil. He went on down to check them out. He was about eight feet away when one of them finally spotted him and snapped to attention, nearly hitting his head on an overhead cable bundle. The other one scrambled to straighten up and dropped his clipboard. Definitely ensigns.

"At ease, gents," George said. He had to almost shout to make himself heard over all the racket around them. "What'ya doing?"

Ensign Sauer started to explain but it was hopeless with all the engine noises. George indicated a nearby hatch. They went through into one of the interior passageways where normal speech was possible. Sauer explained their mission. Way to go, Lieutenant McCauley, George thought.

"What are you finding?" he asked. This time it was Ensign Sweet who replied.

"Well, sir," he began. "The fire-main system is *sorta* like the plans."

"Sorta like?"

"Yes, sir. What we were told to do was take one branch and go back to where it starts, say at a main riser up against the side bulkhead of the hangar bay. Then we trace it all the way to the last branch and outlet where a fire hose could be attached."

"Makes sense," George said, nodding. "How much of the system diagram is accurate?"

Sweet looked at Sauer. "Fifty percent?" he said. "More or less. Unless we're doing it wrong."

Good God, George thought. *Fifty* percent? "Do *you* think you're doing it wrong?" he asked.

"Um, no, sir," Sweet said. "Mister McCauley said to trace the piping hand over hand, and then compare it with the drawings and plans. Where it didn't jibe, correct the plans—in pencil."

He wondered if the cheng was aware of this. "Okay, guys," he said. "Good work. Important, no, *vital* work. When things turn to shit, we *have* to know where to find firefighting water. I'd tell you to go faster, but in this case, accuracy trumps speed. Carry on."

They replied with a pair of aye, aye, sir's, and went back to work. George pulled out his little green wheelbook and noted what he'd just heard. Fifty percent? The captain would have a cow. As he went back out into the hangar bay, he had an irreverent thought: if the captain had enough cows, they could have steaks forever. He laughed out loud, then sobered his face. Fifty percent wrong: Jee-*zus*. What about the rest of it—all the new electronics, the second catapult, the main plant upgrades? Had the captain's constant bitching and moaning in the shipyard led to the realization of that old shipyard union rule?

At that moment he heard the thump of another plane landing topside, except it seemed to come from too far back. The thump was followed by a prolonged screech of metal interspersed with the unmistakable sounds of a propeller chewing its way along the wooden flight deck. Then silence. Then the flight deck crash alarm.

George hurried across to the starboard side of the hangar bay and then up a succession of gallery ladders to get to the flight deck. By then Klaxon horns were blaring and he could hear men running and shouting as he neared the hatch leading to the flight deck. He got out there in time to see the tail assembly of a Corsair going vertical and then right over the port side edge of the flight deck. There was no fire, but there were men down on the flight deck, probably victims of wooden splinters from that enormous prop taking 2800 horsepower bites out of the flight deck. The LSO was waving off the next plane in the pattern, so George made a run for it across the flight deck to the port side catwalks. He had to hop over an arresting wire that was coiling its way back to the landing area. He spotted the plane in the carrier's wake as soon as he dropped down into a catwalk. Its nose was underwater and its tail was standing up. There was just enough chop in the sea that he couldn't make out whether the canopy was open, and, of course, the carrier was already leaving the scene at twenty-seven knots. One of the escorting destroyers was closing in on the plane in the water, shooting off a big plume of steam from her stack as she crashed back to full astern in order to stop in time. Then they were just too far away to see what was happening back there.

George knew the carrier wouldn't stop—there were still more planes waiting to get aboard. If they delayed landings, the remaining airborne planes might have to abort due to low fuel and return to port. That would screw up the schedule big-time. If the pilot had gotten out after his crash landing the tin can would have him. If not, well, the show must go on. He decided to get out of the way and head to the bridge. He'd experienced one ditching in his torpedo squadron days. He vividly remembered the rib-crushing belly punch of the sudden stop, his forehead smacking the console as his plane stood on its head, that heavy engine seemingly anxious to play submarine, the mental confusion, the blood in his eyes, and then banging away at his strap release as water filled the cockpit and the ambient light began to turn green.

"Was that another Goddamned Marine?" the captain bellowed at him as soon as he stepped into the pilothouse. His face was redder than usual and the bridge watch team were studiously not looking anywhere near in his direction.

"I'll find out, sir," George said. "Lemme call PriFly."

"Then find out who that LSO is. That guy was too low, *much* too low. *Anybody* could see that. We're Goddamned lucky we didn't have a ramp-strike. Tell Boss to resume flight operations. I haven't got all Goddamned day. And get another LSO out there. *Now,* got it?"

"Aye, aye, Captain," George said, as the captain strode back out onto the port bridgewing.

George called PriFly, identified himself, and asked for the boss. "Yes, sir, XO?" Billy answered, obviously upset.

"Captain says to resume flight ops and get the rest of this gaggle aboard, Billy. Was that a Marine Corsair?"

"Yes, sir, it was. He was too low, firewalled the throttle and the engine hesitated. One second, but that was enough with his sink-rate. We're lucky we didn't get a ramp strike."

"Exactly what the captain said," George said. "And he wants a new Paddles out there. Any word on the pilot?"

"They got him," Boss said. "He's got a broken nose and he's pretty shook up, but they got him back. Nugget, of course."

"Yeah, I assumed that. Okay. Anybody going dry up there?"

"No, sir, not yet. They filled up at Hickam, so they should be good for another hour at least."

"I recommend you extend the interval, Billy," George said. "Pretend we're off P-Cola and that these are *all* nuggets."

"Pretend, XO?"

"Okay, yeah, but get 'em all down in one piece, and then we'll work on speeding up the land-launch cycle. Is the Marine squadron commander aboard yet?"

"Affirmative."

"Get him up to PriFly; put him on a land-launch circuit. Let him coach his shaky-Jakes."

"Understood, XO."

George hung up and went out to the port bridgewing, where the captain was watching the flight deck crew reset the arresting wires and sweep all the bits and pieces of wood off the flight deck. The wind coming across the flight deck was so strong that all they had to do was throw the splinters and pieces into the air and they were overboard in an instant. He looked into the sky and saw about twenty aircraft orbiting lazily outside of the pattern, waiting for the orders to land. That's when he realized that there was indeed no pretending: the air group, just like the ship, was made up of lots and lots of new guys.

Peachy, he thought.

9

J.R. had been down in the Log Room when the Corsair crashed on deck. He was far enough down in the ship that he didn't hear the actual impact, but the sailor manning up the sound-powered phones to PriFly suddenly yelled: "DC Central, aye!" and then turned to J.R. and told him the bad news.

"Is there fire?" was J.R.'s first question. The talker relayed the question to PriFly.

"Negative, sir. Bang down and then over the side. There are casualties on deck."

"Okay," J.R. said, relaxing just a bit. There was actually nothing *he*, as fire marshal, needed to do at this moment. There were crash crews pre-positioned on the flight deck as well as two medical teams. Something like this would have had a destroyer racing to pilot-rescue quarters, but on the carrier, if the crash hadn't sparked a major conflagration, PriFly and the flight deck crews would have it under control pretty quick. The sad truth was that although a crash on deck was definitely an inconvenience and sometimes a precursor to a really big mess, if a plane wiped out *and* went over the side, the major effort then became one of search, rescue, and recovery of the pilot, which was not the carrier's job. Flight ops would resume just as soon as the flight deck was cleared of any debris and the arresting gear declared ready to work again. J.R. knew that the fact that one of their brethren had crashed was certainly of poignant interest to the other guys still up in the pattern, but so were their gas gauges.

His duty now as fire marshal was to inspect the firefighting equipment on the flight deck to see what had been damaged. He grabbed his steel helmet, which had the words FIRE MARSHAL stenciled in red on it, and headed for the flight deck. The general rule aboard an aircraft carrier was that, if you didn't have a specific assignment on the flight deck during actual flight operations, you didn't go out there. His showy helmet would help him avoid questions from the guys who did belong out there. He'd make a quick survey and then report to the cheng. He hoped they'd rescued the pilot but he couldn't let thoughts about the pilot distract him. Death was a constant companion on an aircraft carrier, and one of the first things every man had to learn was how to carry on when a shipmate standing right next to you lost his life.

He prepared to step through a hatch onto the flight deck when it opened in front of him. Two plane handlers were helping a third man, whose face and jersey were spattered with blood from a scalp injury, over the hatch coaming and into the relative quiet of the island.

"Where'd he go over?" J.R. asked.

"Port side, just aft of the deck-edge elevator, sir," one of the men responded, and then they were gone, headed down three decks to sick bay.

J.R. stepped through the hatch and dogged it behind him. The wind across the deck was nearing fifty miles an hour and he had to lean into it to stay upright, just like every man out there. He made his way through the densely parked planes waiting for their elevator rides, going hand over hand along wing edges and under the propellers with their hold-down straps attached. The rule was a strapped prop *shouldn't* suddenly spin into motion, so it *should* be safe to walk under it. Wisdom dictated a quick look up into the cockpit before doing that. He glanced up at the signal halyards bowing aft from the ship's mast, where he saw the Fox flag fluttering furiously at the dip. That meant that flight ops were suspended for the moment so there shouldn't be anyone landing, although he could hear multiple engines out there in the landing pattern above the rushing wind.

Once across the flight deck he headed aft along the deck-edge catwalks, with their AA guns securely wrapped in gray canvas shrouds. The deck-edge elevator had been in use when the crash occurred, so there were steel stanchions linked by safety chains around the notch in the flight deck to keep people from walking off the edge. With the elevator down, he had to walk around the notch, and that's when he saw the brutal gouges in the wooden flight deck where the plane's propeller had clawed its way over the side. He spied some medics down in an adjacent catwalk, tending to more bleeding crewmen, victims of the murderous splinters that prop had torn out of the deck and flung everywhere right about face level. There was a piece of horizontal stabilizer jammed into a catwalk where the plane had pitched over and down into the sea. A 20 mm gun mount was dangling by its cables from the deck edge. Fortunately, none of the ship's guns had been manned, not when they were this close to Pearl.

He saw a fire-main riser that had been torn out of its mounting, its twin bronze receptacles gleaming in the sunshine. Then he saw something else: down at the bottom of the catwalk, where the structure made a ninety-degree turn back into the edge of the flight deck, there was a bundle of red rags. He blinked, his brain trying to determine what it was looking at. Then he knew: one of the flight deck crewmen, a yellow shirt, except that now it was a blood red shirt, crumpled into the corner of the catwalk. He looked around to see who was nearby, but everyone he saw was busy. He dropped down into the catwalk and approached the body, for that was what it surely was. His gorge rose as he beheld the tattered remains, cut to pieces by that smashing propeller. Lungs, intestines, ribs, bright white bones, all coiled in a heap. He leaned over the catwalk and vomited at the sight. He hung over the side for a long moment, breathing but trying not to. Then he stood up. He'd come aboard in Bremerton right after the kamikaze attack; he'd never seen a dead body before, and that was not what he'd expected one would look like.

He steadied himself and then went back along the catwalk to where the medics were treating one of the injured. He stood there for a moment, not knowing what to say. When one of the docs, a chief petty officer, looked up, he inclined his head in the direction of the dead man. The doc gave him a puzzled look and then understood. J.R.'s pasty face and thoroughly shocked expression had given him a pretty good clue.

"Okay," the medic said. "He dead?"

J.R., who couldn't trust his voice yet, just gulped and nodded.

"Right," the medic said. "But *this* guy isn't and he needs to get below. We'll take care of it, Lieutenant." He paused for a second. "First one?" he asked.

J.R. nodded again. For some reason, he thought he was about to cry.

"Wish I could tell you that you'll get used to it," the medic said. "But the truth is, you don't. And we ain't even in WestPac yet."

10

Gary Peck had been so far down in the main engineering spaces that he was unaware of the crash until the alarm came over the ship's general announcing system, called the 1MC. He was sitting in Main Control, otherwise known as number one engine room. Everyone stopped what they were doing, waiting to see if the ship was going to go to general quarters. When that didn't happen, he resumed his inspection of the water king's boiler water report. It wasn't that he wasn't concerned for the pilot or the people on the flight deck. He was, but there were several hundred men poised to take care of that situation during flight ops and there was literally nothing he could contribute. The water king was a senior chief boilertender named Harold McKenzie, whose sole job was to monitor the feedwater circulating in the ship's eight boilers. He had twenty-five years in service and probably knew more about the ship's 600-psi boilers and main steam systems than anyone aboard except the chief engineer.

Water was the key ingredient to any marine steam plant. The boilers turned it into main steam, which was then piped to huge steam turbines, which were themselves directly connected to the ship's reduction gears and through them to the ship's propellers. This wasn't tea-kettle steam. This was a superheated vapor under 600 psi of pressure and heated to 850 degrees Fahrenheit. Pressurizing it and superheating it made it possible for the steam to transport enormous amounts of energy, which the turbines converted to a mechanical force capable of making the ship's twenty-two-foot-diameter propellers turn at 300 RPM. It was imperative that the boiler's steam-generating banks, made of high-quality steel tubing, were fed only the purest water possible. This meant that there could be no contaminants, such as dissolved oxygen or, even worse, salts of any kind. A boiler operating at ambient temperature and pressure could withstand contamination. A boiler operating at 600 psi and an 850-degree temperature could not. A minute amount of dissolved oxygen would immediately begin to create pits in the metal surfaces. A pit could lead to a hole, and a hole could lead to a boiler explosion. Salts could accumulate on the metal of the tubing and create scale, under which an invisible chemical reaction would begin, again leading to a hole and the failure of a boiler tube. Since all the ship's water was distilled directly from seawater, salt intrusion was a constant threat.

"Looks good, Chief," Gary said after studying the reports. "Where do we stand on reserve feed?"

"Sixty percent, Mister Peck," the chief replied. "Fresh is at seventy. Evaps are working really well."

"Great," Gary said. "We'll have to see how well they hold up out in WestPac. Ask Chief Dyer to come around. I need to see the refueling plan for when we get back in."

Chief Dyer was the oil king, the counterpart to Chief McKenzie, only for fuel oil—and aviation gasoline. *Franklin* carried 6,300 *tons* of Navy Special Fuel Oil, allowing her to steam for 17,500 miles. She also carried 230,000 gallons of super high-octane gasoline for the airplane engines. Dyer had three jobs: keeping track of both the fuel and gasoline inventories, ensuring there was no water in any of the fuels, and pumping the stored inventory to various tanks throughout the ship to keep her level at all times as fuel was expended. Dyer's kingdom included all the fuel tanks, the underway replenishment gear by which *Franklin* could be refueled or refuel other ships at sea, the fuel and lubricant labs, and the master flood and counterflood station, by which he could deliberately alter the trim of the ship.

Today Dyer had a problem: the diagrams for the CO_2 fire-suppression systems didn't seem to match the actual installations. There were aviation fueling stations on both sides of the hangar deck and the flight deck. These were connected to central pumping stations down below in the auxiliary machinery rooms. If an enemy attack was expected, the topside fueling lines were drained down into the deep tanks and the lines themselves were then filled with CO_2 gas. Dyer said that the gas lines weren't matching up with the pumping station risers. Gary decided to call J.R., keeper of the damage control diagrams.

"You're not all alone with that problem," J.R. told him. "Looks like Hogan's goat drew up my DC diagrams."

"Crap," Gary said. "I guess I better tell the cheng."

J.R. told him what he'd set in motion to get his diagrams straightened out. "They're ensigns, but they're getting good at it. My new problem is that I'm gonna have to realign all the controls in that conflagration station, now that I know how all dem bones are connected."

"I don't wanna hear that," Gary said. "Where the hell am *I* gonna find ensigns?"

"When in doubt, ask your chief," J.R. said. "*He's* the Oil King. Gotta go—Cheng's called a meeting on the flight deck damage."

"That guy get out?"

"He did. One of the tin cans has him. We probably won't get him back until after we go back in to Pearl. I hear we're headed west pretty soon."

"'Bout time," Gary said. "All this training. I'm ready to go fight some Japs."

"Careful what you wish for, shipmate," J.R. said. "I hear those bastards fight back. Hard."

George knocked on the captain's stateroom door and then went through. The captain was sitting in an upholstered chair in a voluminous white terry-cloth bathrobe, which made him look even bigger than he was. George banished the thought of Moby Dick in a bathrobe. The captain was reading a thick sheaf of naval messages encased in a steel clipboard. He'd obviously just had a shower, and a long, hot one at that, considering the pink color of his face.

"What'cha got, XO?" he asked, not actually looking up.

"I understand from the ops boss that you don't want to go back into Pearl," George said. "That you want to depart for WestPac directly from the op-areas?"

"That's right," the captain said. "We have plenty of fuel, most of the air group on board, and stores enough to get to Guam. I've asked for a tanker to come out of Midway so we can top off. Last thing we need now is shore leave in Honolulu."

"You're worried about the crew losing their edge?"

"What edge?" The captain snorted. "They're barely qualified as it is. Besides, all those shore-duty headquarters pukes will want to fiddle and fine-tune until for Goddamned ever. At this rate we'll miss the end of the war. I want to go *now*. The WestPac Service Force is awash in parts, people, fuel, and ammo. This way we don't break up the training with a boozy weekend in Honolulu."

George couldn't really argue with that. There was, of course, the matter of all those replacement personnel, spare engines, fresh food, four more Corsairs, the latest aviation charts, etc., all waiting on the pier for the *Franklin* to come back in after her shakedown period. On the other hand, the captain was right about a three-day weekend in Hawaii, although he didn't dare mention his own real concern: that even more unhappy crewmen would jump ship. Morale wasn't exactly wonderful just now. It wasn't that the crew hated being on the ship. All they had to do was watch one of their escort destroyers crashing, pitching, and rolling through rough seas to appreciate their relatively comfortable circumstances. Nor was it a case of the crew despising or disliking the captain. There were probably no more than two dozen people who came in personal contact with the captain out of the 3,600 people on board.

George thought it was the pace of operations since leaving the yard. A carrier never slept. If the ship wasn't operating airplanes, then it was operating *on* airplanes, which required constant maintenance just to keep them flying, much less fighting. Then there were the endless hours of training and drilling. You couldn't just put the high school class of last year out on the flight deck and expect them to keep their heads, literally; George figured more than half the crew—officers, chiefs, and enlisted—were new to *Franklin* and equally new to carrier aviation. The people who did know their way around carrier ops had to train the newbies and thus did double duty. People were tired, really tired, and now the captain wanted to head west without even a weekend off. George had no illusions about the tempo of operations en route. It would get worse.

"Do you want me to make an announcement, then?" George asked.

"No," the captain said. "The four replacement planes are flying out later this afternoon. Once they're aboard we're gonna turn into the sunset and chase it. People will figure it out soon enough. I don't believe in babying the crew, XO: they go where I tell them to and do what I demand of them when we get there. I want Admiral Nimitz to know that we're not only ready to go back to war, but that we are *eager* to go back to war.

The Navy didn't man this thing to have people sitting around, polishing brass and passing inspections. Victory over the Goddamned Japs is in sight and I, for one, don't plan to miss out on that. I didn't take a step back in rank to sit out here in pineapple land looking at Diamond Head, got it?"

"Yes, sir," George said with a sinking feeling, thinking about all those loose ends flapping in the wind which he'd hoped to get some help with back at the Pearl Harbor shipyard. Like the problem of figuring out the actual configuration of the firefighting piping, or the CO_2 system diagrams and controls. He hadn't yet briefed the captain on these problems because he wanted to have a solution fully in view before he raised the problem.

"Anything else?" the captain asked.

"No, sir," George said. "Engineering is chasing down some documentation problems in the damage control systems, but—"

"But, what?" the captain said. "You mean like the conflagration station controls don't match the actual piping configuration?"

George's surprise must have shown because the captain barked an unpleasant laugh. "Yeah, I know all about that. I know all about the other problems, too. I also know you've got people working on it. I get around, XO, because nothing beats personal reconnaissance. I talk to people, I ask questions. Then I wait. I figure you'll tell me when you've got both the problem identified *and* a fix in hand. I understand that. But don't ever try to hide anything, XO. Got it?"

"Absolutely, Captain, and I certainly wasn't trying—"

"Yeah, yeah, I know. I was an XO, too—don't forget that. You're doing fine. Now, I've got messages to read. I'll speak to the crew in the morning once we're safely on our way."

George got back to his office, wondering if his cheeks were still red. He should have known. Of *course* he should have known, if only because of some complaints he'd heard. The captain was accompanied by two Marines—one in front and one behind—whenever he left his cabin, even if he was only going up to the bridge. There'd been a lot of grumbling about how those Marines acted whenever the captain approached a doorway or hatch. The leading Marine would bellow "Gangway!" in a tone of voice that made it clear that it was not a request. Anyone about to step through the doorway had to leap back out of the way so that the captain and his guards could stride right through.

The captain had overheard a couple of the Marines wondering if they should maybe tone it down a little. He had summoned the Marine detachment commander and told him not to change a thing. "You can see that I'm a big bruiser," he'd said. "I don't want to bowl someone over and hurt 'em just because I'm in a hurry. And I'm always in a hurry." His orders had been somehow widely circulated, adding to the crew's growing awareness of their imperious new skipper's abrasive personality.

The ship's doctor, Commander Sam Levine, Medical Corps, USN, was waiting in George's office with a report on the pilot who'd gone into the drink. He'd survived the ditching with the usual cuts and bruises, but then had had a bunch of skin flayed off his back when a wave dragged him along the destroyer's barnacled-covered side while the deck crew were trying to hoist him aboard. He'd have to go back to the hospital at Pearl for some skin grafts. George indicated that the doc should join him in his stateroom, which was next door to the main ship's office, and then closed the door.

"We're not going back into Pearl, Sammy," he said, once they had some privacy. "We're going to head west tonight. Right from the op-areas. The captain will inform the ship's company tomorrow morning, once we've put some miles between us and Pearl. Next stop will be an at-sea refueling near Midway, and then we're on to Guam."

Sammy swore. "I was depending on going back in one last time. There's a whole bunch of medical supplies waiting at the Supply Center. Two new docs, up-to-date meds, and some of this new penicillin stuff. Plus, I've got some people in sick bay who need to see a specialist or two."

"I know, Sammy. I've got about thirty crew replacements waiting on the dock. The departments have all sorts of stuff waiting for them, too. But the captain is adamant: We're headed west tonight. Guam will be the next port where we can onload anything of consequence. The WestPac Service Force is just gonna have to stage everything and everybody all the way across the pond."

Sammy stared at the deck for a moment, shaking his head. "I've got a bad feeling about this trip, XO," he said. "This guy, he's—"

George raised his hand. "That's enough, Sammy," he said. "He's the captain, remember? Look at it this way: he may know something that the rest of us don't, including me. The big bosses ashore wouldn't allow him to do this unless there was an overarching need. So: regroup. I'll see what we can manage at Midway when the tanker comes out to refuel us. But if I were you, I'd plan to see your people and stuff in Guam. Or maybe even never."

"What the hell does that mean, George?" Sammy asked.

George had surprised himself, saying that. "I'm not quite sure I know, Sammy. There's so many things happening as America and its allies close in on Japan itself, that the sheer scale of it all is driving the forces, not the other way around. Anyway, turn to and commence ship's work."

"Aye, aye, sir," Sammy said, but as he left, George saw an obviously worried man. He decided to summon the chief engineer, let him in on the big secret, and ask him where they were with the firefighting systems' schematics problem.

12

The next morning, right after morning quarters, the bosun's call sent its ear-piercing all-hands whistle throughout the ship from the 1MC station on the bridge. Everyone aboard paused what they were doing to listen up.

"This is the captain speaking." That announcement provoked some interesting pantomimes in various spaces throughout the ship, all of them well away from the prying eyes of officers.

"As some of you may have noticed, we are headed northwest, which is why the sun came up astern this morning. We're on a course for the vicinity of Midway Island, where we will rendezvous with a fleet tanker before continuing on to Guam. We'll refuel again at Guam, embark a flag officer and his staff, and then join Task Force 58. Soon after that we'll commence strike operations against the Japanese home islands."

There was a brief moment of surprised silence.

"I don't need to tell you that the Japs are becoming desperate. After three-plus years of total warfare, we've pushed them back into their home defenses. They are facing the certain knowledge that their destruction is imminent. The kamikaze is one of the few weapons left to them that actually works as a ship-killer. I am confident that our next encounter with the kamikazes will turn out better than our last, but to that end we will continue to conduct training operations en route at the same pace we've been maintaining during shakedown.

"These constant drills, general quarters at all hours of the day and night, and hands-on training are aimed at doing things again and again until they become second nature. It's hard. I know it's hard. But that is the only way we can prepare for what's coming as the Japs realize their treacherous yellow backs are up against the wall. Understand something: their whole damned nation is one big death cult. They believe that the *best* thing that can happen to them in life is to die in battle for their so-called god-emperor. You and I should agree with that: *we* think the best thing that can happen to the Japanese is for them *all* to die, in battle or otherwise. The problem is, when a warrior has nothing to lose, you can no longer negotiate with him, deter him, or scare him away. A pilot with a death wish is going to keep coming at you unless you literally blast him from the sky.

"That requires a team effort: our attack planes strike their air bases and destroy as many of their aircraft on the ground as possible. But when their remaining planes come, and they *will* come, it'll be the long-distance combat air patrols who'll get the first crack at 'em. Then the close-in CAPs. Then our escorting cruisers, destroyers, and even the battleships. But since only one of the bastards getting through all that can destroy this ship, *you* become the last but most important line of defense. Therefore, *you* must be the most intense, vicious, furious line of defense, despite all the previous help from our many defenders. So: We're going to practice that. A lot. We'll practice that to the point where you will *hate* it, but at the same time, you'll be able to do it practically in your sleep.

"Last thing: We are now committed to all-out war at sea. Not dedicated, but committed. Do you know the difference? A chicken is *dedicated* to the production of eggs. A pig is *committed* to the production of bacon. Stand by to stand by. That is all."

George listened to the captain's little speech, increasingly in awe. Hate him or love him, there was no arguing with anything he'd said. He decided at that moment to rebuke even more sharply anyone bitching about the captain and his unforgiving ways. Japan *was* a cornered animal now. The memory of the kamikaze strike last October was still fresh in his mind, but over half the crew literally had zero appreciation of what might be coming. He realized that for some months, he had been acting somewhat as a buffer between the unpleasant new commanding officer and the ship's company George knew and respected. But now, as they finally headed west into what Navy messages blandly described as "the war zone," it was probably time to take an even strain, hew to the company line, and stop worrying about hurt feelings or bruised morale. A bruised ego was preferable to a dead sailor.

13

"XO, is it true that Admiral Nimitz himself is up on that hill?" one of the bridge lookouts asked as the ship closed in on Apra Harbor. Several tugs were waiting inside the breakwater to take her to the bulkhead pier. The young seaman was pointing to a small cluster of white buildings on a hill overlooking the harbor.

"That's the word," George said. "Moved here last month from Pearl for the final act."

"What *is* the final act, XO?"

"Ultimately, the invasion of Japan," George said. "But first we have to beat on 'em some more, you know, kinda like tenderize 'em before we send in the Marines and the Army."

"Are we close to Japan here in Guam?"

"Around fifteen hundred miles," George said, scanning the rising headlands behind the harbor through his binoculars. The Japs had held Guam and the rest of the Marianas since early in the war. Judging by those hills, taking it back must have been a tough fight. The green hills around the headlands were covered in splotches of blackened and cratered rock. "That's three days or so sailing from here," George continued.

"But we're gonna be a whole lot closer in about a week. Like about *one* hundred miles."

"Wow," the lookout said. Then he saw that the captain was headed for the bridgewing and quickly raised his own binoculars.

"XO," the captain said. He had dark circles under his eyes and was flat burning down a cigarette. "I'm going ashore for a briefing at PacFleet headquarters once we tie up. I want you and the air boss to come with me."

"Aye, aye, sir. I'll let Billy know."

A pilot boat eased alongside the carrier's starboard side. The harbor pilot climbed up a long chain ladder to the after sponson deck and began the long ascent to the bridge. Fifteen minutes later there was a sudden chorus of tugboat horns from under the edges of the flight deck as the pilot began directing the tugs to their assigned tie-up positions. They'd make up and then be dragged along by the carrier until they were abeam of her assigned berth, after which they would begin the final sideways push to bring Big Ben alongside the pier. *Franklin's* four escort destroyers glided by to port in a neat column, headed to moorings farther up in the harbor.

The captain wasn't the only one with circles under his eyes. George was seriously tired from the round-the-clock GQs, flight deck drills, fire drills, and gunnery exercises. The captain had driven everybody hard, including himself. He'd told them they were going to hate it. George told the captain this morning that he'd succeeded in that. They did indeed hate it—the constant drilling, the captain, the officers, the Japs, the war, and even the weather. Right where I want 'em, the captain had responded proudly.

George didn't think that hate was the best basis for honing the operational tenor of a ship, but he knew he'd have to wait for his own carrier command to try out any other theories. He'd often wondered if the captain's sometimes savage attitude toward his officers and crew was the result of how he'd been treated as a junior officer. He'd longed to talk about that with the department heads, but as the second-in-command, he not only had to toe the captain's line but do it enthusiastically, at least outwardly, tolerating no criticism from his subordinates. They could think what they wanted to, but they'd better keep their opinions to themselves.

Far to the south a typhoon was making its way just north of Luzon in the Philippines. It posed no threat to Task Force 58, but it had generated a thousand-mile-long train of deep, muscular swells that had set the carrier to rolling more than usual as they closed in on Guam, leading to widespread seasickness on top of all the drills. George was very much looking forward to forty-eight hours of level decks, and, hopefully, some much needed sleep. There would be no liberty here in Guam, which George thought was just as well. Most of the crew would prefer sleep right now to standing in long lines at a beer canteen, pretending to have a good time.

A police whistle sounded over the 1MC, announcing that the ship was officially moored. George sighed. Now all he had to do was oversee the onloading of fuel, aviation gasoline, an entire pier full of crates, replacement engines, another four Corsairs still in their crates, about a hundred replacement personnel, tons of food, medical supplies, bombs, rockets, torpedoes, and gun ammunition, and, hopefully, mail. Maybe a nap sometime this afternoon, he thought. Then he remembered he needed to go roust out a clean and pressed set of khakis for that meeting at the fleet headquarters.

"XO, sir, urgent phone call from the supply officer."

He sighed again. And so it begins, he thought.

The headquarters "briefing" turned out to be a sit-down in one of the rooms of the newly built fleet command center up on top of what was being called Nimitz Hill. Two lieutenant commanders, one an aviator, the other a naval intelligence specialist, did a tabletop presentation on the strategic and tactical situation farther west. A surprising amount of time was taken up with explaining the fleet logistical system that was spooling up in preparation for the eventual invasion of Japan, thought to be planned for early 1946. The word vast almost didn't cover it, George thought, as the briefers spoke in amazing numbers: *dozens* of aircraft carriers and their escorts, thousands of aircraft, along with the hundreds of ships comprising the fleet's logistical tail: oil tankers, cargo ships, amphibious ships, troop transports, ammunition ships, and hospital ships that were being marshaled in places like the Ulithi Atoll or right here in Guam. Even more ships were coming in from the States to begin building up the vast supply depots for the invasion.

"But before any invasion," the senior briefer said, "we need to attrite the homeland defenses through a combined Navy–Army Air Forces bombing campaign. That will require taking two more islands to provide closer bases and emergency landing fields for the B-29s. Okinawa—here—and then Iwo Jima—here. The Japs consider both of these to be 'home' islands, so we're expecting an exceptionally tough fight for each of them. All of those Japs who survived our drive up the south and central Pacific and who actually made it home are waiting for us."

"What's *Franklin*'s specific role in all this?" the captain asked.

"*Franklin* will join Task Force 58 three days after you leave here, with Rear Admiral Davison embarked. He will command a two-carrier division, Task Group 58.1, consisting of *Franklin* and *Hancock*. That will give your air group and the flag staff operations folks three days' time to consolidate air plans and flight ops schedules. There will be seven big-decks and ten light carriers in operation for the pre-Okinawa phase. The Navy's mission will be to attrite airfields and aircraft on the ground. The Army's B-29s will be hitting cities and Japan's industrial capacity. Our subs have just about snuffed out all but intracoastal seaborne commerce around the home islands, so, hopefully, their ability to replace lost planes, airfields, factories, refineries, and repair facilities will be severely reduced. Just about all of the industrial materials they need to wage war have to come in by sea, and not much is getting through these days."

"*Seven* big-decks," Billy observed. "That's gonna require some really complex air traffic control."

"Yes, indeed," the briefer said. "That means the task force will have to balance the need for concentrated defensive formations with the need to avoid mid-air collisions as multi-carrier strikes go out and then return, day and night. We've had the PacFleet wargaming team working out ways to stagger the launches while keeping the ships tight for overlapping anti-air defense. You're going to see some ships, mostly cruisers, that have been designated solely as radar advisory control stations, with AA defense a secondary mission. You'll be able to pick 'em out—they'll have as many as four radar antennas."

George found that amazing, too. The last time he'd been a part of a carrier strike formation, air traffic control had been mostly a matter of keeping one eye on your instruments and the other out the canopy, with the gunner, if you had one, acting primarily as a lookout until the fun started. Now they would have entire ships dedicated to preventing air traffic problems, friendly-on-friendly engagements, and Jap planes slipping into returning formations. That last function was called delousing.

The two briefers took one more hour, and then they broke for lunch. The captain was invited to the flag mess for lunch with Admiral Nimitz's deputy, Vice Admiral Towers, and other senior staff officers; George and Billy-B sat down for a beer and a sandwich at the outdoor, all-hands canteen located next to the headquarters building.

"*Seven* big-decks," Billy mused. "Long way from '42 in the Solomons, isn't it. We had, what, one, maybe two carriers left after Coral Sea? Now look at us."

George nodded. "Our air group is gonna have to get a whole lot better at landings and takeoffs for—what'd that guy call it? Cyclic ops?" he said.

"Yeah," Billy said. "I gotta bone up on that one. Sounds like they'll have four carriers on the line doing strikes while three take a day off to recover, rest, and fix stuff. Did you see that one chart? We're gonna be operating only *ninety* miles off Japan itself? That sounds like a kamikaze field day in the making."

"I think that's the point of the round-the-clock strikes," George said. "Keep tearing up their air bases and their planes until the suiciders have nothing left to fly. That one intel report said they only had a couple thousand planes left, anyway. The B-29s are hitting their factories day and night, and it's not like they can disperse a whole airplane factory. By the way, scuttlebutt says the war in Europe is almost over, too."

Billy finished his beer and then sat back, looking out over the blue Pacific Ocean. "We've been at war since December 1941," he said. "Now here we are, three-plus years later, knocking on the emperor's door with the biggest fleet the world's ever seen. Why in the hell can't these fuckers just give up?"

"Because Japs *never* give up," George said. "They've got a population of, what, sixty, seventy million? If it comes to it, they'll give every man, woman, and child in those islands a rifle, or a sword, or a damned stick and tell them to dig in and die for the emperor. And those bastards'll do it, too. I heard it's gonna take a *million* troops to finish this thing. Carnage on that scale doesn't bear thinking about."

Billy looked at his empty beer glass. George looked at his, but they both recognized that if they had another, they'd get tipsy after all those dry weeks at sea. Then they saw the captain coming out of the headquarters building, carrying two briefcases.

"Ten-hut," Billy muttered, disrespectfully.

"Onward and upward, shipmate," George reminded him as they got up to head for the waiting staff car.

Back at the pier the ship looked like an anthill that had been kicked over, with long lines of men moving all manner of supplies on board, using two brows, the ship's aviation crane, and three conveyor belts to the hangar bay. It was warm enough, even in late February, that most men had stripped down to dungarees and T-shirts.

George met with the department heads to get an update. The ship had completed refueling. Aviation gasoline would come from a barge that night, when it would be cooler and thus safer. The other department heads had similar reports, all of which indicated that things were going pretty much as they should. One bit of news was well received: the ship would be delayed for two more days beyond their scheduled sailing date while awaiting the arrival of Rear Admiral Davison and his staff. Sleep, George thought. Maybe, maybe. Then the captain called; he'd made a quick inspection of the flag cabin and wanted it repainted immediately. It hadn't been used since the kamikaze strike back in October, and it was absolutely *not* ready.

Well, hell, George thought after he hung up the buzzer phone. Repaint the admiral's cabin. Nothing else to do.

14

One day out from the big join-up with Task Force 58, Gary and the rest of the engineering department officers and chiefs assembled in one corner of the forward officers' wardroom for a meeting with the chief engineer. There was a definite stir of anticipation in the air, especially after three light cruisers had appeared this morning to beef up *Franklin*'s AA escorts. Word was out that they'd begin launching strikes the day after tomorrow, and, for the first time, serious American naval air would be hitting mainland Japan.

"Okay, everybody, listen up," Lieutenant Commander Forrest announced. The chatter around the table subsided. Everyone realized this must be important because the cheng was not known for holding many all-officers-and-chiefs meetings. Gary sat next to his buddy, J.R. McCauley. The two had become friends after joining forces to figure out some of the schematic discrepancies. They were both surface ship officers in an aviator's world, so there was a natural bond.

"Tomorrow we'll join Task Force 58, Admiral Raymond Spruance commanding," Forrest began. "We'll be part of a two-carrier division, designated Task Group 58.1, one of three big-deck CarDiv's. The admiral who embarked in Guam will command our division. His name is Rear

Admiral Ralph E. Davison; his chief of staff is Captain James E. Russell. As snipes, I suspect none of us will ever lay eyes on either one of them. Unless of course they need their rooms painted."

Everyone laughed. The story about the "emergency" paint job had certainly made the rounds.

"Once we're on station we'll be in range of Jap air again. Those of you who were with us in the Philippines last fall know what that means. To the new guys: welcome to the Big Time."

He paused for a few seconds, as if gathering his thoughts. "Word is that the Japs are licked," he said. "In a strategic sense, that's probably true— they can't 'win' this thing. Task Force 58 stretches across fifty miles when it's assembled in a transit formation. The problem is, somebody forgot to tell the Japs, and that's a problem because the Japs who're left are the survivors—the battle-hardened survivors of all those island campaigns from the last three years—who figure they've got nothing to lose in terms of doing crazy stuff. The craziest tactic of them all is the kamikaze, and the *only* thing they exist for is to hit our carriers."

"This probably isn't news, I know, but I want you to consider this: in terms of what we snipes do every day and night, which is mainly keeping our machinery turning and burning, it won't be any different from what we've routinely been doing since we joined the Big Blue Fleet. The Heroes topside, well, they're looking at the real McCoy now—actual dogfighting, high-level bombing runs, and strafing runs in the face of real AA fire. Up to now their major challenge has been landing and taking off without crashing. All those dramatics will fade into the background noise compared to actual combat. My point is, we snipes won't see much of anything different down in the main holes. The pilots, the flight deck guys, and especially our air-defense gunnery folks absolutely will.

"Unless: one of those lunatic Japs gets through the screen and crashes aboard or drills a coupl'a bombs or torpedoes into us. The old hands can tell you all about what happens next. If that does happen, we snipes acquire a second mission besides keeping the steam coming: damage control, and especially firefighting. *Major* firefighting. So: I want all the khaki in this department to spend every minute of training time on damage control procedures and, principally, firefighting. The khaki needs to *know* where the DC gear is in your general quarters space *and* the spaces next to you. You need to *know* how to put on, light off, and do stuff while wearing an OBA. Where the extra cannisters are stored, and how to change one out *during* a fire. And then you need to make sure every man jack in your division knows as much as you do.

"You need to *know* how to rig casualty power cables between the main holes. You need to *know* how to line up and bring an eductor on the line if we're flooding. How to start up a P-500 or a P-250 gasoline-driven fire pump. How to get gasoline to that pump—through a fire. How to do immediate-action first aid. How to rig a sound-powered phone circuit between watertight compartments. You get the idea.

"For you main-hole snipes: you need to make sure every man in your space knows how to light off a boiler, in the dark, surrounded by steam leaks, smoke, oily water up to your knees, electrical arcs, and horribly burned shipmates. For you auxiliary guys: you need to think about and talk about how to rig work-arounds in cabling, potable water, compressed air, sewage, and low-voltage electrical service systems."

He took a deep breath and then let it out. "Look: the point I'm trying to make is that you can't afford to be a specialist when it comes to save-the-ship-scale damage control. I don't expect a machinist mate to *know* how to parallel a ship's service turbo-generator with the ship's load, but I want every machinist mate to be shown how to do it at least once so, if nothing else, he can help an injured electrician's mate do it. Stuff like that. Make time for doing that—it's called cross-rate training. Do it while we're waiting for the Heroes to get back from kicking ass over Japan.

"For the officers: Look around your GQ station and figure out what you don't know how to do with whatever machinery or equipment is in that space, and then get yourselves trained up. If all the people assigned to that GQ station are down or out of action, you may be the only one left to save the day." He paused. "Even if you're an ensign."

He paused again to let the chuckles subside and then smiled. "Sorry if it seems like I came up here to scare you. Truth is, war at sea is real hell, because, unlike the Army or the Marines, we can't retreat to safer ground. Either you sink the other guy or he sinks you and then you swim with the sharks. That's just the nature of our business."

He looked around at the faces of the fifty officers and chief petty officers staring back at him with expressions that ranged from bleak resigna-
tion from the chiefs to wide-eyed alarm from the junior officers.

"That's right, friends and neighbors, the bogeyman is inbound. On the
plus side, consider yourselves lucky to be snipes: we live and work *under*
the armor belt, which is the hangar deck. Everybody else lives and works
on or under that layer of Douglas fir they call the flight deck. They get to
be outside in the fresh air, and see sunup and sundown on a regular basis.
They also get a chance to go face-to-face with a Jap suicide plane coming
at them at four hundred miles an hour and sporting a big-*ass* bomb."

He paused again. He even closed his eyes. Gary wondered if he was
recalling the horror of the kamikaze attack last October. The burning
airplane, dropping bits and pieces of wings and fuselage as it descended
through a veritable curtain of anti-aircraft fire to crash on board at 400
miles per hour. He, himself, hadn't seen it, but one of the cameramen up
on vultures' row had filmed it right up until the resulting fireball burned
him to a crisp. The camera had survived; everyone who eventually saw
the film wished it hadn't.

Forrest looked up and took a deep breath. "Okay," he said. "That's enough,
I think. Chins up. Pay close attention to what you're doing and what's going
on around you. And otherwise, turn to and resume ship's work."

Gary and J.R. scored some somewhat sludgy coffee from the wardroom pantry afterward and then started up to the hangar deck. They'd
felt the ship coming up to full power while the cheng had been talking,
so flight ops were probably in the offing. J.R. had told Gary all about the
conflagration station in the hangar bay and Gary wanted to see it. His
appreciation for firefighting usually involved a fuel leak at a boiler-front.
He couldn't imagine what it would be like to fight a big fire within the
confines of the hangar.

They stepped out into the forwardmost bay and then jumped back
into the hatch. The hangar was full of airplanes in motion, with their
attendant yellow-gear tractors roaring here and there in what seemed
like a demolition derby. They appreciated that what they were seeing was
actually a carefully choreographed operation aimed at getting each individual plane to an elevator and thence to the flight deck just in time to

be pushed into its "spot" position for the upcoming launch. Some of the planes were already fully fueled and armed. Their wings literally sagged under the weight of bombs and rockets. There was an enlisted plane captain in each cockpit and a wing-walker guarding either wingtip. No engines were turning, because propellers spinning in that pulsing traffic jam would have had fatal consequences.

The hangar's announcing system was also going full blast, inviting individual aircraft by their side numbers to one of the three elevators, where the yellow-gear would push or pull the plane onto a steel square suspended from sixteen large cables. Four-foot-high steel stanchions threaded with cables to make a temporary fence would then be inserted into the elevator's deck, and then the elevator would rise the fifty feet to the actual flight deck, admitting an all-too-short blast of fresh air into the hangar. The plane would be moved off, and then the elevator would descend to a chorus of Klaxon warning horns, ready to pick up the next warbird.

Gary looked at J.R. There was no way they could cross the actual hangar deck to get to the other side where the conflagration station was, so they gave up. They headed aft to a ladder well under the island, which could take them up through the island to vultures' row. This was going to be the first actual carrier strike against the Japanese homeland, and while the thought of bombing Japan, proper, was somehow savagely satisfying, few had any illusions about what would happen next.

They made their way up to vultures' row in time to watch the first of the Corsairs lumber down the flight deck to the bow, where it appeared to drop off the front of the ship. The loaded planes would literally sink out of sight for a few seconds before reappearing, those enormous props carving visible condensation circles in the cold, wet air, and then slowly gain altitude until they were a half mile out in front of the carrier. Then they would bank carefully to the right to clear the pattern and head for their join-up position with the rest of their squadron. Gary was amazed they could even fly with all that ordnance hanging off their wings.

Three more got off in good order, but the fifth plane to launch suddenly was enveloped in a cone of yellow-white spray emanating from that elongated engine as its engine oil blew out from a ruptured shaft seal. They stared in horror as the plane's propeller shuddered to a stop; nose-heavy, especially with ordnance, the Corsair flipped its tail up and disappeared out of sight under the forward edge of the flight deck. The crash alarms blared out on the flight deck as men ran to both sides of the ship to see where the plane was. The carrier, ploughing through the sea at thirty knots, didn't have time to maneuver to avoid the ditched bird. Flight deck crewmen on both sides were throwing up their hands, unable to catch a glimpse of the plane. Gary knew what that meant: the carrier had run right over the top of it and was about to chew it to bits with those four enormous screws turning at full power. A destroyer darted out of its escort station and headed toward the carrier's broad wake, its two stacks pumping smoke and then a cloud of steam as she backed down hard in an effort to stop right in the carrier's track.

Gary and J.R. just stood there, utterly shocked at what had happened. *Franklin* had lost planes before, but this was the first time either of them, being snipes, had actually witnessed it. Even more shocking was the fact that the next plane in line for launch revved up to full power and then trundled down the deck as if nothing had happened. The plane after that quickly took position at the front of the line and began spooling up its engine to full power.

"God*damn!*" J.R. exclaimed, with a sick expression on his face. Behind the carrier the destroyer's mast was still stopped in *Franklin*'s wake, but the carrier was going so fast that it was now impossible to see what was going on back there. Gary decided he'd had enough of watching flight ops and headed for the hatch. J.R was right behind him, equally eager to get back inside. Below them yet another Corsair howled off the flight deck, its engine battering the morning air with a determined roar. Gary now understood why the snipes called the pilots Heroes.

Gone. That guy had to be just—gone. He'd seen those propellers in drydock. As they stumbled down the interior ladder toward the gallery deck, they encountered a disturbing scene in the vestibule. A plane captain was squatted down in a corner of the vestibule, his hands on his head and bawling like a baby. Crouching next to him was Father Joseph T. O'Callahan, the ship's Catholic chaplain. Father Joe was probably the most popular officer in the ship. Anytime someone needed him he always

seemed to have known about it already. If there was a flight deck accident with injuries, he'd be there with the emergency crew, humping a
fire hose if they needed help. He was a Jesuit priest with several graduate
degrees who'd joined up in 1940 and served in the North African campaigns aboard a carrier. Everyone in the crew felt that he was their friend,
especially when he stood up to the new and unpopular captain. This time
he was comforting the plane captain of the Corsair that had just gone in.
The plane captain apparently thought the engine failure had somehow
been his fault. It hadn't, but that was the nature of plane captains.

They took great pride in tending to their aircraft. They were important enough that their names were stenciled on the fuselage right beneath
the pilot's name. From the moment a plane landed and the pilot climbed
out, it was the plane captain who climbed into the cockpit and rode the
plane down the elevator to its tie-down spot on the hangar deck, where
he then would begin a multipoint inspection of the entire aircraft. If
the pilot had mentioned a gripe he was the one who called the maintenance guys over and made sure the problem got into the maintenance
planning system, and, if they were slow getting to it, he was the guy who
would bird-dog the gripe until it was cleared or the aircraft was officially downed for repairs. And finally, the plane captain was the guy who
handed the plane over to its pilot saying she was ready to fly. Gary knew
that those words were now tearing this poor guy's heart out.

15

George had been out on the port bridgewing when the Corsair went in, and he slumped when the plane just disappeared without a trace under the bow in the early morning light. No explosion, no splash, no indication whatsoever that a 12,000-pound aircraft had just dropped into the sea right in front of a 36,000-ton ship.

"That one of the Marines?" the captain asked from inside the pilothouse. He was standing on the port side, where he could watch what was happening down on the flight deck.

"Corsair," George said. "Probably Marine."

The captain shook his head. "Can't land, and now they can't take off, either."

George thought the comment was unduly harsh. That yellow cloud streaming out of the engine cowling had to have been the result of a sudden massive oil leak, not pilot error. On the other hand, the captain's distaste for the Marine squadrons embarked was well known. George had often wondered what was behind that. Perhaps some conflict during an earlier tour of duty. He tried to ignore the frowns on the bridge crew's faces when the captain made his nasty remark.

"Quartermaster," the captain called. "How far are we from Japan?"

The quartermaster, one of the ship's navigator's team, consulted the chart and applied a pair of dividers. "One hundred twenty miles to Kagoshima, Captain. That's on the island of Kyushu."

A message came up from PriFly that the launch was complete and that the flight deck was being respotted for the eventual return of the strike aircraft. George had attended the morning briefing for Rear Admiral Davison down in flag plot, along with the captain and Commander Phil Gardner, the carrier's embarked air group commander, or CAG. This morning's strike was aimed at a collection of airfields around the city of Kagoshima. The intel briefer, a lieutenant commander from Naval Intelligence, had told them that Admiral Spruance was still making up his mind about the size of the strikes on the home islands. One plan had all of his carriers attacking one target area in successive waves for several hours; the other had two-carrier divisions attacking geographically separated target areas. Today's strike was one of the former, the theory being that waves of attacks would slowly but surely grind down the target's defensive capabilities to the point where the final wave ought to have free rein in the target area.

"What's the expected Jap reaction?" the admiral had asked.

"Fill the skies with kamikazes and fly out here to return the favor," the briefer had replied. "They have snoopers in the area between us and Kagoshima, so they'll know when we launch. They'll try to get as many planes into the air as possible before our guys arrive over their fields, so midmorning attacks can be expected."

"I was told in Guam that the Japs have lost so many planes that they can't keep that up," the admiral said. "That still the official position?"

The briefer hesitated. "Well, Admiral, personally I think that remains to be seen. Photo recon shows they've dispersed their planes all over the countryside. Any paved street or road can be used to launch a fighter or a Navy carrier bomber, and any barn can hide one. I think it'll become clearer after the third day of strikes—if the same number of kamikazes come out on day three as came out on day one, today, we might have to revise our estimates."

"After-the-fact estimates," the admiral grumped. "Those are the accurate ones, right?"

There'd been chuckles in the room, but George knew that the admiral's question had been uppermost in just about everyone's mind. The Japs had lost almost all their operational carriers, either by sinking or by the fact that they'd run out of both fuel and trained carrier pilots. But now they had unsinkable aircraft carriers—the home islands, themselves. If they had stashed thousands of planes instead of hundreds, life was going to get rough and everybody on the operational side knew it. He'd seen the cruisers, battleships, and destroyers closing in around *Franklin* and her division partner, USS *Hancock* (CV-19), at first light just before flight ops had started.

The 21MC, the command intercom, squawked to life in the pilothouse. "Bridge, Flag Plot."

The captain leaned forward and pushed the talk switch down. "Bridge, Captain," he said, calmly.

"From the admiral, sir. Warning red, set condition one. Multiple raids inbound."

"Bridge, aye," the captain answered and then nodded at the boatswain mate of the watch, who twisted the red handle to sound the general quarters alarm. George hurried off the bridge, grabbing his steel helmet and life jacket as he passed by the GQ gear rack. His GQ station was at a place called secondary conn, which was a much smaller version of the ship's main pilothouse. That way if the bridge got hit and the captain was disabled or killed, the second-in-command in the ship could take over from his station 250 feet back from the bridge.

George hated being back there on what was essentially just an open-air platform, surrounded by four phone-talkers, a single lieutenant junior grade, a light steel gun-tub-style railing, and a gale. There was a small combination steering wheel and engine-order telegraph stand, a radio-handset panel, a sound-powered telephone switch box, and a first-aid box. Directly behind the platform was the top of the upper mount of the after five-inch gun battery. The island towered directly in front of the platform, so if they ever had to actually steer the ship from secondary conn, they would be able to see both sides and the stern, but nothing forward. It sounded like a dumb design except for the fact that any ships operating near an aircraft carrier would be doing everything in their power to stay out of its way, especially if she was damaged and possibly out of control. It was axiomatic in the fleet: an aircraft carrier always had the right of way, even if by maritime rules she didn't. The axiom was reputedly based on the unwritten Law of Gross Tonnage.

His team was on station by the time he got there. The lieutenant, provided by the ship's operations department, was there to act as relief officer of the deck. The four phone-talkers were connected to the major sound-powered phone circuits dealing with maneuvering the ship. One circuit was connected to the bridge, the signal bridge, PriFly, and the Combat Information Center. Another talked to Main Control, the central station for the engineering department, controlling the boiler rooms, emergency diesel generators, and the engine rooms. A third talked to Damage Control Central down in the Log Room. The final circuit connected with a space called after-steering, where a team of twelve men were stationed who could position the ship's rudders by hand if steering control from the bridge was lost due to battle damage. George had exercised the secondary conn system during the ship's workup after the yard. It seemed crude, but it was obviously a vital station if things went off the tracks. Plus, crude equaled simple, which was always an asset when a ship got hit.

The ship began a wide, slow turn to starboard. Her clutch of escorts turned with her, bristling with guns, carefully maintaining their assigned stations. The prevailing winds had had the ship headed northeast, away from Japan, to maximize wind over the deck for takeoffs. Now that the launch was complete, she was turning around, headed back toward the target area in order to shorten the flight for returning strike aircraft. Turning through the wind momentarily enveloped the ship in her own eye-watering stack gases. Eddies of boiler smoke whipped down from the top of the island. Behind and below the secondary conn station the train-warning bells started to ring on the two after twin five-inch gun mounts as the gunners made transmission checks with main battery plot down on the third deck.

There were still men working down on the flight deck, moving some parked aircraft to different spot positions. Damage control teams were verifying that the flight deck aircraft refueling stations had been drained down and refilled with CO_2 gas as a fire prevention measure in case of damage. Literally hundreds of men were manning up the gallery gun-tubs, where 40 mm and 20 mm anti-aircraft guns bristled down both sides of the flight deck, along with four more five-inch single open mounts. The ship's four radar-controlled twin five-inchers could reach out nine miles, but if an attacker made it through that barrage, he'd be met by a hail of hot steel all the way in to the ship from the packed gun galleries.

George scanned the western skies for incoming aircraft. The various combat air patrols should already be thinning them out, beginning at about seventy-five miles distant from the carriers, just as the captain had described. There were three concentric rings of fighters stationed at 25,000 feet at ten-mile intervals to intercept unknown radar contacts. A radar contact was called a bogey. A visible enemy plane was called a bandit. There were also some fighters loitering down low in case the Japs tried to come in on the deck, below the ever-searching American radar beams. Both heavy and light cruisers made up the fourth line of defense, using their own five-inch AA guns and sometimes even their main battery guns of six-inch and eight-inch. The final ship line of defense were the individual destroyers assigned to protect each carrier, stationed close in and packing multiple five-inch and three-inch guns. The whole idea was to make sure no bogey or bandit got close enough to *any* of the carriers as to require them to use their own guns.

George remembered his own war experiences in a carrier torpedo bomber earlier in the war. Some missions had been virtual suicide runs because the Navy's early aircraft-dropped torpedoes had been unreliable, and, worse, required the torpedo bomber to fly straight and level at low altitude and directly at their target for up to a minute before launching. That made them sitting ducks for their target's AA defense guns. If it got too hot, the pilot had the option of aborting the run and trying again from a different direction or going for a different target. This option assumed the attacking pilots wanted to survive the attack.

The dawn of the kamikaze had changed all that. A suicide plane had no reason to break off an attack, because its pilot had already committed himself to die. George had seen Jap planes with both wings shot off and trailing sheets of fire keep coming, controlled only by their tail surfaces, to smash into American ships. They carried bombs, too, but they didn't drop them. The pilots would arm their bomb just before impact, adding the explosive power of a 500-pound bomb to the fiery explosion created by the plane's own crash.

"Ack-ack, bearing zero two five, relative," one of the phone-talkers called out.

George pointed his binocs off to starboard and saw the tiny black puffs of anti-aircraft fire blossoming in the clear morning air, several miles away. The bogeys were invisible but the outer screen was obviously giving them hell. Occasionally a plume of fiery black smoke spiraled out of the sky. After a minute he began to hear the thumps of the nearer cruisers' guns, and then both the five-inch mounts right behind his station swung out and lifted their barrels. He grabbed a sound-powered phone headset and clamped it over his ears. Then the close-in destroyers opened up, and now George *could* see the bandits—*lots* of bandits—headed in, enveloped in airbursts as hundreds of guns sought them out in a firestorm of anti-aircraft fire. *Franklin*'s five-inchers finally got into it, blasting away no more than fifty feet behind them, hammering the air so hard that one of the phone-talkers sported a sudden nosebleed. The two-gun mounts spat expended brass powder cans onto the surrounding deck. The air was filled with gun smoke and burnt cork wadding, making it hard to breathe even up on the secondary conn platform in the open air.

George finally saw what *Franklin*'s guns were shooting at, a cumbersome-looking twin-engined bomber coming in right on the deck, already trailing smoke but not wavering from its approach. All the gallery guns started in on him now, tearing pieces off the plane until finally, and much too close, he thought, a wing came off and the bomber rolled violently, shed its other wing, and smacked into the sea, followed by the explosion of its bomb load, which was big enough to send a visible shock wave right over the ship.

Almost immediately, the five-inchers whirled around to a new bearing and began shooting again. The air was so filled with smoke and gun-flashes that George couldn't see anything, so he gestured for his team to sit down on the deck behind the meager protection of the shield wall. He felt a little foolish, but there was nothing he and his team could contribute until all the shooting stopped unless something happened to the bridge. Based on the increasing roar of gunfire, that possibility was getting stronger. The burnt powder-can wadding settled over them like a black snowfall. He felt the ship begin another turn, this time to port, and this one wasn't all that gentle. He wondered if the captain was trying to avoid a torpedo, because sharp turns had the potential to roll any untethered aircraft right off the flight deck and thus were rarely executed.

They all felt a large thump from somewhere down on the flight deck. George peered over the shield in time to see a flaming twin-engine Jap bomber screeching across the flight deck and then slanting over the side, where it threw up a tremendous splash, followed a few seconds later by its internal bombload going off underwater. That'll wake the snipes up, he thought. A firefighting crew was already smothering the trail of avgas flames on the flight deck. He marveled at their coolness. Every gun on the ship seemed to be shooting at something, but the chief in charge of the D/C team was standing there, hands on hips, his steel helmet cocked back on his head, shouting orders to his hosemen as if it was just another drill. And that's why you drill, over and over, George thought.

The carrier steadied up on a new heading, and then immediately began another turn back to starboard. He's weaving, George thought. Making it harder for the torpedo bombers. The two five-inchers had stopped firing, probably waiting for more ammo to come up the hoists from the deep magazines. He watched as one of their escort destroyers literally tore a Jap plane to flaming pieces behind them and thought he actually saw the pilot cartwheeling through the air until he smacked into the sea along with the remains of his plane.

Kamikaze, he thought. These people are truly alien beings. Then he realized that all *Franklin*'s guns had stopped shooting, except for the single pops and bangs as gunners cleared rounds out of red-hot barrels to prevent them from exploding inside the barrel. The five-inch mount down on the flight deck level swung out to seaward and cleared both of its barrels with short rounds, which were powerful enough to blast the live projectiles out of the barrel but only for a few hundred yards. The short rounds were followed by a prolonged blast of 3,000-psi air down each badly charred barrel to sweep out any burning debris.

George scanned the seas around the close-in formation. There were several columns of black smoke rising from the water where Jap planes had gone in and left a pyre of burning avgas. One of their own escorting destroyers had a pretty big fire going up on her forecastle, of all places. He watched admiringly as the tin can's skipper put the helm over and steamed directly into *Franklin's* huge wake, creating an enormous wave over her own bow, which instantly snuffed out the fire. Otherwise, none of the carriers appeared to have been hit. He felt the ship turning again just as the bridge phone-talker waved his hand at him. George plugged his headset into the brass barrel switch and selected the JA circuit.

"XO here," he said.

"This is the captain; we're going to secure from GQ for the moment, but I'm setting Condition Two, not Three—our radar picket destroyers say there's more coming. I want all guns manned and ready, but the crew needs chow."

"Aye, aye, sir," George said.

"And I need that flight deck cleaned up and ready ASAP. We've been running southwest to close the returning strike. We'll have to go back northeast as soon as we get planes in the pattern. Got it?"

"Yes, sir, got it," George said. He got a sudden whiff of woodsmoke, which was somewhat incongruous this far out at sea. He looked down at the flight deck and saw a plane tractor making successive passes while pulling a spiked steel mat over the long scorch mark in the wooden deck. The deck hadn't actually caught fire but the dying bomber had left a blackened furrow across the deck, deep enough to bounce a returning plane high enough to miss the arresting wire. The steel mat was slowly turning the charred furrow into a long, shallow dent. He also saw medics down in the gun galleries, tending to gunners who had been wounded when the plane went over the side. He saw body bags, too, so they hadn't gotten off scot-free. Back aft the LSO was manning up his platform and he could hear the arresting wires scraping across the deck as they were being tensioned for recovery. He scanned the ship's wake and imagined he saw black specks way out behind the ship as the first of her strike aircraft made their way back to "Mother."

An all-hands call came over the 1MC, which then announced the setting of Condition Two. This meant that half the crew would remain at their GQ stations, while the other half got a chance to get some food, rest, and maybe even some sleep after all the shooting. This also meant that a six hours on, six hours off watch-standing routine was imminent. Set long enough it would slowly exhaust the crew, but with Jap snoopers still out beyond the perimeter of the massive carrier formation it was better to be safe than sorry. Condition Two was a compromise between the maximum security of Condition One, or general quarters, and the relatively minimal protection of Condition Three, where only some of the guns were manned and ready. It was the clearest indication yet that they were well into Injun Country, and yet, almost perversely, they were still headed back *toward* Japan.

16

Six decks below the flight deck, Gary settled himself onto a steel stool in Main Control. He'd come down from the wardroom mess to the engine room after an early dinner of the Navy's notorious green-tinted canned ham, reconstituted powdered mashed potatoes, and canned baked beans. He planned to make a quick tour of his boiler rooms before the nightly general alarms started, but first he'd stopped in Main Control to get some decent coffee. The engine rooms had the best coffee in the ship because they made it with low-pressure steam instead of water. The water king had handed him a metal message board with the most recent feed-water reserves and tests from the ship's eight boilers. Lieutenant Commander Ed Moran, the main propulsion assistant, was the engineering watch officer, in charge of the entire plant for the next six hours.

Everybody was tired. There'd been two more general quarters alarms after the morning attack as the formation fought off a surprising number of Jap aircraft. The enemy had pretty much ignored *Franklin* during the early afternoon attack, but then seemed to seek her out during the sundown visitation. Gary had lost track of when his next watch was scheduled, which is why he'd gone below. Between the GQs and the frantic rush to get aircraft struck below from the day's second strike and then fresh ammo to all the gun stations, Gary felt he'd been lucky to get fifteen minutes to grab some chow. He'd passed J.R. on the way to the ladders leading down to the "main holes"; when he asked him how it was going, J.R. could only shake his head.

"Every time we go to GQ all the repair-party guys have to suit up and stand by," he said. "So, nobody's getting any downtime. And then, when it's over, we gotta restow all the hoses, pumps, *and* the breathing gear, *and* reset the flight deck fuel lines. I'll tell you what: it's been a level bitch topside."

"Well, for us main-hole snipes, it's been pretty much business as usual, just like the boss predicted," Gary said. "Go fast, slow down, go fast again. Hopefully the bastards will take the night off. I'm thinking of finding a quiet corner in one of the firerooms and sleeping there tonight."

"Sounds good to me," J.R. had said over his shoulder. "Sleeping *any-where* sounds good."

Gary finished reviewing the feedwater reports and signed the forms. Reserve feed was getting a bit low again with all the high-speed land-launch runs, but if things slowed down tonight the ship's evaporators could catch up. None of the boiler-water tests had indicated salt intrusion. He finished his coffee and then hung his mug up on the coffee board, unwashed. Snipes prided themselves on their coffee, so anyone who stood main-hole watches had an inscribed porcelain mug hanging in their work spaces. It was an engineering department axiom that if you ever washed your coffee mug, you'd ruin it forever. He didn't take it with him because all of the firerooms and engine rooms were separated by reinforced watertight bulkheads. To get from Main Control to the nearest fireroom he had to climb two decks' worth of ladders, walk a hundred feet down a hot passageway, and then go back down into the adjacent space via more ladders. There were four firerooms; that meant a whole lot of ladders. Besides, as boilers officer, he had a personal mug in each fireroom, too.

He made a quick inspection of number one fireroom, then went back up, across, and down into number two fireroom, directly aft of number one. He was talking to the chief on watch when the GQ alarm went off again. Gary's GQ station was in Main Control with the chief engineer, but there was no way he could get back there before all the watertight hatches would be dogged down. He wasn't worried about that: as long as he was physically present in one of the main holes, he could direct emergency actions in case there was damage to a fireroom or one of the boilers started to act up. He found a steel stool next to the log desk in a corner of the fireroom, mostly to stay out of the way of the GQ crew that was manning up the space.

A normal steaming watch would have four men at the boiler-fronts and control stations. At GQ, there were eight. One of them finally brought Gary his steel helmet, gas mask, and a life jacket. He donned the helmet, buttoned down his shirtsleeves, stuffed his khaki trousers into his socks, made sure he had a flashlight, and then hung the life jacket and the gas mask close by—it was much too hot down there to wear either one. The chief boilertender then distributed oxygen breathing apparatus sets, known as OBAs, around the space so that each man could grab one if needed. An OBA could give a man forty-five minutes of breathable air if the compartment suddenly filled with smoke, less if the man had to really exert himself in damage control. Or panicked and started panting.

And then they waited. The fireroom was sealed in by watertight hatches two levels up. Ventilation had been secured throughout the ship *except* in the main holes, where men would die of heat stroke in about twenty minutes without it. The exhaust system blowers were set on high, while the supply blowers were on low. That way if a fire erupted, the vent system would begin vacuuming the smoke out of the space, assuming the vent motors still worked. The chief joined Gary in his corner by the DA tank. The fireroom crew basically had nothing more to do, since both boilers were already on the line, other than to watch for problems and monitor speed-change orders from the bridge.

"I'm getting tired of that damned GQ alarm," the chief said, lighting up a cigarette. Smoking was forbidden during GQ, but the snipes figured that with eight oil-fired boilers blazing away, a cigarette didn't pose much of a hazard. Gary didn't smoke, although he enjoyed the smell of good tobacco.

"Apparently the Japs just keep coming," Gary said. They both had to shout a bit to be heard over all the machinery noise. "And if they don't make an actual attack, if they even turn toward us, the whole task force goes to GQ."

"Good way to tire your enemy out," the chief observed. "Make sure he doesn't get any sleep."

"Well, I heard we've got these night-fighters now," Gary said. "They've got a radar. Creep up on 'em from below and flame their asses before they even know our guy is there. But I gotta say: whoever predicted they were running out of planes was flat-*ass* wrong. Word is we've shot down over two *hundred* planes in the past two days, but the CIC officer said you'd never know it, looking at the radar screens."

They both heard the engine order telegraph repeater jingle. Twenty-seven knots being ordered up. The chief got up and walked to the steel alley between the two boilers to make sure the crew responded to the increased steam flow demand from the engine rooms. As the engine rooms opened their turbine throttles, the steam pressure in the boilers would begin to drop. The boiler techs would then open up the fuel regulator valves to regain pressure. The chief was watching to make sure they didn't go overboard with that effort and cause the boilers to overpressure and lift their safety valves.

Gary could feel the hull begin to tremble as the carrier came up in speed, its four enormous propellers churning the sea and leaving a wake that stretched out for two miles behind the ship, probably visible even in the dark. There was a rudder-angle repeater next to the engine order telegraph dial, and he watched as the rudder swung left five degrees to put the ship into a port turn. Gary couldn't really feel the turn down here in the bowels of the ship, unlike on his destroyer, where even a five-degree rudder order at twenty-seven knots would heel the ship fifteen degrees and send coffee mugs flying.

He also couldn't hear the ship's guns way down here unless the five-inchers got into it, and then only as distant double-thumps. Either way, there was nothing he could do about what might be going on topside. It was the Heroes' time to shine. The snipes wouldn't really fear bombs, being this far below the armored hangar bay deck. Jap torpedoes, on the other hand, were a whole different story. They were monsters, even the air-dropped variety. There was a steel honeycomb of tanks and voids built along the sides of the ship, placed there to absorb torpedoes, but those Jap Type-93s came in at almost fifty miles an hour, packing nearly a half ton of explosive and time-delayed fuses. They were fully capable of smashing into the sides of a big ship and penetrating all the way into a vital space, such as a fireroom, and then going off. It just didn't bear thinking about.

The thump of the five-inchers finally did penetrate the machinery noise. Gary decided to loosely don his life jacket, and then picked up his OBA and began to strap it on. He wouldn't activate the cannister unless something actually happened, but he wanted it ready to hand. If *Franklin's* own guns were in action, that meant something had gotten by all those night-fighters, CAP stations, the cruiser line, and their own escorts. There still wasn't anything for the eight-man crew to do other than to watch gauges and adjust steam throttles on the bigger pumps. He saw men hand-oiling bearings and tightening valve handles that were weeping steam. All probably unnecessary, Gary thought, but it was important to keep busy when the ship was maneuvering and the guns were speaking. He would have almost preferred to be out on one of the gun galleries, blasting away at an incoming suicider, than sitting here waiting for the unknown. Almost; there was some comfort in knowing that the armored deck was above him. He shifted his perch to get directly under a vent and tried to stay awake.

17

J.R. waited out the first nighttime GQ in the secondary Damage Control Central station up at the very front of the hangar deck. It was a mini version of the main DC Central, with the same charts and sound-powered phone terminals, but with none of the records and admin spaces. J.R. was in charge of a crew of four phone-talkers, who were in communication with the repair parties, the conflagration control station, DC Central, and Main Control. J.R. personally manned a sound-powered phone circuit connected to the bridge and the captain's phone-talker. He, too, was dressed out in his GQ uniform, as were the phone-talkers. Everyone had an OBA on. The main Damage Control Central station was called simply, Central, on the phones. J.R.'s station was called Central Two. Their mission was to back up the main station in case it got cut off for any reason.

Actual damage control was performed by eight repair parties, which consisted of twenty men each with a chief petty officer in charge. They were stationed next to their repair lockers, which contained all the fire-fighting, de-flooding, and smoke control equipment, as well as emergency electrical power cables, axes, sledgehammers, portable lanterns, portable fire pumps and generators, extra hoses, five-gallon cans of firefighting foam concentrate, and lockers full of OBAs and backup cannisters. The members of a repair party were dressed out in fire-resistant overalls, anti-flashburn hoods, and asbestos-lined gauntlets. Their OBAs were strapped on, with only the mask dangling loose. The repair lockers were spread out throughout the ship, including the two crash-crew lockers on the flight deck itself, embedded into the island.

J.R. had been spending his time during all the GQ sessions correcting his Damage Control diagrams. It was tedious work to be sure, but there wasn't anything else to do. The ship was buttoned up, all the guns and radars manned, flight deck fuel lines in safe mode, and the repair parties sitting and sweating side by side in their hot passageways. There were no air ops in progress and all the planes down in the hangar bays would have been defueled. The air group's pilots had gone to their ready-rooms for GQ, but they had reclining chairs and air-conditioning so they could sleep. J.R. had wondered about the wisdom of so many of the pilots be-ing concentrated on the gallery deck, which lay between the flight deck and the hangar deck. If anything really big got going on the hangar deck, those spaces on the gallery deck would become ovens. On the other hand, berthing compartments above the waterline were not especially secure against fire, smoke, or flooding, either, so in a way, it was kind of a toss-up.

At least they weren't doing drills. The captain had called GQ constantly during the transit out from Guam, which meant that the repair parties had to leave their lockers and go fight imaginary fires throughout the ship. It was good and, indeed, vital training, but after a while, it became hard to generate the go-get-it enthusiasm and aggressiveness needed for effective firefighting. He subscribed to the rule that there was no such thing as too much training, as the captain never tired of pointing out. He also knew the bleary-eyed crewmen who had to hump all that firefighting gear might have taken issue with that.

The five-inchers began to boom and some loose fittings in the over-head shook and danced in approval of each salvo. The five-inchers could shoot effectively at a target range of nine miles, J.R. remembered. It still wasn't personal at nine miles, and with this new radio-fused ammo, their five-inch shells only had to fly close to the target in order to go off. He'd been proudly explaining that while trying to reassure one of his new firemen one day when a passing gunnery officer pointed out that nine miles slant range was only about five miles horizontal distance. "Time is what's important," he'd said. "A suicider five miles away diving at three hundred knots will be here in one minute, which isn't much time for the smaller guns to do any good." Fortunately, the fireman hadn't understood a word of it; if his lieutenant was confident, then so was he.

He felt the ship start into another turn and begin to increase speed. He recalled all the tactical lectures conducted during the outbound transit. A destroyer at twenty-seven knots could whip through a complete reversal of course in under a minute. A 36,000-ton carrier took a lot longer to make a 180-degree turn unless it was willing to shed all the planes up on the flight deck, but a carrier executing a big circle was a lot harder to hit from the air. He heard the word "flares" over his phones. There was no telling who'd said it, but that meant that the attacking Japs were close enough to begin lighting up the carrier task force with air-dropped magnesium parachute flares. The rattle and bang of the shorter-range guns began, including the two quad-mounted 40 mm's right up under the forward end of the flight deck, just ahead of his station. That meant there was something coming from dead ahead and low on the water, because those guns couldn't shoot *up*. The five-inchers also stopped shooting, because they couldn't shoot down.

The ship steadied up for a moment before tilting ponderously in the other direction as the conn put her into a narrow sinuous weave. Everyone in the space tensed for a long minute; attacks from dead ahead usually meant torpedoes. The Japs would come in from thirty degrees on either side of the bow and drop those fearsome Type-93 fish; either way the carrier turned, one or the other should get a hit. The only tactic that could be used against that was to steer straight between them, allowing the target ship to thread those fifty-knot monsters.

The forward-pointing forties went quiet and everyone held his breath and then finally relaxed when nothing happened. The ship began turning again and the five-inchers resumed their steel-thumping cadence. J.R. wondered if everyone locked up within the ship's hundreds of compartments felt as trapped and helpless as he did. He tried to imagine the scene topside: the huge, fully darkened ship twisting and turning in the dead of night while being illuminated by long vertical tentacles of burning magnesium descending on parachutes out of the clouds; the night sky shredded by hundreds of white and red tracers coming from dozens of ships, all urgently seeking airborne metal; and, hopefully, the spiraling orange flames of kamikazes or bombers tumbling out of the sky, shedding burning wings and other debris on the way to their all-important honorable death, followed by a soundless splash and then the roar of its bomb going off underwater. He looked around his crowded little space as the lights flickered in time to the deadly rhythms of the massed gunfire. Everyone seemed to be avoiding eye contact, as if to conceal how afraid they all were.

Then all the noise died out. The ship stopped turning. It felt as if she was steadying up for a change. One of his phone-talkers spoke up.

"They're calling for more ammo topside," he said. "CIC says three more raids are inbound."

Great, J.R. thought, we're gonna be here all damn night. He passed the good news on to his little crew of phone-talkers. When the ammo resupply party came through, his talkers each took turns going up to the open forecastle deck and urinating over the downwind side.

18

The following morning, George sat at the wardroom table stabbing disinterestedly with his fork at his powdered eggs and slippery tinned sausages. General quarters had been sounded a total of four times through the night and his eyes were sandy with fatigue. The wardroom was fairly full, even though it was almost 0500 because there was a major strike launch planned for 0600. He knew he needed food and he was painfully aware that a lot of the crew hadn't had a chance at hot chow for almost thirty hours with all these constant probes and attacks. He planned to talk to the captain this morning about maybe staging people through the messdecks all day and night instead of sticking to rigidly fixed meal hours. He expected the usual gruff no, not regulation, but he thought it worth a try. The captain would declare that fighting off Jap planes was more important than full bellies right now. George would have loved to point out that he, the captain, had a personal steward who managed to keep him fed, whether he was in his stateroom or up on the bridge, and the admiral had a whole herd of stewards doing the same thing for him.

His fork failed to penetrate one of the rock-hard sausages. He'd been eating so slowly that his breakfast was now cold. He gave up. Billy-B Perkins came by his table carrying what looked like a fried Spam and ketchup sandwich that was barely contained in some greasy paper napkins.

"You gonna die, you eat that mess," George observed.

"Probably," Billy responded. "But at least it's portable."

"Big deal today?" George asked him, reaching for the coffee pitcher.

"Yes, sir, we're throwing the whole damn air group at 'em this time. I think all the carriers are. Spruance is getting tired of these all-nighters."

"Me, too," George said. "I'm dead on my ass, and I'm afraid the whole crew is, too."

"We're sending so many planes today that we've had to arm and fuel some of them in the hangar bay 'cause there's no room on the roof. I hate to do that, but—"

"If you have to, you have to," George said. "Captain's not gonna want to hear about any delays in the launch."

"That's for damn sure," Billy said. "I guess this is what we get for stirring up the home-islands hornet's nest. Gotta go."

George stopped by his office to get a quick read on the morning's message traffic before heading for the bridge. He half expected the hateful buzzer to go off. He was becoming convinced that the buzzer knew when he came into his office and informed on him to the captain, but apparently the captain had other people to annoy right now. He heard flight quarters being sounded at 0600 and then came a surprising announcement over the 1MC: set Condition Three with the exception of gun batteries, the bridge, and CIC. The messdecks will remain open until all hands have had a chance to get chow. Gun crews authorized to send one-third of their crew to chow on a rotational basis. That is all.

He felt the ship turning into the wind to begin the launch. That order must have come from the captain, who must have been thinking along the same lines as George about the crew not getting fed. He heard the passageway outside his office fill with men hustling down to the messdecks. He felt rather than heard the first of the fighters rolling down the flight deck toward the bow. Tired of paperwork and already getting sleepy in the warm office, he decided to go to the bridge to watch the launch. He actually preferred to watch from PriFly, but the captain would wonder why he wasn't up there on the bridge. With him.

George grinned mentally at the thought of his self-deception as he threaded his way through the throng of hungry sailors. He decided to go out to the flight deck briefly before heading upstairs. Maybe that cold air streaming across the flight deck would help him wake up.

The noise nearly overwhelmed him as he stepped through the island hatch and into the light-locker leading out to the actual flight deck. Two dozen bombers were packed together back aft with their engines turning and wings drooping with bombs and rockets. Between the engine exhaust smoke and the noise, he wondered how the flight deck crews could even think, much less coordinate the steady movement of planes from their spots to the launch position, all the while prancing about the flight deck almost on their hands and knees to avoid the whirling propellers. The wind was blowing hard. He looked up to the signal halyards, where the Fox flag was two-blocked and standing stiffly in the relative gale. At least forty, maybe even fifty knots of relative wind over the deck. Good, he thought. It would help those overloaded Corsairs waddle off the deck. He, himself, had to hang on to a stanchion to stay upright in that baby gale howling down the deck.

He looked back aft to see what the gang was taking to Dai Nippon today. Some of the bombers carried the big stuff internally, with a couple of incendiary 100-pounders strapped to the wings. They'd drop the crowd-pleaser and the fire sticks together. The bomb would create wreckage; the incendiaries would start it on fire. Others had five-inch rockets, three to a wing, instead of bombs. These were the train-chasers, who'd find railroad tracks and fly down them until they found a train and then rocket the engine. With the engine disabled, they'd turn around and fly back down the line, strafing the freight and tank cars to finish the job. Still others had those murderous Tiny Tims, much bigger rockets with large, 500-pound warheads. These were used to smash into big factory buildings like steel mills or aircraft hangars. All the planes, fighters and bombers, also carried guns, and once they dropped their main armament, they'd turn around, get low, and strafe the hell out of whatever was left, especially all the people running for their lives. George had spent more than a few nights at bases in the Solomon Islands subject to Jap bombing raids and even battleship bombardments. This whole picture was immensely satisfying.

Okay, he thought. Time to go face the ogre and make nice. But as he turned to go back into the light-locker, something way above the flight deck caught his eye. His brain at first rejected what he was seeing, but then he realized he *was* seeing it: a lone Japanese bomber, green-skinned with a greenhouse structure for a cockpit, those big red meatballs staring back at him, flying directly over the carrier, from bow to stern, and going like a bat out of hell. A *Judy!* He was forming the words WHAT THE HELL, when there was a flash of reddish-white light and he was blown off his feet and all the way forward along the sides of the island, where his body then rolled through the space between the two forward five-inch mounts and right into the lifelines. He was frantically grabbing for something to stop himself from going right over the side and falling eighty feet into the sea when his head hit something truly hard and he blacked out for a moment. When he came to, the end of the world was upon him in all its fiery glory.

19

J.R. was in the forward wardroom, finishing every bite of his "gour-met" breakfast, which this time consisted of oatmeal, limp strips of canned bacon, and freshly baked cornbread on the side. He hadn't eaten since lunch the previous day and the cornbread, awash in syrup and but-ter, was a real treat. He was reaching for the coffee pitcher when some-thing happened. For an instant he wasn't sure what he'd felt, but then realized that whatever it was, it was really serious. It was like a bump, but a mountain-sized bump. Then there was a second one, this time farther back in the ship. The overhead lights flickered, came back on, and then buzzed into darkness.

He looked around the wardroom. Everyone had the same expression on his face: What the hell was *that*? And then came the roar of an explo-sion, followed immediately by another and another, all somewhere above and behind them. Some of the light fixtures fell off their mounts as the air filled with dust. The cascade of explosions was strong enough to shake the entire ship. Ominously, the battle lanterns came on and projected trem-bling beams of yellowish light into the wardroom. Those ponderous blasts got even louder and more frequent until J.R. had to grab the wardroom tablecloth just to stay upright. Then came a truly enormous explosion from what had to be the hangar deck, right above them.

J.R. jumped out of his chair and ran for the forward door to the ward-room passageway. Other officers were also getting up, some headed for other doors, others just standing there, mutely trying to comprehend the growing crescendo of stomach-thumping blasts behind and above them. J.R. ran forward in the passageway and then went up one ladder to the hangar deck level. He opened a watertight door that led out into the hangar and was confronted by what looked like a blast furnace to his im-mediate left. The entire hangar, deck to overhead, was a mass of gasoline flames, which were boiling forward and directly toward him in a lethal yellow and orange incandescent cloud, pursued by white-centered ex-plosions farther back in the hangar deck. The fire was compressing what air was left in the hangar bay and before he could fully comprehend what he was seeing the overpressure forced the hatch back into the hatchway, pinning J.R. behind it against the bulkhead, which actually protected him from the bolus of flames that pushed into the vestibule, looking for someone to burn.

He instinctively pushed back and slammed the hatch shut before having to let go because his hands were being burned. The hatch began coming back open and he quickly sat down on the deck and used his legs and shoes to push it shut. One of the dogs dropped into place, which held the door long enough for him to get back up and gingerly secure the other dogs.

Great *God,* he thought. What the hell's happened? Then came *more* explosions from the aft end of the hangar deck, each one shaking the steel bulkheads and sending clouds of steel fragments rattling and pinging the length of the hangar deck. It sounded like all the shipyard needle guns in the world were at work on the other side of that hatch after each explo-sion. He stared in horror as some fragments punched dimples in the metal on *his* side of the steel bulkhead.

He knew he needed to get forward to Central Two, his GQ station. Normally he would have gone out onto the hangar deck, hurried forward toward the ship's bow, and then gone through two hatches and into the secondary DC station. But now? Then came a truly terrifying sound: what sounded like a large rocket came howling by the hatch on the other side and then exploded forward, in what had to have been his GQ station. The bulkhead, which held the hatch, was beginning to deform from the heat of the fire on the other side, and suddenly the vestibule began to fill with thick, black smoke, forcing J.R. to retreat back into the passageway behind him. To his horror, every ventilation outlet in the passageway was pumping hot, black smoke, thick enough to obscure the battle lanterns. He had none of his battle gear—no helmet, and, most importantly, no OBA. He did have his gas mask, which he stopped to don. He had to drop to his knees to do so. It gave him some relief from the acrid oil smoke, but no additional oxygen. He knew he *had* to get out of this passageway *now* or he was going to suffocate. Another rocket came blasting forward, screeching along the hangar bay bulkhead before hitting some immovable object and disintegrating in a shower of heavy metal fragments. Its motor must have been pointed right at the bulkhead because a red spot began to glare at him in the steel. When he saw metal bubbles forming, he began scrambling forward, away from all those explosions.

20

Gary was jarred awake by the sound of two powerful explosions. Guns? Wait a minute, he thought: we're not at GQ. And those *definitely* weren't guns. Then came a whopper of a blast that sounded as if it involved the entire length of the hangar deck. It was strong enough to rattle all the ventilation ducts, which showered the fireroom in dust and soot particles.

Oh, shit, he thought: we've been hit. As if to confirm that thought other things began to blow up above them in an ascending crescendo of disaster topside. Then he heard the forced-draft blowers begin to overspeed. Two of the boilertenders jumped to take them off the line as the chief shouted instructions to pull fires and then secure the two boilers in the space. Without forced air for their fireboxes they would fill with atomized fuel and blow up. In quick succession the burners were secured at the boiler-front, followed by the main feed pumps and their boosters, the fuel pumps, and the main and auxiliary steam valves, which routed steam to the engine room behind them. When those were closed the boilers were momentarily overpressured from residual heat in the firebox, causing the safety valves atop the boilers to lift with an ear-punishing roar of escaping high-pressure steam going up the stack, rendering the explosions above them into deckplate-shaking thumps.

Gary got on the amplified sound circuit that connected all the main holes and called Main Control. He thought he heard a garbled response but the safeties were still bleeding steam so he simply shouted that they'd lost combustion air and were securing the space. The sudden loss of power as generators tripped off the line threw the fireroom into momentary darkness and also killed all ventilation. Battle lanterns popped on but there was a lot of steam-heated haze in the space now, so they glowed rather than illuminated. The temperature began to rise rapidly.

The chief was frantically trying to make sure everything that needed to be secured *had* been secured when one of the huge, rectangular-shaped steel ducts that brought combustion air down from the tops of the island bulged outward and then split lengthwise, immediately filling the fireroom with hot black smoke, punctuated by pulses of fire as gasoline fumes, entrained in the stream of air being pulled downward from above by the still red-hot boiler fireboxes, ignited in snapping balls of fire across the fireroom overhead. There was still negative atmospheric pressure in the fireroom even with all the ventilation fans knocked out because of the hot updraft in the secured boilers.

Gary stared in horror at those fireballs racing across the fireroom overhead, but then training kicked in. All hands on the upper level of the fireroom dropped down ladders to the lower level to get away from the spontaneous combustion going on across the tops of the two boilers, while struggling to don and activate their OBAs. The machinery noise had subsided by now as the shutdown took effect. The two boilers had pretty much drained themselves of steam through their safety valves. The growing silence in the space only amplified the thunderous explosions going on several decks above them. Right above them, on the upper level, that seething black cloud was getting bigger and bigger from the ruptured air supply intakes. They could feel its heat radiating through the upper-level deck gratings, and each time one of those whumping fireballs ignited every man jumped. Gary knew that if enough combustible fumes made it down into the fireroom the whole thing would go off like the fuel mixture in the cylinder of a gasoline engine.

Then a new phenomenon manifested itself: water. There was suddenly a muscular stream of water pouring down into the fireroom from somewhere above them. Gary was about to order his team to light off the bilge pump, but without steam or electrical power, that wasn't possible. Eductor, he thought. He checked the fire-main gauge, which still showed about 80 psi. That would do, he thought, and sent two men into the bilges to align the necessary valves.

The in-line eductor was basically a horizontal Y-shaped suction tube with no moving parts other than valves at each end. The men opened the two valves, thus connecting the eductor to the ship's fire-main stream, which meant that there was now water at 80 psi flowing through the long leg of the Y. That flow created a vacuum in the short leg of the Y. They then attached a hose, which ended in a debris screen basket and dropped that into the bilges, where water was visibly rising. They then opened one final valve, which allowed the water being sucked up out of the bilges to push overboard. They gave the chief the high sign: eductor was taking suction.

Gary figured that the cascade of water pouring down through various air ducts was probably firefighting water. He wished he had three more eductors, but the good news was that an eductor shouldn't have to be constantly tended—just as long as there was fire-main pressure, it would try to empty the bilges underneath the lower-level deckplates. If the fire-main pressure did fail, there was a check valve in the basket that should prevent the system from operating in reverse. Should. Eductors were notorious in the fleet for flooding spaces if not checked frequently. The chief was pointing up and giving Gary a look that said: we can't stay here.

Gary looked up again and could now no longer even see the upper-level deck gratings. That boiling, rumbling cloud of heavy oil smoke was now blanketing the entire upper level. The fireballs had quit, probably for lack of oxygen, but that meant it was time to evacuate. He shouted the order. The men dropped what they were doing and scrambled for the emergency escape trunk, a steel shaft that was four feet square with a ladder welded to one side. The shaft led up to the third deck, where there was an air lock chamber through which they could exit to a passageway. One man opened the escape trunk hatch. Thankfully, the trunk appeared

to be smoke free. Battle lanterns were shining at ten-foot intervals to il-
luminate the thirty-foot climb.

Gary made sure he was the last man out. He'd tried to pass the word
to Main Control that they were bailing out, but the intercom system was
dead. As he climbed into the trunk and dogged down the door behind
him, another terrific explosion shook the entire ship. Dust and tiny bits
of insulation rained down on the men as they climbed toward whatever
disaster was unfolding above them. Gary had followed procedures up to
now, but suddenly he was really afraid of what they might encounter the
closer they got to those ear-hammering blasts going off above them. Dear
God, he thought, as every steel surface around him bucked and heaved.
They got us. *Franklin* was in her death throes.

21

The bright stink of high-octane gasoline roused George from his momentary daze. For a few seconds he didn't know where he was, but for some reason he was covered in water. He was lying on his back, with one leg all the way through the lifelines, and he couldn't hear anything at all. Eyes, he thought. Open your eyes. He felt rather than heard the punishing blasts coming from the other side of the island and then he saw the towering cloud of black smoke rising over the aft end of the ship some two miles into the air. He rolled his head to the right, toward the bow of the ship. There appeared to be hundreds of people on the flight deck, some of them scrambling to unroll fire hoses, others just staring in shock. Then he looked up to see if PriFly was still manned. PriFly wasn't there anymore. All that remained were blackened cable ends, twisted steel stringers, and a strip of melted windows dangling in the wind along the top of the island. Billy-B, the mini boss, their entire team, and anyone who'd been out on vultures' row had been simply obliterated.

He lay there for a long moment, trying to gather his wits. He watched as a crowd of about thirty men unreeled three fire hoses, rigid now with fire-main pressure, and began to haul them back toward the aft end of the ship. They got about fifty feet before a wave of bright fire, propelled by a large bomb blast from somewhere abaft the island, mowed them down like stick figures. A few badly burned men tried to get up but were then smacked down to the deck by yet another bomb blast. The explosions were coming every few seconds now, followed by a slashing phalanx of air-to-ground rockets that came screaming up the flight deck at waist level, thinning out the crowd of men hunkered down at the bow, cutting men in two before howling off the bow and down into the sea, where they exploded in dirty fountains of water right in front of the ship. The charged fire hoses were writhing around on the flight deck like angry snakes.

Gotta get up, George told himself. Okay, his legs said: *you* do it because we can't. He took a deep breath and then retracted his leg from the lower lifeline and rolled onto his left side. It was hard, but he realized he wasn't in real pain. He checked himself for bleeding: not bleeding, either. Well then, what the hell are you doing, lying here like some kind of slacker?

He hunched his back, rolled, and got up on his hands and knees. And capsized immediately, skinning his cheek on the deck. Then there were gloved hands helping him to his feet. He caught a glimpse of a red cross on the steel helmet of one of his helpers, who was asking him in a barely audible voice where he was hurt.

"I'm not," he shouted, unaware that he was doing so. "I must get to the bridge. What the hell happened?"

"A Judy got in on us, XO. One, maybe two bombs, right on the flight deck. Half the strike was back there, gassed and loaded. That's what's blowing up right now."

"God*dammit*," George said. "Someone help me up to the bridge, please."

Two sailors propped him up as he gradually found his sea legs again. The awkward trio staggered into the island on the seaward side while the explosions continued back aft. There'd been at least two dozen bombers spotted back there the last time he'd looked, every one of them filled to the gills with gasoline and loaded with bombs and rockets. And then he remembered what Billy-B had said: we had to arm and fuel some planes in the hangar deck, because we're sending the whole air group. *That's* what was slowly but surely tearing the ship to pieces. Now we're getting a taste of what the Japs went through at Midway, he thought.

He was still very unsteady on his feet but the two strong young men helping him pushed him up three flights of ladders until he could get out onto the seaward catwalk that led to the bridge. The whole time they'd been going up there'd been a constant needle-gun sound as waves of metal fragments kept hitting the flight deck side of the island. He tried not to wince each time he heard it, but didn't entirely succeed.

Two bombs, he thought. One had obviously set off a major conflagration on the flight deck. Where'd the other one gone? Oh, God. The two sailors delivered him to the starboard bridgewing. He grabbed onto the wooden bullrail and tried to get his wind back. His helpers then hustled back down below.

George took a moment to gather his equilibrium. Ahead was a clear sky and a slate-gray sea. There were still escorts and carriers all around them, right where they should be. Some of them were shooting at things in the sky. Another carrier—he couldn't tell which one—was also burning. Then he turned around.

Oh, Jesus, he thought. The entire horizon astern of the ship was obscured in the largest column of smoke and fire he'd ever seen. It was rising above the ship like a bulging black mountain, with spherical yellow and red flashes at its base propelling the hot cloud ever higher. Fiery objects were being blasted into the air and over the side every few seconds. He recognized plane parts, flight deck tractors, and what had to be human bodies. For an eternal moment he was glued to the deck, trying to comprehend what was happening. And not succeeding.

A quartermaster in full battle gear came out on the bridgewing, recognized him, and hustled him inside the pilothouse, where everyone appeared to just be in shock. Just like me, he thought. Then he saw the captain, over on the port side of the bridge, white-faced and staring down at the carnage on the afterpart of the flight deck. The admiral was standing next to him, talking to him. He could barely hear their voices but then the captain said no, shaking his head emphatically. A blast down on the burning flight deck momentarily deformed the entire bridge structure and turned the bridge windows into crazed panes of cracked glass. Someone was gripping his right elbow, trying to get his attention.

"XO," he was saying. "The admiral wants a destroyer to come alongside and take him and his staff off. What do I do?"

George focused on the frightened young face in front of him. The officer, a lieutenant, was wearing a steel helmet with the letters OOD stenciled on the front. Officer of the Deck. Scared out of his mind. "Get on PriTac and ask the nearest destroyer to come alongside to starboard for personnel transfer," he said. "Forwardmost sponson."

"Aye, aye, sir," the OOD said in a high and tight voice. George recognized his face but couldn't recall his name. The thumps and booms coming from the afterpart of the flight deck seemed to be gathering strength, and then he saw the forward centerline elevator bulge and then blow right out of its shaft, pursued by an evil bolus of bright orange flame. Oh my God, he thought. The whole hangar bay must be on fire. And the gallery deck? All those waiting pilots? That must be an oven by now.

"XO?"

It was the captain. His face was gray and his hands were shaking. "The admiral is transferring his flag to *Hancock*. Get a highline team down to the starboard side."

"How?" George asked without thinking. There were probably 500 men huddled on the forward part of the flight deck, most of them sitting or even lying down to stay out of the way of flying ordnance that was blasting out in all directions from the catastrophe behind them. But if the hangar bay was totally enveloped, none of them would be able to get down to a sponson, which were accessible only from the hangar deck.

The captain blinked several times, almost in time with the thunderous explosions erupting back aft. He was used to giving orders, not telling people how to carry them out. George realized his mistake.

"I'll try to get below," he said. "But we're gonna have to make it skin to skin. Bring the destroyer alongside, tell him to push his bow under the sponson and then they're gonna have to jump for it."

"Admirals don't jump from ship to ship, for Chrissakes," the captain exclaimed.

"It beats swimming," the admiral said, appearing behind the captain. He was gray-faced, just like the captain. "Think about what I said, Dick," he said. Then he turned to George. "Find us a safe route to the forward sponson, get someone to lead the way, and tell your escort exactly what to do, just like you said."

"Aye, aye, sir," George said, suddenly realizing that the ship was doing a very slow, ponderous roll. Shit, he thought. We're slowing down. Probably going to go dead in the water. The OOD was talking on the radio handset, so one of the emergency generators must have kicked in. He walked over and signaled that he wanted the handset. The OOD handed it over, almost gratefully.

"It's the *Smith Thompson* who's coming alongside," the OOD said. "Call sign Red Dog."

George keyed the press-to-talk button. "Red Dog, this is Rumble XO. Come alongside my starboard side and press your port bow against my hull under the forwardmost sponson and hold it there. We are going DIW. The admiral is transferring his flag to Warlord, over?"

The destroyer responded immediately. "This is Red Dog; WILCO. Out."

WILCO, George thought. Short for "I will comply." Good. That had been the destroyer's skipper on the other end because only a ship's captain could say WILCO. He tried using the electrical intercom, lovingly called the bitchbox, but then saw the red light was out. He then asked the terrified phone-talkers which one had DC Central. A sailor with 1JV stenciled on his steel helmet raised his hand.

"Tell Central I need a clear route from the bridge to the forward sponson, starboard side," he ordered. "A destroyer is coming alongside to take off the flag and his staff."

The talker repeated the message. Then he told George that Central needed to speak to him directly. George picked up a sound-powered handset, rotated the selector dial to 1JV, and then said: "XO here."

"XO, this is Bill Harris, DCA. The normal route to the forward sponson is through the hangar bay. The entire, I repeat, *entire* hangar bay is on fire. We'll get Repair One to rig a chain ladder from the forwardmost starboard side gun gallery down to the sponson. They'll have to go down to the flight deck level *in*side the island, exit on the seaward side, go forward to the 20 mm nests in the catwalk, and then climb down the chain ladder to the sponson platform."

"Okay, I'll get the JOOD to lead them down." He winced when three large explosions went off, big enough to shake the entire island. The bridge's clock fell off its mount and shattered on the deck. "What's the status on the gallery deck?"

There was a pause as Harris checked with his plotters. Then he was back. "There's been approximately three hundred feet of deck heave, starting from the conflagration station and going forward. What's left forward of that is being cooked."

"Were the gallery deck spaces evacuated?"

"No, sir. Not as far as we know. It happened too fast."

Jesus H. *Christ,* George thought. There would have been *hundreds* of people on the gallery deck, many of them pilots waiting for the order to man their planes. The term "deck heave" meant that the floor of the gallery deck had been crushed upward into the ceiling.

"XO, aye," he sighed. "Inform the bridge when that ladder's ready."

"Central, aye."

George walked back across the pilothouse to tell the captain about the arrangements being made to get Rear Admiral Davison and his people off. As he did so, there came a roaring noise from down on the flight deck. George got a momentary glimpse of a Tiny Tim rocket going forward up the flight deck at twice the speed of sound, climbing gracefully and then thundering off into the sea ahead of the ship, where it raised a big splash worthy of its warhead. Two more followed, one skewing sideways off the ship and blasting off in the direction of the *Hancock.* The second one slashed its way forward right down on the flight deck, carving a path of death and destruction through the pack of crewmen gathered on the extreme end of the flight deck at the bow. It disappeared off the bow, went skipping like a flat stone several times on the sea surface, and then exploded about a mile in front of the ship. George felt a thump on the ship's starboard side.

"XO," the OOD called. "*Smith Thompson* is alongside."

He looked right and saw the radar antenna on the mast of a destroyer practically level with the bridge. He grabbed the junior officer of the deck's elbow, gave him his instructions, and indicated to the admiral to follow him. He then called flag plot and instructed the staff to go down to the seaward side of the island at the flight deck level. Central called and said that Repair One had the ladder rigged and were ready to assist the admiral and his staff down to the sponson platform. At that moment, two more Tiny Tims lit off. One went off the ship to port and into the water. The other came forward, actually scraping along the flight deck side of the island in an unearthly screech before disintegrating just forward of the bridge. George saw the warhead section then go end over end down the flight deck, missing the forward five-inch mounts and the gun gallery where the admiral was headed by only a few feet, and then into the sea.

He looked back across the bridge to see the captain standing there, clenched hands at his side, obviously stupefied by the scale of what was happening. At that moment the shattered windows along the port side of the bridge were battered by a spray of seawater. George ran to the port side, overlooking the flight deck, and was amazed to see a makeshift fire-fighting crew struggling with a two-and-a-half-inch fire hose, trying to get it pointed back down into the raging gasoline fires behind the island. He looked for the chief in charge but then saw that the ragged crowd was being led by no other than Father Joe O'Callahan, his distinctive figure easily recognizable as he harangued men to join the effort and even helped wrestle the hose himself. A second firefighting team followed the chaplain's lead and was trying to get their hoses close enough on the other side of the flight deck. Once again, there was a sudden, surreal smell of woodsmoke blowing through the bridge, but this time the flight deck itself was burning.

George felt a sudden wave of panic, but quickly got ahold of himself. The enlisted men standing around the bridge with their oversized sound-powered phone helmets tethered to phone lines were wide-eyed and looked, to a man, ready to bolt. They weren't exactly reassured when screeching noises came from the starboard side as the destroyer tried to keep her bow plastered to *Franklin*'s sheer steel sides. George had never felt so helpless in his entire life. Flying a torpedo bomber against a Jap ship formation—that had been a piece of cake compared to this. The JA talker was signaling that he had a message.

"Captain, XO, light cruiser *Santa Fe* has been assigned to come along-side and render assistance."

The captain acknowledged this news and went to the starboard bridge-wing to see how the flag transfer was coming. Then he looked up at the signal bridge to see if they'd hauled down Admiral Davison's two-star flag. Protocol, at a time like this, George thought. He looked out through the damaged bridge windows for the *Santa Fe*. She was passing down their port side at a range of about 1,000 yards, headed astern, where she'd then make a 180-degree turn and come up alongside the *Franklin*'s starboard side after the destroyer broke away. As he watched her maneuver, a volley of six rockets spat out of that huge cloud of fire and smoke back aft and rained down in *Santa Fe*'s wake. Welcome alongside, George thought.

Something behind him caught his eye: it was the mast of the *Smith Thompson* pulling away from *Franklin*. She'd backed away and then come ahead, accelerating to get in front of the carrier, cross her bow, and then head for the *Hancock,* some two miles distant. The captain returned to the centerline pelorus. He took off his helmet and wiped his forehead with a handkerchief. The expression on his face indicated he felt as helpless as George did.

"Tell *Santa Fe* we need firefighting water into the hangar deck," he said. "There's nothing to be done for the flight deck."

George was about to respond when a particularly nasty blast erupted aft. It sounded like a 1,000-pounder going off. A moment later parts of the ship's enormous air-search radar antenna came crashing down on top of the signal bridge in a clatter of broken metal, while shards of red-hot bomb casing whined down the length of the flight deck and took out yet more of the helpless men huddled at the bow.

"We've *got* to get those people off the flight deck," George told the captain, shouting now to make himself heard over the constant blasts behind them. "But they can't go down into the ship. Gallery deck's gone, and the entire hangar is afire. How's about we get *Santa Fe* to do what *Smith Thompson* just did—come alongside and marry up. Those people trapped on the bow can go down ropes to her upper decks."

"I *will* not abandon ship, XO," the captain retorted. "No matter what the admiral said. If the rest of the crew sees that they'll think the abandon-ship order's been given."

George took the captain's left wrist in his right hand. "Listen to me, Captain," he said. "The rest of the crew is either dead or trapped *in*side the ship," he said, bluntly. "They're not going to see *anything* that's happening up front."

The captain glared at him, but then relented and nodded. "Very well," he said. "Make it so. Evacuate all nonessential personnel and anybody not necessary to saving the ship to *Santa Fe*."

George got on the radio to the cruiser, which was approaching cautiously up *Franklin*'s starboard side. Cautiously because every cruiser skipper remembered what had happened to the cruiser *Birmingham* when she came alongside the stricken carrier *Princeton* at Leyte Gulf. When undetected fires reached *Princeton*'s magazines, the ship blew up, shredding everything and everyone along *Birmingham*'s starboard side. In just trying to help, the cruiser lost 229 men killed and more than 400 wounded.

Santa Fe's damage control teams, collected on her upper decks, were already playing two-and-a-half-inch fire hose streams into the carrier's open sponson doors from 100 feet away while periodically ducking as flaming fragments showered down upon them. As he watched, one of the *Santa Fe*'s firefighting crews had to drop their hoses and run for it when a sudden waterfall of burning gasoline swept across one of the sponson platforms and cascaded into the sea between the two ships, casting a ghoulish orange glow onto the sides of both ships.

22

J.R. now found himself crawling on the passageway deck, along with a crowd of sailors. He was frantically trying to remember the damage control diagrams for this part of the ship. They were on what was called the second deck, directly underneath the hangar deck. The invisible fires raging just above them were beginning to melt the cableways over their heads. Blobs of paint, fused insulation, and even molten copper were dropping on everyone's head and shoulders.

Down, he thought, frantically. We have to get down, one more deck. He pushed his way through the crowd of huddled men to get to the head of the line. When someone objected, he said: "Fire marshal. Lemme through and I'll get you out of this."

That seemed to work. If his memory served him, there was a ladder about 100 feet ahead of their location that led down into the crew's mess passageway on the third deck. It would have been dogged down for GQ, but GQ had been relaxed just before the bombs hit. With any luck, it might be open or at least undogged. He kept pushing, reciting his fire marshal mantra until he arrived at what was blocking the passageway: a waterfall. A really big waterfall, stinking of gasoline fumes and engine oil. There was another companionway leading up to the hangar deck right there, and thousands of gallons of water were crashing down into their passageway. He realized his shoes were already submerged. They couldn't see the hatch above them because of all the smoke, but he thought he felt the beginnings of a starboard list coming on.

"Listen up," he shouted. The hubbub in the passageway subsided, which made the sound of the bombs going off even scarier. "Guys at the front: Feel around the deck for a hatch coaming. There's a way down to the messdecks in this passageway. Find it. It's probably just ahead."

Several men went down onto their hands and knees and frantically felt along the deck, which was now submerged in at least a foot of water that was clearly rising.

"Here," a voice yelled.

J.R. scanned the bulkhead to find a dogging wrench. That suffocating smoke cloud was down to within four feet of the deck. Everyone was hunched over, gulping what was left of the breathable air. He knew that the wrench would be mounted higher than that. "Find the dogging wrench," he yelled. "Feel for it on the bulkhead. It's higher, in the smoke. You find it, sound off and don't drop it."

Thirty seconds passed. It was getting harder and harder to breathe. And hotter. Much hotter. Then a voice yelled: "Yo—I got it."

Two men then attacked the submerged top of the hatch, one using the wrench to loosen the dogs under the rising water, the other getting them completely off until they said they had all the dogs undone.

"Bear a hand," J.R. ordered. "This hatch is under a foot of water. Get around it and heave it up."

As if glad to be told what to do, a crowd surged forward and bent their shoulders to lift the hatch. It didn't budge.

"Check the dogs," J.R. shouted. "Hand over hand. See if we missed one."

Two men felt around the edges of the hatch under the rising water, then one called for the wrench and undid the final dog.

"*Heave,*" the crowd yelled. The smoke was almost in their faces now, thick, heavy, oily, and tasting of sulfuric acid. The water was halfway to everyone's knees.

Then the hatch came up, instantly creating another waterfall down into the ladderway. Below there was battle lantern light and, most importantly, no smoke. J.R. crouched down against a bulkhead and shouted for them to go, go, go! No one needed encouraging. He heard shouts of alarm from below as over a hundred men came scrambling past and then went dropping and even falling down that ladder, accompanied by a muscular flow of water. When the last head disappeared below the hatch coaming, J.R. stepped down onto the ladder, took two steps, and then pushed the hold-back latch off its hook. The hatch came down, faster than he expected, pushing him down the ladder hard enough that he basically fell down its entire length. But with the hatch down, the waterfall subsided.

J.R. looked around. He was in the vestibule that led to the messdecks. He saw a crowd of men looking back at them from the messdecks, which was lit only by battle lanterns. There was a haze of steam and smoke hanging just below the overhead. The nearest man was a chief petty officer.

"I sure hope you know a way out of here, sir," the chief said quietly. "Everything's burning forward, and I think we're gonna run out of air."

23

Gary and his Number Two Firehouse crew stepped cautiously out of the companionway vestibule and looked around the dark passageway. The air was hot and smelled dangerously of gasoline fumes. The passageway stretched back aft a few hundred feet into total darkness, where Gary knew there were storerooms, the reefer decks, the crew's galley, and the Marine detachment berthing. There were only two battle lanterns shining that he could see, but there appeared to be a dull but fierce red glow all the way at the very back end of the passageway. They were now above the fireroom, and they could hear and feel the detonations on the flight deck and, even closer, the hangar deck. Every time a bomb went off, Gary saw that red glow way back there brighten momentarily, as if applauding.

"What *is* that?" his chief asked, staring into the darkness.

"Really hot steel, I'm afraid," Gary said. "There must be the fire to end all fires on the other side of that hatch."

"Jee-*zus*," the chief said. "*Now* where do we go?"

Four big booms came in succession, starting a rain of dust from the cableways stretched along the overhead. One of the men began coughing uncontrollably. The others were too busy being scared to death to notice.

Gary turned around to look forward. There were no battle lanterns shining, but there seemed to be a low current of hot air coming toward them from the darkness.

But no red glow, Gary told himself. Good deal. But then came a blast that sounded like it was at *their* level in the ship. Gary caught a split-second glimpse of a thin yellow-white rectangle in the distance, about the size of a watertight hatch. Then came a fireball headed straight at them.

"*Do-w-w-n!*" he yelled at the top of his voice. They all hit the deck and then were treated to a momentary session under a broiler as the fireball whumped down the passageway in search of that glowing hatch. Suddenly it was really hard to breathe. Gary realized that the fireball had consumed precious oxygen. There was only one thing to do.

"Back *down* the escape trunk," he yelled. "Hustle—air's going fast."

The two men nearest the escape trunk hatch just stared at him, but then the chief was right there, spinning the dogging wheel and then lifting the round scuttle. He then grabbed the nearest man by the shirtfront and shoved him into the hole. The rest quickly followed until Gary, the last man remaining in the rapidly rising heat of the passageway, dropped through the scuttle and pulled it shut behind him. He held on to the brass handle to catch his breath but then had to let go and grab for the ladder when the wheel began to singe his hands. He looked down. His entire crew was hanging on the ladder in various poses, their frightened faces illuminated by flickering battle lantern light. They looked like pieces of laundry with their OBA masks dangling off to one side of their soot-covered faces, one hand on the ladder, the other covering their faces.

Great, he thought; we're now trapped in a thirty-foot-long steel tube, with a smoke-filled fireroom beneath us and a big-assed fire above. The thump of explosions way up above continued unabated, each one rattling the ladder on which they were hanging. It was clear to everybody that every damned bomb, rocket, and gun magazine on the flight deck was going to have its day in the sun before this was over. The men on the ladder had the same expression on their faces now: we're well and truly screwed *and* we're gonna die.

Gary took a moment to think. There was breathable air in the escape trunk. It was warm air, but not lung-searing hot air, *and* there was no smoke. He wondered if maybe, just maybe, when the fireroom ventilation system finally lost power, the smoke from whatever the hell was going on topside stopped being drawn down into the engineering spaces. In which case, they might be able to re-man the space. Hell, maybe even get a boiler lit off. Besides, there was clearly no going up. So down it was.

"All right, people, listen up," he called down to the string of pale faces looking up at him. "We can't get out by going up, so we're gonna have to go back down. There's no smoke here in the escape trunk. It's possible the fireroom can be re-manned, okay? We're gonna go back down and see what we got on the other side of that bottom hatch. If the smoke has dissipated in the fireroom, we'll re-man the space. We'll be about as far away from all those fires topside as we can get. Maybe we can even light off a boiler and get some damned steam up."

"What if it ain't?" one of the younger men asked. "What if it's just like we left it?"

Gary frowned but then saw that the man intended no insubordination. He was merely asking the only question that mattered.

"Figure that out when we get there, Fireman. One step at a time. Start down, people. First man down, feel the hatch; sound off and tell me what you got."

They began to climb down the ladder until the first man to reach the bottom stopped and raised his hand to test the dogs.

"Hot," he said. "But not very."

"Okay," Gary said, his voice sounding unnaturally loud in the confined escape trunk. "Now listen up. That fireroom may be filled with explosive gases, just waiting for some oxygen. So we're gonna *crack* that hatch—but not open it, not until we *know,* okay? Undog all dogs except one, and then we'll ease that puppy open. Get extra hands on the hatch to hold it back. Ready?"

There were murmurs from below him. The man at the hatch looked up at him. Gary nodded. The man loosened and removed all the dogs but one and then barely released that one. Everyone in the escape trunk felt their ears pop as the pressures equalized, but there was no other sign that an explosion was imminent. Then a big boom from up above startled all of them. The chief, sensing panic, started down the ladder, passing each man below him by swinging around to one side of the ladder. When he got to the bottom, he cracked that hatch, looked inside, and then closed it.

"Smoke," he said. "Lots'a smoke. Full'a smoke. Couldn't see shit."

God*dammit,* Gary thought. Now what. Then he had an idea. "Chief?" he called. "I'm gonna go back up and crack the top hatch. When I do that, you crack open the hatch down there. Maybe what's going on top-side will suck all that smoke outa there."

The chief gave him a thumbs-up. Gary climbed wearily back up the ladder to the passageway hatch. He gingerly felt the scuttle-wheel. Warm, but no longer burn-you hot. He took a deep breath and then spun the wheel. When the dogs retracted, the scuttle bounced up a little, indicating lower pressure in the passageway than in the trunk.

"Open the hatch," he called down. The chief did.

Immediately a thick cloud of black oil smoke came boiling up the escape trunk, so fast that it nearly dislodged the men hanging on the ladder. Everyone stuck his face into his armpit in an effort to breathe, but the smoke quickly thinned out and then was gone, replaced by a rising column of hot air, stinking of fuel oil and steam. Gary closed the scuttle.

"Okay, get down there before this shit changes its mind," he yelled. The men didn't hesitate, and, one minute later, they were all back in the fire-room. As they gathered on the lower level, bent over, trying for a breath of good air, a cascade of water began to thunder down the trunk from up above. There was so much of it that it took the chief and three men to get the escape hatch closed again. At that rate, Gary thought, the escape trunk would fill in about two minutes, so here, in the fireroom, they would stay, one way or another.

He sat down on the deckplates with the others and looked around. It was dark, with only a few battle lanterns showing. The air was extremely humid; the space had become something of a steam bath. But—there was breathable air, no fire, and no serious smoke. The rumble of disaster four decks up was no longer so loud, either. Plus, there were no fireballs chasing them anymore.

"Okay," he announced. "We're back where we belong. Go through the space, see what we've got. Chief, see if you can find power, anywhere."

The chief nodded and then took three men up the ladder to the upper level. Gary took a moment to gather his wits and assess their situation. This beats being on the flight deck right about now, he thought. We're hot and dark, but there's no major flooding and no visible damage. If the air holds, we can start being snipes again.

Another serious explosion vibrated all the metal and machines around him. Great God, he thought. What happened to us? And how much more of this can the ship take before she just rolls over and goes down?

24

George and the captain watched *Santa Fe* come alongside and basically bounce off the much larger carrier with an ugly screech of rending metal that was audible even over the rumbling booms coming from back aft. George could see that the captain of the cruiser was personally conning the ship alongside, trying hard to keep the afterpart of his ship splayed out at an angle to avoid the cataracts of flaming gasoline spilling over the carrier's deck edges. *Franklin* now had a substantial list to starboard, meaning that everything up on the flight deck that could roll, slide, or fall—burnt-out aircraft carcasses, fuming bombs and torpedoes, push-tractors, and even bodies—was starting to drop into the water between the two ships. George gasped when he saw a four-pack of 500-pound bombs on a deck-dolly come rolling off the deck edge from just behind the island, but then exhaled when he spotted that their nose and tail safety cables were still attached just before they disappeared into the sea.

Santa Fe backed away and then made a second approach. This time her skipper forced the cruiser's port bow up against the carrier's tilting hull and held it there with engines and rudder. *Franklin* was by now dead in the water, but there was a seaway that was working against his efforts.

The noise of the two ships rubbing against each other was excruciating, a gigantic version of chalk going the wrong way across a blackboard, but the cruiser held her place, and there were now highline messenger ropes being shot across from *Franklin's* forward flight deck down to *Santa Fe's* number two six-inch gun turret and her midships replenishment station. George couldn't see who was in charge down there until he once again spotted Father Joe, who seemed to be everywhere at once, exhorting shocked men to bear a hand, rigging the highlines, then tending to the wounded, then giving last rites to the dead or clearly dying, before once again wading into the chaos on the flight deck. George could see other officers down there but they seemed to be just huddled with their people, probably still in shock at what they'd witnessed out on the flight deck. Within minutes, the first stretcher-baskets were riding the highline trolley down to the cruiser's deck, where *Santa Fe's* docs removed the wounded and hustled them below. Other *Franklin* crewmen were escaping down long steel ladders hanging from the starboard side gun-tubs and dangling over *Santa Fe's* number two six-inch gun turret. George winced when he saw men dropping onto the armored steel top of the turret and then tumbling out of control down onto her armored main deck, breaking God knows what.

He looked at his watch. It had been three hours since the first explosions. He thought that the noise was beginning to subside, as there could not have been much left to burn or blow up back there. Then he heard other noises and looked up. The skies around them were filled with black puffs of AA fire and the occasional flaming plane tumbling out of the sky. The noise from the flight deck had been so overwhelming that he hadn't been aware there'd been a major air attack in progress for the last thirty minutes. He realized that the Japs, smelling *Franklin's* blood, were desperately trying to finish the job. Ships all around the task force formation were heavily engaged in driving off Jap planes. There were now twice the number of destroyers arrayed around *Franklin* as there had been, every one of them blasting away with their five-inch guns.

"How far are we from Japan?" the captain asked, eyeing all that flak. George thought he sounded really frightened.

"Fifty-five miles, sir," one of the quartermasters called out.

"Too close, *much* too close," the captain muttered. "XO, get on the horn, see if they can send us a tow."

George headed aft into the island structure to the radar plotting room behind the bridge. It was a miniature version of the Combat Information Center down below, but that had been burned out in the first hour of the conflagration. He put a radio call into the task force commander's flagship and requested a tow. One minute later the USS *Pittsburgh,* a heavy cruiser, was detached from her task group and ordered to take *Franklin* in tow. George went back out onto the bridge, reported this news to the captain, and then had a talker alert the forward deck division to prepare to receive a towing hawser. They would do that all the way forward, using one of the ship's anchor chains.

The anchor handling machinery was located on an open deck below the forward edge of the flight deck, so they should be safe from whatever rockets might be left. *Pittsburgh* would maneuver to a position directly in front of *Franklin* and then shoot a messenger line attached to an eight-inch Manila hawser over to the open deck where *Franklin*'s anchor windlasses were. *Franklin*'s crew would have to pull the messenger line and then the end of the actual hawser through the carrier's bullnose, break one of the ship's anchor chains, and then attach that chain to the Manila hawser. They would then signal *Pittsburgh* to begin retrieving their hawser, which would rouse the anchor chain up out of *Franklin*'s chain locker and out into the open sea between *Franklin*'s bow and *Pittsburgh*'s stern. Once four hundred feet of chain had come up from the chain locker, *Pittsburgh* would go ahead at bare steerageway to begin pulling *Franklin* east, away from all those air bases in Japan.

George went back to the starboard bridgewing once he was confident the forecastle crew were ready to receive the towing hawser. There were two highlines between the ships in full operation now. Men from that battered crowd huddling way up at the front end of the flight deck were still gently placing the wounded, covered in red and white bandages, into wire-mesh stretchers, hooking them to the highline trolley, and then signaling for the cruiser's highline crew to haul away. George was amazed that they'd managed to get two highlines going, but there were still an awful lot of stretchers laid out on *Franklin's* flight deck and the carrier's starboard list was making it even more difficult to work the highlines. Father Joe was still ramrodding the entire operation.

He saw a surprisingly large number of men down in the water between the two ships. Many were struggling to reach the sides of the *Santa Fe,* whose crew had streamed dozens of Manila lines over her sides. But a disturbing number were just floating, held up by their life jackets. Then he saw what had happened: the men who were just floating all had their helmets still strapped on. George swore. If you jumped from a big ship with a life jacket *and* your helmet strapped on, the impact with the sea would break your neck. Those men who were just floating were probably already dead.

He went back over to the port bridgewing and looked aft. To his dismay, the fires appeared to be getting even bigger. On the inboard edge of the flight deck, closest to the island structure, the wooden flight deck was burning with a flame front advancing like a grass fire. As he watched, two rockets came out of the towering clouds of flame and smoke, skipping along the flight deck in a shower of sparks and crumpling fins before breaking up abaft the island and then showering the highline crews with fragments and flaming chunks of smoking warhead explosive. Everyone on the flight deck reflexively flattened themselves but then Father Joe got them back up, exhorting them to re-establish the highlines. George could see that the rows of white-bandaged stretchers had not diminished very much, and now there would be even more wounded to get off.

He looked for the captain but couldn't immediately see him on the bridge. He stumbled as he headed back across the bridge and actually had to catch himself on the helm console. He looked at the inclinometer. *Thirteen* degrees? What the hell was causing that, he wondered. And then he understood: all that firefighting water being played on the flight deck, the hangar deck, and the sponsons was going *down,* into the ship. He grabbed a sound-powered phone, called DC Central, and ordered counterflooding to reduce the list. The chief engineer got on the phone.

"We can't counterflood because there's no power," he said. "We, ourselves, are trapped here in the Log Room. Both passageways outside are full of burning fuel."

Shit, George thought. He was pretty sure that the ship's hull hadn't been penetrated below the waterline, at least not to his knowledge, but if they didn't do something about this list she could capsize. *Franklin*'s stability margins had been slim to begin. They'd become even slimmer with all those new guns added along the flight deck. How had he missed the fact that she was heeling thirteen degrees, he asked himself. And where the hell was the captain?

One of the bridge-talkers got his attention and reported that a destroyer following *Franklin* from directly astern was reporting she had over 400 of *Franklin*'s crew on board, all men who'd either been blown overboard or who had jumped into the sea to escape immolation. Well, that was something, George thought. He asked the cheng if there was power available anywhere on the ship.

"The after emergency generator should be running, if it survived what's going on above it," Forrest said. "Don't know about forward. Does the bridge have power?"

"No," George said, but then remembered they still had radios, which meant that Radio Central must have power. He told Forrest.

"The after diesel is set up to power command and control spaces," Forrest said. "Forward diesel normally supplies the main holes. They can swap loads if the right cables are intact and the spaces are manned. Otherwise . . ."

"Okay," George said. "We'll try to get someone into forward diesel."

"The access is through the hangar deck, XO," Forrest said. "Not possible."

"The whole thing?" George asked.

Forrest confirmed that at least half of the gallery deck, which housed several of the air group's ready rooms, had been destroyed by that first titanic gasoline-vapor explosion in the hangar deck. The blast had pushed the deck of the gallery deck up against the bottom of the flight deck. George experienced a wave of nausea at the thought of that calamity. An unknown number of pilots, sitting in their ready rooms, waiting to man their planes, suddenly squashed like bugs against the steel ceiling.

He fought back tears at the enormity of that loss. A coffee mug crashed against the pilothouse deck, reminding George that the ship might be getting ready to roll over. They had to get power from somewhere, but first he had to locate the captain.

25

J.R. told the chief to get a head count—how many men were actually down here on the messdecks. The chief nodded, turned around, and bellowed in a surprisingly loud voice for the men to pipe down and count off. Training took over; there was a sudden silence. Then the man nearest the chief shouted "One." The man next to him: "Two." When they were done the number came to 310. Then J.R. spotted one of his two system-tracing ensigns, Bill Sauer, in the crowd. He gestured for the young officer to join him out in the vestibule. As he did so there was a clatter of falling pots and pans in the hotline pantry, which is when J.R. realized that the ship was indeed listing to starboard. Based on all the wide eyes out there among the tables, he was probably the *only* one who hadn't noticed that it was getting worse. He felt a pang of alarm—his shipboard damage control courses had told him more than he wanted to know about his carrier's vulnerability to flooding, especially a carrier whose stability margins weren't wonderful to begin with. If she capsized now, nobody would get out.

"Okay, Mister Sauer," he said. "I think I know a way out of here, but we're gonna have to do it in bunches. *Disciplined* bunches. I'm gonna go back out through the hatch nearest the scullery. If my memory serves me,

I can find a way out to a deck sponson, assuming there's no fire. Once I confirm that, I'll come back and get the first group. The passageway I'm thinking about can hold no more than a hundred men, so it'll require three trips. You put the word out as to what I'm doing, especially the part about my coming back, and that not everybody can get out in the first trip. Got it?"

"Yes, sir," Sauer said.

"If there are walking wounded in this mob, they come out first."

"Yes, sir, absolutely. Got it."

J.R. closed his eyes and resurrected the damage control diagram for this part of the ship. What he had in mind wouldn't be a straight shot. In fact, it would be pretty convoluted, but he really had no choice—two side passageways and the overhead of the messdecks had fire on the other side. Between the growing heat and the rapidly diminishing oxygen, they *had* to get out, one way or another.

"One more thing," he told Sauer. "Figure out a way to tie men together, one behind the other, so if we have to run through smoke, nobody gets left behind."

Then he had another thought—he should tell the bridge, Central, or someone that he had 300 men trapped on the messdecks and that he was trying to get them out. He looked around for a sound-powered phone station. Then he asked the chief, who said there was one in the serving galley. They found it quickly, and switched into the 1JV circuit. He spun the caller handle. Nobody answered. He dialed another circuit, with the same results. The lines had probably been burned away, like everything else in the ship.

"Okay, we tried," he told the chief. "I'm gonna go exploring."

"Want company?" the chief asked. Sauer also stepped up.

J.R. almost said yes, but then explained to them quietly that if all the khaki went out that scullery hatch, the men would think they were being abandoned. The chief pointed out that Ensign Sauer could remain behind. J.R. just looked at him. The chief grinned back. An ensign. Right. Okay, I'll stay behind.

There were no replacement oxygen cannisters on the messdecks, so he donned a gas mask. If he encountered one of the damage control lockers he might be able to find an OBA, but for now, the mask would have to do. He did acquire a flashlight and a spare from a small fire station next to the serving line. He nodded at the chief, who opened up the scullery hatch, and then stepped into the dark vestibule.

First, he tested the air. The familiar stink of gasoline and burning oil was pretty bad, but he could breathe. The temperature in the narrow passageway was easily over 100 degrees and the sounds coming from the next deck up were not encouraging. The ship's main galley was on this deck but a few hundred feet farther aft. The passageway from the galley to the messdecks, where the men actually ate, was a zigzag affair because the massive boiler uptakes and smokestack pipes were in the way. If he remembered correctly there were two smaller passageways that led out to the ship's starboard side sponson decks from just behind the uptake plenums. When the ship conducted an underway replenishment at sea, steel highlines would be sent over from the supply ship to this sponson. That way pallets of food could be manhandled by working parties directly back to the galley areas where the ship's refrigerated and freezer spaces were. The scullery passageway divided into two branches, one on each side of the uptakes.

He started aft, feeling his way along the passageway, whose battle lanterns had given up the ghost. The thin beam from his flashlight pierced the accumulated smoke, but just barely. As he got closer to where the passageway first divided, he heard a bomb go off and then the clatter of collapsing sheet metal. He felt a sudden pressure drop in the air that made his ears pop and then a noise like wind whipping down a canyon. Before he knew it, he was being sucked down the passageway. He frantically grabbed for a handhold along the bulkheads and finally caught a vertical cableway. There was a roar of fast-moving air now, but it wasn't coming from the passageway. He dropped down onto his hands and knees and crept up to the turn that led to the right, making sure he always had something to hang on to. He made the turn, crept about ten feet, and then began the next turn, to the left this time. Something warned him not to do that, so he jammed one leg against a steel protrusion on the bulkhead. He was barely able to keep himself from being sucked around the corner.

He was aghast when he did finally manage to get a look around the corner. The entire bulkhead had been ripped away, and he was looking into the uptake plenum itself, a steel mineshaft-like structure. There were four large, steel ducts in the uptake space, each one about ten feet square. Two of them carried clean combustion air down from the stack to feed the boilers. The other two took the products of combustion from those same boilers—smoke, superheated gases, steam, and a haze of acidic soot—back up the stack and out into the sea air. He realized he no longer needed the flashlight. He could see and that was because, above him, there was an enormous fire, and that's what was sucking the air out of the ship. Incongruously, there were streams of steaming-hot water sluicing back down the sides of the uptake chamber.

That's the hangar bay way up there, he thought. No wonder we lost all power—with no air supply the boilers couldn't function. Even as he stared up at this horrifying sight, a bright white bolus of flame appeared above him as something blew up in the hangar bay. That Jap bomb had ruptured *all* the uptake chambers. What had followed the Jap's bomb had finished the job.

He curled under himself and clawed his way back into the original scullery passageway. For some reason the moaning darkness was more comforting than seeing the interior of the ship's smokestack chambers. That had been like looking into an active volcano. There were all sorts of objects—airplane engines, wheels, a crumpled wing—tangled up in the plenum chamber stringers, making it look like a charred steel clothesline. No way they were going to get by that mess, he thought. Then he remembered there was a second branch to this passageway. Try the other side, he said to himself, but for just a moment he just sat there on the warm deck, that evil breeze blowing past his head. So, do it, his brain told him. "Gimme a sec," he said, out loud this time. He was being overcome with a feeling of hopelessness, a sense that he should maybe just curl up right here on the deck and grab a quick nap. He was tired, very tired. The cacophony of explosions and rending metal above him didn't help. Maybe for just a few minutes, he told himself. He tried to change position but his leg slipped on something oily and he went down hard. His forehead hit a sharp fitting on the bulkhead and it hurt, really hurt.

Wait a minute, he thought, wiping blood out of his right eye. It's the air, or lack of it. Shit! There's carbon monoxide in this passageway, and *that's* what was lulling him into a quick nap, one from which he would never awake. *Dammit!*

He sat back only to hit that object a second time, hard enough to see stars this time. The sudden jolt brought him completely out of his gathering funk and he was able to focus again. Then he heard something coming—something falling down through the ruined uptake chamber, something big and heavy, banging its way through the spiderweb of steel stringers that supported the uptakes, getting closer, tumbling, bang, bang, crash, and then it punched through the skin of the uptake shaft and crashed down practically on top of him. He had no time to think, move, or do anything at all, and then there it was: the *thing*: a 1,000-pound bomb, its casing seams oozing a brown liquid and little puffs of harsh chemical smoke. Its steel casing was hot, really hot, hot enough to singe his skin. It was missing its fins, and, thank God, the safety wire was still threaded through its nose and—wait.

Oh, shit, there was no safety wire going through the tail assembly, and that little propeller at the back of the bomb was turning in the hot draft flowing through the passageway, but not quickly. Its shaft must have been bent because it gave off a squeak on each revolution. He knew that propeller was a counter. It didn't mean that the bomb would explode when it reached its count, but it might, and the bomb's casing was hot enough to make his khaki trousers smoke.

As he stared in horror at this monster bomb lying practically in his lap, quietly arming itself, there came a really big boom from the hangar deck that seemed to twist the entire length of the ship's hull. The remains of the uptakes rattled like a load of trash cans overturning on the street, and then the damned bomb moved, pinning his right leg to the deck. It felt like a bus had just quietly parked on his leg. For one long, agonizing moment, he watched that little propeller go around and around, one squeak at a time, as its geared shaft withdrew the internal pins that blocked the fusing train within the bomb.

Once again, he experienced a sudden fog, as if he was being mesmerized by that lethal little propeller. Another blast from the hangar deck above, and this time more things came rattling down the uptake plenum, including an aircraft engine that burst through the sides of the uptake and dislodged the bomb. He yelled in pain but then realized he was free. This time he didn't hesitate—he rolled sideways and kept rolling all the way back down the passageway, wind or no Goddamned wind, until he was back at the T-junction. He tried again to gather his wits. The rumble of explosions up on the hangar deck continued unabated, each one contributing a new cascade of burning metal down into the uptake chambers.

Move, move, *move,* damn you, his brain yelled. He did, rolling into the other branch of the passageway, where suddenly it was quieter and not so hot. A piece of his mind was still waiting for that 1,000-pounder to let go, in which case his search for a way out would become academic.

A way out. *That's* what I'm supposed to be doing. Find a way out. Three hundred guys are waiting, hoping, praying that you succeed. *Move!*

Don't want to.

But he did, and within minutes he found a hatch. He undogged it, pushed, and then tumbled out onto one of the sponson decks. The sudden blast of clean, fresh air almost undid him and he staggered around the sloping deck like some kind of drunk. He had to grab a stanchion to stop sliding toward the deck's edge. When he fully opened his eyes, he was stunned to see another ship right there, tight alongside. A cruiser, and there were men not that far away pointing at him and yelling. There were big streams of water coming up from that ship, playing up and down and all along Franklin's blistered sides. A big blast up on the flight deck flung more burning debris all over the place. The firefighters over on the cruiser hit the deck. Instinctively, he did, too, although nothing was falling on or near him until a flaming wing tumbled over the deck edge above, painting the ship's sides with burning gasoline until it hit the sea.

He struggled to stand back up. Men on the cruiser were signaling him to jump, pointing to a tangle of monkey-lines in the water between the two ships. Both ships were apparently dead in the water, so all he had to do was jump and someone would pull him in. All he had to do was just let go.

No, dammit. That's not why you're here.

He had work to do. He put up a hand and then drew the number 300 backward in the air, pointed back into the hatch, took two deep breaths, and forced himself to go back in. It took him an unpleasant thirty minutes to find his way back to the messdecks. If anything, the passageway was even hotter and there seemed to be more wreckage now in his way than on his way out. The fuming bomb—*his* bomb—was no longer in sight. But—there *was* a way out, for the moment, anyway. Now all he had to do was go get them. He realized he'd been going uphill, which meant that the starboard list was getting worse. He tried to hurry through the labyrinth of passageways, vestibules, and hatches leading back to the messdecks but if anything, there was more debris in the passageway. When he finally opened up the scullery hatch, he was hit by a wave of warm air that smelled in equal parts of mortal fear and gasoline fumes.

"Listen up," he shouted at the crowd of men who'd hurried to cluster around the scullery hatch. "I've found a way out, and there's a cruiser right alongside you can get to. First hundred: come with me. There isn't room for any more, so I'll be back. You got my word on that. Chief?"

"Sir," the chief answered.

"You figure out a way to keep them hooked up?"

"Yes, sir, each man grabs the belt of the guy in front of him."

"That'll do it," J.R. said. Then he started shouting again. "Hook up. Some of the passageways are full dark and there's wreckage, smoke, and some really big holes, so just keep moving. Once we get outside, you'll need to bear a hand in receiving a highline, and they'll get you down. All right?"

No one responded. For an instant the only sound was that of the rumbling fire on the hangar deck.

"I said: All *right*?" he shouted.

They responded with a muted "all right." He was facing a virtual sea of terrified eyes. Scared shitless, he thought. And for good reason. Me, too.

"Let's go—first hundred. Follow me."

He felt a hand grab the back of his belt in a death grip. The chief opened the hatch. At first, he couldn't move until the nearest men behind him got the idea and stepped forward. It felt like walking in a nightmare, straining to get the line moving while those frightening orange flares erupted ahead of them and everyone was able to see just how much debris was in the way. But they did move, even if it felt like he was pulling the whole train all by himself. When he finally got to the hatch leading out to the sponson deck, he stepped aside and yelled at them to hustle up. They didn't need much encouraging at that point, and in only a few minutes 300 of them were crowded around the sloping sponson deck.

So much for my great plan, he thought, grinning at the chief and Ensign Sauer as they tumbled out of the hatch bringing up the rear, the last to leave the messdecks. Then some shouting began at the other edge of the crowd. The slanting deck, wet from the cruiser's firefighting streams, made it hard to stand up and suddenly men were tumbling off the edge into the sea between the ships, unable to get their footing on the slippery steel. All J.R. could do was hang on to the hatch itself and watch a slow-motion avalanche of terrified men gathering speed as sliders grabbed the stationary men. Within sixty seconds, almost the entire crowd was down in the water, some men disappearing when other men fell on them from forty feet above. J.R. thought they looked like the swarm in a commercial fishing net when they begin to haul it in.

The cruiser people, God bless 'em, didn't hesitate. Men carrying the ends of lines jumped in and passed their lines to the struggling *Franklin* crewmen. Others up on the cruiser's main deck heaved around smartly and began pulling people out of the water. At one point, J.R. thought there were as many cruiser men in the water between the ships as *Franklin* men. Suddenly, as if to add to the terror, the cruiser's five-inch-gun secondary batteries cut loose, firing at a Jap plane that was trying to crash into the once-in-a-lifetime target of two ships tied together in the open ocean.

J.R. suddenly had to just sit down on the wet steel as his brain became completely overloaded. The chief was hanging on for dear life at the other side of the sponson. Ensign Sauer had apparently joined the human waterfall going over the side. J.R. hooked the back of his belt to a tie-down fitting in the deck and decided it was finally time to take a little nap. He was helped along by a roaring noise in his ears, which he hoped wasn't something about to fall on him. Or another Jap bomber. Exhausted, he simply passed out.

26

George still didn't know where the captain was, so he headed back into the passageway behind the bridge, bracing himself against the starboard list. A quarter mile directly ahead *Pittsburgh* was painstakingly maneuvering to get her stern right under the bows of the stricken carrier to begin the business of passing the heavy towing hawser. She was hampered by the fact that the hawser was sinking as it absorbed water, putting it right in the way of the cruiser's backing propellers. They had to pull it back aboard *Pittsburgh,* wait and hold it while the ship put on a backing bell, then stop it, and then let it slip back into the sea. It was taking over sixty men just to hold on to it. Then the *Franklin's* forecastle crew would have to heave around, by hand since there was no power to the winches, to bring the bitter end ever closer to the bullnose.

He glanced sideways at the inclinometer as he left the bridge. Thirteen degrees. Well, actually, it was more like fifteen degrees now. He just kept going. If Central couldn't get some counterflooding under way pretty soon they'd all be swimming. At least all the fires would go out, he thought, cheerily.

Santa Fe had ceased firing on nearby bogeys, for which George was grateful. The noise had been terrific, amplified as it was between the steel sides of the two ships. Twenty feet back was the captain's sea cabin. George knocked on the door and then tried the handle. Locked. He knocked again. Then the anti-air gunfire next door started up again, and this time it included 40 and 20 mm guns. George stood there in the passageway, holding his breath. He finally heard the sound of an aircraft engine, howling at redline RPM, pass close over the ship, followed by what he recognized as the determined growl of a Corsair engine accompanied by 50-caliber fire. Then all he heard was the staccato banging of small-caliber AA ammo cooking off down along *Franklin's* flight deck. *Santa Fe* must have ceased firing to let that Corsair take care of business.

He banged on the sea-cabin door one more time, then pressed his ear against the thin metal of the door. He thought he heard something inside, but couldn't make out what it was. But he was definitely in there. Then a talker was calling for him from out on the bridge. He gave up and hurried back out into the pilothouse. The talker was pointing down onto the flight deck forward, where dozens of men were desperately trying to take cover as more and more of the ready-service ammo lockers, bathed in the remains of a lake of burning gasoline trapped in the portside catwalks by the ship's list, cooked off with increasing ferocity, shooting armor-piercing incendiary tracer rounds in all directions, including some that punched through the backside of the port bridgewing and killed one of the lookouts. The hapless man grunted in pain and then folded onto the deck gratings, bleeding horribly, but still holding his binoculars.

George closed his eyes yet again to banish the sight, but then opened them in time to first hear and then see a Tiny Tim rocket arcing high over the flight deck, its rocket going half-blast. It got up to about 400 feet, then arced over and headed directly toward the *Pittsburgh*. George found himself mouthing the words: no, no, *no*, as he watched the rocket, its back end still spitting flaming smoke, fly right over the cruiser's after eight-inch gun director and then disappear somewhere abeam of the ship. They're gonna get tired of that, George thought, remembering the previous rocket. Two bloodstained corpsmen appeared out of nowhere to tend to the bloody mess on the bridgewing.

He looked back down at the flight deck and saw that the remaining men up there had given up on taking the highline. There was a continuous stream of men sliding down monkey-lines or chain ladders into the water between *Franklin* and *Santa Fe,* where the light cruiser's crew worked frantically to get them out from between the two ships. He reluctantly went over to the starboard bridgewing and looked down. Some force of wind and sea was slowly pushing the two ships closer together, creating a closing wedge of looming steel that threatened to crush the frantic swimmers thrashing below.

One of the talkers piped up with the news that several men were going over the side all the way aft, at the very end of the flight deck that was called the round-down. The fires had become so intense that they could no longer hold on back there. George couldn't see that end of the ship because of the volcano erupting between him and the round-down, but he could see what looked like *two* destroyer masts poking up to one side of that gigantic smoke column. They had probably nosed in right up against the carrier's stern to rescue as many men as possible from the water right behind the ship. Once again, he thought that the fires aft *had* to be finally diminishing, except for the fact that there was a column of pure flame blowing out of the ship's starboard side hangar bay doors like a giant acetylene torch. There might be not much left to burn *on* the flight deck, he thought, but inside, there were a quarter-million gallons of high-octane aviation gasoline available to keep this catastrophe going for damn near ever. Then the captain appeared. His face was flushed, and his eyes were bright, almost wet, as if he'd been weeping. He strode uncertainly to the front windows.

"Where are all the men who were forward, on the flight deck?" he asked in a tight voice.

"Down there," George said, pointing at the still considerable crowd of heads down in the water. "Trying to get pulled aboard *Santa Fe* before the ships drift together."

"They abandoned?" the captain said, his voice rising. "They *abandoned* ship? Who gave that order? *You?!*"

George shook his head. He explained about the anti-aircraft ammo cooking off and how that had made the flight deck untenable.

"Get 'em back," the captain roared, but at that moment there was an awful screeching of metal forward as *Santa Fe,* her port bow still pressed hard against *Franklin's* starboard side, began to ever so slowly drift back. Her skipper's efforts to use his engines to keep the ships from pinching together had somehow put sternway on the smaller ship, and now the chorus of terrified screams from down in the water was as loud as the screeching sounds of the two ships' hulls dragging against each other. At that moment, a Jap plane came screaming down out of nowhere in a vertical dive and sliced into the water right between the two ships, about a hundred feet astern of the island. It came down so fast that no one actually saw more than a flash of metal and then it was gone, leaving behind only a cruciform of foam in the sea. As hundreds of men on *Franklin* and *Santa Fe* stared in stunned surprise, the Jap's bomb went off underwater, as it always did. The plane by then had to be a hundred feet down, but the shock wave from that explosion, trapped and then focused by the two ships' underwater hulls, created a fleeting, bright white shock-circle in the water, after which the sounds of the men thrashing about in the water diminished.

Santa Fe's guns then resumed firing; this time joined by the cruiser's six-inch main batteries. She jerked backward to get away from *Franklin*, gathering sternway with what looked like every one of her guns blazing away. George finally saw why: way down on the near horizon, flying just above the surface of the sea, four enemy torpedo bombers were headed in. They were instantly obscured by all the anti-aircraft shells from *Santa Fe*, her guns firing so low that some of the shells were skipping out like flat rocks before tumbling into the sea and exploding. George held his breath as the oncoming planes were swallowed up in a storm of AA fire from both *Santa Fe* and the two destroyers trailing the carrier. He heard booming from ahead of the ship and saw that *Pittsburgh* had joined in with her AA batteries, even as she was backing the last few feet toward *Franklin's* bow.

It was all over in a few seconds. The cruisers ceased firing, and, as the smoke cleared, nothing remained of the torpedo bombers.

"*Torpedo*, starboard side," one of the lookouts screamed, pointing down into the water. George looked down and actually saw the incoming wake, passing just ahead of *Santa Fe* and headed straight for *Franklin's* starboard side. He unconsciously braced himself for the impact, and then actually felt the thing hit amidships, a one-ton killer going almost fifty miles an hour. He squinted his eyes and felt his toes and fingers curling in anticipation of a blast, but nothing happened. A dud. Thanks be to God.

He looked around for the captain, who was now standing by his chair in what looked like a total state of shock. Four Corsairs came ripping over the forward flight deck from port to starboard, causing the men clustered on *Pittsburgh*'s upper AA gun mounts to hit the deck.

Pittsburgh, he thought. She had backed in so close that he could no longer see her stern or even her after eight-inch turret, because her stern was now practically right under *Franklin*'s bow.

"Fo'c'sle reports they've got the hawser through the bullnose," one of the talkers announced. "They're requesting permission to veer chain when ready."

George turned to the captain. "Captain? *Pittsburgh* is ready to make the tow."

The captain looked back at him blankly for a second, and then nodded. Then something blew up behind the island. It made a different sound from the bombs. George whirled around in time to see an entire twin five-inch gun mount go flying across the remains of the flight deck and then off the ship's port side, dropping a trail of burning powder cans as it went down and out of sight into the sea. For one brief, frantically painful instant, George just wanted to jump off the bridgewing and follow that mount into the calm, soundless depths of the sea.

27

The chief came back after fifteen minutes and declared the fireroom to be totally devoid of electrical power. "Everything's deader'n a doornail," was the way he put it.

"Why isn't there emergency generator power?" Gary asked. "We've got two of 'em, Goddammit."

"Ain't no way to tell if either one of them's up and running, not from here," the chief said. "One's all the way forward, the other's all the way aft."

Forget about aft, Gary thought. There'll be nothing left aft. But, maybe, if he could reach the bridge by sound-powered phone, they might be able to send someone down to check on the forward emergency diesel generator. It lived in a compartment on the second deck, right below the hangar deck, all the way forward, so it might have survived the fires. He went over to the nearest phone selector switch and dialed in the 1JV circuit. He tried every station and got nothing. There was a second barrel switch next to the one he'd tried. The circuit selections on the brass switch were not familiar, so he tried one marked *JX* and heard voices. Excited voices. It sounded like the signal bridge, or maybe one of the emergency radio-rooms. When there was a momentary pause, he pushed the talk button. "This is two fireroom; I need to talk to anyone on the bridge, and my normal line is down."

"What?" a voice asked angrily, as if suspecting a stupid prank.

Gary tried again. "This is Lieutenant Gary Peck, boilers officer. I'm in the number two fireroom. All my normal comms with the rest of engineering are down. This fireroom is tenable. Please get word to the bridge that I need a dedicated sound-powered phone circuit and emergency electrical power. We're trying to raise steam and I desperately need power."

"Don't we all, Lieutenant," an older voice said. "Stay up this circuit. I'll see what I can do."

Gary ordered one of the firemen to strap on a sound-powered phone headset, plug into the JX circuit, and listen for a call.

Maybe, just maybe, he thought.

28

"XO!"

George blinked and then looked around to see who was calling him this time. It was one of the phone-talkers.

"Radio Central reports there's some snipes down in the number two fireroom. They say if they can get some emergency power, they can light off a boiler. They're on the JX circuit."

Radio Central? George wondered. Hunh? But then he went to the phone selector, dialed JX, and called number two fireroom, identifying himself as the XO. A scared-sounding fireman answered him.

"Let me talk to the senior officer down there," he ordered. A moment later a voice said: "Lieutenant Gary Peck, B-division officer, sir."

"Mister Peck, we were told that all the main holes had been smoked out; what's your status down there?"

"Hot, with some smoke, but the holes in the uptakes are letting the smoke *out* now for some unknown reason. If I can get emergency power, I can probably light off a boiler, although first we gotta get about four feet of water or so inside the fireboxes pumped out."

"I can probably get some emergency power cables lowered down to you, but as best we know, there's only one diesel generator available now and that's carrying Radio Central and the bridge. What little fire main we have is coming from those portable gasoline fire pumps."

"The forward emergency diesel generator should have survived all this, XO," Gary said. "It's all the way forward and one deck below the hangar deck. If it can be started up and connected to its switchboard, I should be able to tap it down here. If I can get a boiler going, we can make real power for the whole ship."

"How the hell can you do that?"

"One of the ship's service generators lives in number one engine room, XO—right behind this fireroom. If we can get steam up, we can probably re-energize that engine room, de-smoke it, and roll that generator."

Wow, George thought, listening to a distant barrage of anti-aircraft fire. Wouldn't that be nice. "We'll give it a try, Mister Peck. We've got a whole crew up on the fo'c'sle. The cruiser *Pittsburgh* is trying to take us under tow. Lemme work it."

"Aye, aye, sir. Standing by. That generator room is one deck down and a bit aft of the fo'c'sle. And I can tell whoever goes down there how to air-start the generator and line it up to the board."

"Got it, Mister Peck. I'm not gonna ask how you got a crew back into a fireroom, but very well done."

The captain came over and asked George who he was commending at a time like this. George told him what he'd learned. The captain nodded, but George wasn't sure he'd actually understood. They walked out to the port bridgewing. Back aft the explosions had quit except for some small-caliber ammo. The flight deck fires had pretty much run out of fuel, but underneath, on the hangar deck and the crumpled gallery deck, there was still an ominous rumbling.

"*Santa Fe* is getting ready to stand off," the captain said. "Our long-distance pickets are reporting a large raid forming up over Kagoshima. He wants to be able to maneuver when they show up."

"Can't blame him; fo'c'sle reports they've made *Pittsburgh*'s towing hawser to our starboard anchor chain; they're starting to veer chain to set up the tow."

"Very well," the captain said. "Just in time; what took so damned long?"

"They had to pull the hawser in by hand, sir," George said, patiently. "It's six hundred feet long; eight-inch Manila."

"So why didn't they call for more men?"

"There aren't any," George said, gesturing toward the forward flight deck.

The captain, obviously startled by what George had just reported, started yelling. "What? *What?!*" he shouted. "What the Goddamn hell does that mean?"

George wanted to slap him. Where the hell had *he* been for the past five hours? As he tried to formulate an answer the captain pointed a finger at him. "If I find out you ordered abandon ship, I'll—"

George set his face. "You'll what?" he growled, inspiring a nearby lookout to scamper back into the pilothouse.

The captain's eyes widened. Nobody, *no*body, in his entire, if short, tenure as CO had ever stood up to him. George bored in.

"You need to get a hold of yourself, Captain," he said quietly through clenched teeth. "We have only fragmentary casualty reports from GQ stations around the ship. Most of the sound-powered phone circuits are out. We've got fire-main pressure only because of those handy-billys, and maybe, just maybe, the after emergency diesel generator is running. There's no ship's service power—anywhere. All the main holes had to be abandoned when the uptake spaces were breached. I'd guess—and that's all I got right now, is a Goddamned *guess*—that we lost one-quarter of the crew and most of the air-wing that was still aboard in the first hour. Lost, as in killed. I'd *guess* over a thousand crewmen went over the side rather than burn to death on the flight deck. I don't know how many got picked up—the destroyers came in pretty fast. I saw several hundred men go over the side to *Santa Fe* when exploding ammunition started to strafe the flight deck. If we have six hundred men left aboard I'd be surprised, and of those, half will be wounded."

The captain's face went white. "Six hundred?" he gasped. "Out of a ship's company of thirty-six hundred?"

"Yes, sir. I assumed you knew. I assumed you've witnessed the same disaster that I have."

"Six *hundred*?" the captain said, ignoring the insult. Now it was almost a whisper.

"The only reason we're afloat is that all the damage—so far, anyway—is *above* the waterline. This list has most likely been caused by firefighting water getting down below. I've ordered Central to commence counter-flooding, but that takes pumps, and pumps require power. And by the way, Central itself is completely isolated. They're basically trapped in there until we can get repair parties down into the interior passageways. So right now, yes, I'm working to get some Goddamned electrical power."

The captain stood there, all six foot three of him, staring at George like a wounded ghost. George had seen that look before during the Solomons campaigns back in '42 and '43. He changed his tone of voice and suggested to the captain that he go sit down in his chair, get some food and coffee. *Santa Fe* had sent over some cargo nets filled with emergency rations for the past hour—mostly bread, cans of Spam, and jerry cans of potable water. Without the steam plant or electrical power there was apparently no fresh water available anywhere in the ship. There'd been a few rain squalls during the afternoon, which had inspired the men huddling on the flight deck to catch rainwater in their helmets. The skies were overcast even now as evening approached. Good, George thought, as he shivered in the biting wind blowing through the cracked portholes. Harder for the Japs to find us.

The captain turned obediently around and went to his chair, where he sat down, staring into the gathering darkness. George called the forecastle crew about that emergency generator. *Pittsburgh* was taking a strain on the towing rig but the carrier was so much bigger than the cruiser that the larger ship's bow was actually pulling the smaller ship's stern all over the place. They were moving, at perhaps one knot, but they were getting nowhere. And, crappy weather or not, George knew the Japs by now knew how bad off the *Franklin* was and were determined to finish the job.

29

J.R. came to and discovered to his surprise that *Santa Fe* was gone. He sat up to make sure, dislodged that all–important belt loop, and began to slide down the tilted sponson deck toward the water. He quickly rolled onto his side, wide awake now as the deck edge approached, until his belt buckle caught on something, spun him around, and brought him up short. He was cold, wet, and sore, and the daylight was fading rapidly. He couldn't see the horizon anymore. He looked around the sponson deck to see if anyone was there, but there were only small mounds of wet clothes here and there. There was a Corsair propeller assembly at the far corner of the sponson, held in place by one of its blades, which had punched into the deck.

He realized the ship was rolling a bit. Nothing violent, but a definite pendulum movement in ponderous slow motion. As he took that in, he saw one of those mounds begin to slide toward the deck edge, leaving a dark slick. He caught a glimpse of a human rib cage as it toppled into the sea. He closed his eyes, squeezing hard to banish that picture.

Where the hell is everybody, he wondered. All those people in the water, and the others up forward, shinnying down monkey-lines and going hand over hand down the tilting radio antennas in an effort to get down to the cruiser's decks. Oh, *shit,* he gasped. They've abandoned! I'm here all alone and she's gonna roll over and go down. But then a cold rain squall swept in, soaking his clothes and bringing him back around. The ship was moving. Slowly, but she was definitely moving. He'd seen her insides—a tow. They'd sent another ship to take *Franklin* in tow. He turned sideways on the sloping deck and looked up at the island. He thought he saw indistinct faces out on the bridgewing. He looked forward again, beyond where all those men had gone over the side. There *was* a ship up front, a cruiser from the shape of her top hampers. He felt instantly better. Gotta get inside, he told himself. This whole thing was just nuts: running from fire and brimstone one moment, longing to get warm and dry again the next. Jee-*zus!*

He untangled his belt and crawled upslope to the hatch through which he'd brought everybody out. The actuating handle was only warm, so he opened it and swung it back. He was immediately bowled over by a blast of hot gases that reeked of burning electrical insulation. He tripped over his own feet and then fell backward, sliding faster and faster toward the deck edge again until he was able to grab a stanchion and stop just short of going overboard. Then the stanchion broke. He went over with a yell but managed to grab on with both hands to a fragment of snaking that had been blown down from the flight deck earlier. He hung there for a moment and wondered if things could get any worse. Then he felt a blaze of searing heat across the backs of his hands as all those pent-up and nearly incandescent gases, trapped in the passageway, discovered there was fresh air available and exploded in a jet of flame that shot out over his head and extended fifty feet off the side of the ship like a momentary blowtorch before extinguishing itself. He tried not to cry out when that fireball burned the backs of his hands. Thankfully it was over in an instant, but not before he got a whiff of his own broiled skin.

Open your eyes, he told himself. He did.

He was hanging on to a snarl of snaking, which was a weblike band of marlin woven into a diamond lattice and stretched along the bottom rungs of the ship's lifelines to provide a final handhold for someone about to be swept overboard in a seaway. The deck edge of the sponson was in his face while the rest of his body dangled over the cold sea below. For one giddy instant, he was tempted to just let go. This was all too God-damned *hard*! But then he saw one of the ship's fifty-foot-long whip antennas, still connected to its insulator base on the edge of the flight deck but now leaning down across the forward edge of the sponson deck. There were black bloody handprints all along its length.

He began to swing his legs back and forth like a pendulum until he could catch an ankle on the deck edge and heave himself back up onto the sponson. He relaxed for a moment after that big effort, only to realize he was beginning to slide right back over the side again.

"No!" he yelled, and then started clambering like a frenzied crab across the deck, skinning his hands, knees, and even a cheek on the steel surface, until he was able to grab that antenna.

It moved, starting a slow arc back toward the edge with the sudden weight. He yelled again: "No, no, *no!*" and then started kicking like a sprinter rising from the starting crouch with an amazing burst of adrenaline-inspired strength, until he'd pushed that antenna all the way to the top of the sponson, when he finally ran out of steam.

He lay there, gasping for breath, but now his seaboots were wedged against the deck so everything—himself, the antenna—had stopped moving. He looked up the length of the aluminum antenna, which resembled a fly-fishing rod. Its glass insulator base was mounted on the very edge of the flight deck, and that's where he needed to be. The angle from the sponson to the flight deck catwalk was about sixty degrees. Not vertical, but near as dammit. He commanded his scorched hands to hold on and then he rested for a minute. The ship was moving around enough for him to feel it. It was getting really dark and there was a cold, wet wind blowing spray against his face. He knew there was no way he was strong enough to inchworm his way up that slender metal shaft.

Belt, he thought. Take off your belt, take a turn around the antenna shaft, grab the two ends, and then shove it upward and pull. And repeat. Let the antenna take your weight. Use your strength to pull yourself up the incline, one tug at a time. Become an inchworm.

Five painful minutes later he was able to roll off the antenna base and into a sagging catwalk. Where am I, he wondered. Starboard side. Forward of the island and the two forward five-inch mounts. He lay there in the catwalk, catching his breath.

Where the hell *is* everybody? he asked himself again. Three thousand, six hundred people on this ship, and now the only indication that he wasn't completely alone was the glow of red lights in the pilothouse way up there on the top of the island. There was water in the catwalk, deeper on one side than the other due to the ship's list. For a moment he submerged his face in it, letting the cold water refresh him. Then he soaked his hands.

"Okay," he said to himself. "You're not really wounded. Your arms and legs work. Time to stand the hell up and go forward."

No, his brain argued. Go back to the island. Get inside. Rest.

No: *forward,* all the way to the bow. That's where there'll be people. *Some*body had to be up there—they'd rigged a tow. Behind him was only death and destruction. The wind whipping over the darkened flight deck moaned through the remaining deck stanchions, making an almost anguished sound. You and me, brothers, he whispered. Then he stood up, weaving like a drunk.

He stumbled forward, holding on to both sides of the catwalk, until the catwalk itself ended. There were steel steps leading up to the actual flight deck. He struggled to climb them and then tried to stand upright. The starboard list made that hard, but the flight deck surface kept him from slipping. He went all the way forward and down a ladder into a small catwalk, where he found an open hatch that had been locked back. There was black soot all around the hatch coaming, but whatever fire had done that was no longer present. The smell coming from the vestibule was nauseating. A passageway inside led forward to yet another vestibule, where a hatch in the deck led down one level to the ship's open-air forecastle and anchor windlass machinery platform under the flight deck overhang. The very front of the flight deck overhung the forecastle by about sixty feet.

A heavy cruiser was off the port bow about six hundred feet away. There was a small group of boatswain mates keeping an eye on the anchor chain, which was now threaded through the bullnose instead of its hawsepipe. The chain was tending toward the cruiser, but J.R. got the impression that the carrier was jerking the cruiser around every time a deep swell slapped up against her bow and blew salt spray all over the forecastle. A boatswain mate first class spotted him.

"Where'd you come from, shipmate?" he asked. Then he realized J.R. was wearing khaki. "Sorry, sir, I meant—"

J.R. waved him off. "I've been inside, getting people off the messdecks. Where the hell is everybody?"

"On the *Santa Fe* or one of those destroyers out there. Or just gone. The rest of my guys were sent down to see about an emergency diesel generator. Bridge is desperate for power, but my guys are all deck apes, you know?"

"I'm a snipe," J.R. said. "Can someone lead me down there? I couldn't recognize where I was in that passageway back there."

"Take you myself, Lieutenant," the bosun said. "And if you think that passageway is bad, wait'll you see the hangar bays."

Five minutes later he was standing in the forward emergency diesel generator compartment, where, to his astonishment, the big 250,000-watt generator was humming happily away. The bosun explained to the small crowd of deck seamen that someone from engineering had arrived. They appeared to be greatly relieved. J.R. spotted one of them wearing a set of sound-powered phones.

"Who you talking to?" he asked the seaman, who appeared to be about fifteen years old.

"The bridge, sir," the kid said. Then his eyes widened. "Sir? The XO's on the line. The XO, himself."

J.R. took the headset and put it on. He called the bridge. George answered immediately. "Who's this?" he asked.

"Sir, this is Lieutenant McCauley, fire marshal. I just got here from amidships."

"How?"

"The hard way, XO. The *really* hard way."

"Okay," George said. "They're telling me that generator is *running*?"

"Yes, sir, it is, but it's running at no-load. Its switchboard's been cleared. I can put it on the line, but we'll have to limit the loads—this engine can't carry the whole ship."

P. T. DEUTERMANN • 154

"Right," George said. "Here's the deal: We've got a skeleton crew in number two fireroom. They think they can get a boiler lit off, but they have no electrical power. Can you make that happen?"

"I think so, XO," J.R. said. "Gimme a minute to ID the circuits this thing can supply."

"Standing by, Mister McCauley."

J.R. told the bosun he could take his people back up to the forecastle. They did not linger. The emergency diesel's main breaker was easily identifiable, but the individual circuit breakers were not labeled except with a number. He went around to the side of the switchboard to examine the breaker chart. He knew there was a better-than-even chance that electrical supply cables running from the forward emergency diesel had been burned away. He was hoping to find a breaker labeled number two fireroom, but instead there were breakers for Radio Central, sick bay, the bridge, one twin five-inch mount, and the Combat Information Center. No help. He stared down at the chart and then realized he was looking at the chart for the *after* diesel. He went back around to the front of the switchboard. There was one large breaker with a red tab on it at the very end of the breaker row, marked M.E. Back to the chart. Wrong chart, his tired brain told him. No breaker labeled M.E.

He looked some more, then spied a three-ring binder hanging on a small stand-up desk beside the switchboard. It contained wiring diagrams for the forward diesel switchboard. The spidery lines on the chart went fuzzy the more he looked at them. He sighed. This was electrical gang stuff. He flipped through the pages of crisscrossed lines and arcane symbols until he came to the last page. He stared, mentally yelling at his eyes to focus. The title of the page was Main Engineering Bus. Main Engineering: M.E.

The diagram below was as simple as it could be: one red line running through all six main engineering spaces, from the forward auxiliary through numbers one and two firerooms, number one engine room, numbers three and four firerooms, number two engine room, and, finally, the after auxiliary space. There were switchboards in each of the spaces, which could be fed from either the forward or the after emergency generators. J.R. was pretty sure that the after emergency diesel probably no longer existed, since everything aft of the island had been turned into an open-hearth furnace. But—if he closed the M.E. breaker, number two fireroom's switchboard should go hot. That meant they could light off a boiler. Then a team would have to get into number one engine room, and bring that space back to life, including the big ship's service turbo-generator that lived there. That would provide 1,500,000 watts of power, enough to get the rest of the plant going.

This all assumed that the main engineering bus was intact, and, even more worrying, that the crews abandoning the eight main spaces had taken the time to clear their switchboards. If all six main spaces' worth of electrical demand suddenly lit up, the forward emergency diesel would trip right off the line and probably jump overboard. He slumped down into a crouching position. His very bones ached. He decided to call the XO again.

"Do it," George said after listening to J.R.'s explanation of what they were facing. "And here's why: if any given main space's switchboard senses that the voltage is inadequate, it will trip its main breaker. Then all two firehouse has to do is re-energize their board."

"Yessir," J.R. said, in a distinctly if-you-say-so voice. "Can you inform two firehouse to man their board?"

"Yup," George said. "And very well done, Mister McCauley. If you can make your way to the bridge, do so. The chief engineer and a lot of his people are trapped in the Log Room because of passageway fires and smoke. I need a snipe up here."

"Aye, aye, sir," J.R. replied, and then threw the M.E. breaker.

Nothing happened. The generator didn't try to jump off its pad and the diesel engine barely wavered. That meant one of two things, J.R. thought: either the generator wasn't actually physically connected to anything at all, or the main space crews *had* cleared their boards. Training, he thought. Well, we're gonna find out.

30

hat's that?" the chief asked, looking over Gary's shoulder. Gary
turned to see. There was a dim yellow glow coming from the
upper level. It was hard to see because there was still a wet, smoky haze
enveloping the upper level of the fireroom.

"That's our switchboard," Gary said. Then the talker confirmed that
the forward diesel was sending power to the main spaces.

"Hot damn," the chief said. "Let's go to town."

They then went up to the fireroom switchboard. It was hotter and
harder to breathe on the upper level, and there was a strong, sickening
stink of oil smoke, producing instant headaches. That yellow light meant
there was power available from the M.E. circuit. They closed the board's
emergency power breaker. A red light then glowed above the board's main
breaker.

"Now," Gary said. "Let's make this whole board hot and get two-Baker
lit off."

"Okay," the chief said. "Just one thing: where we gonna get combustion
air? The uptakes are torn all to hell."

"The lightoff blower will tell the tale, Chief," Gary said. "The boiler doesn't care where the air comes from. The real problem will come when the boiler starts making smoke. That shit's gonna go everywhere."

"How would anybody know?" the chief asked.

Gary just stared at him. How indeed: after what had been happening all day, a little boiler exhaust would be hardly noticeable. The chief was grinning at him, albeit with a fine white line of hysteria in his eyes. Gary punched him lightly in the chest. "Turn to and go make us some God-damned steam," he ordered.

"Goddamned steam, aye, sir," the chief replied.

For the next hour the chief had his crew cleaning out the firebox of 2B boiler, which had the least amount of water in it. Two men had had to crawl through a burner front with swabs to dry down the brickwork and get the last of the standing water out of the firebox. Others had had to disassemble burner assemblies to rid them of saltwater residue. The light-off blower fan motor was completely grounded out with salt, so they had to take a motor off another, dryer pump and swap that out with the grounded one.

Once the switchboard went hot, they had lights, which, for some reason, improved everyone's attitude. There was still no ventilation because Gary wanted to make sure he didn't overload that diesel generator up forward. Finally, they were ready. The light-off blower was lined up to the air registers. The burner assemblies were in place and lined up to the fuel manifold, just waiting for pressure from the light-off fuel pump. Ordinarily they would have taken the time to pass the fuel oil through heaters, because Navy Special Fuel Oil was extremely viscous. But when Gary had ordered the fuel oil heater lit off, the lights had dimmed. They were just going to have to make do. Like they'd done with feedwater. Again, ordinarily they would have filled the boiler with pure, distilled water. As it was, they'd tapped the closest feedwater bottom in order to fill the boiler. The quality of that water was necessarily unknown.

Lighting off a marine boiler was a bootstrap operation. Start with small pumps and blowers, fill the boiler, close the main steam line stops, and throw the torch in. Once steam pressure began to rise, they'd gradually switch over to the bigger, steam-driven pumps—fuel oil service, feedwater main booster, and, eventually, the turbine-driven main-feed pumps and forced-draft blowers for combustion air. As these bigger auxiliaries came on the line, they'd create low-pressure auxiliary steam from their turbine drains. Once that was available, they could light off the deareating feed tank and use what they called aux steam to scrub any entrained oxygen out of the incoming feedwater. Eventually, the boiler would reach 600 psi and then they'd cut in the superheater burners. Main steam, 600 psi and 850 degrees hot, would become available after about twenty minutes.

The initial "customers" for main steam would be the turbine-driven main-feed pumps and the forced-draft blowers. Next would be the 1,500-kilowatt ship's service turbo-generator sitting in the number one engine room right behind them. Once that generator's board went hot, there'd be serious power available throughout the plant. Other main spaces could be re-manned and lit off. As for the rest of the ship, everything depended on whether or not the cabling ship-wide was still intact. Gary knew that couldn't possibly be the case, but one step at a time. And finally, with main steam being produced in a fireroom, the nearest two main-engine turbines could be brought back to life, which in turn would mean two of the ship's four propellers could be rolled.

Gary knew it would take hours—perhaps even all night—to get just this boiler room up and running. But when that torch went into the firebox and produced the familiar whump, he knew *Franklin* now might just have a chance to escape. The next step would be to get a crew into the number one engine room, so that the machinery then could be warmed up and made ready for main steam. His gang was looking around and nodding at each other. There was fire in the box, the steam gauge needle had trembled off its pin on its way to 600 psi, and one of the young firemen was holding up a cannister of coffee-makings. What more could any snipe want?

31

George exhaled in relief when the word came up that fires had been lighted under number two boiler. He walked over to tell the captain but found him asleep in his chair. His steward had brought him a sandwich and some coffee; he'd eaten half the sandwich and then fallen asleep. George decided to let sleeping dogs lie, but did relieve the captain of the other half of that sandwich and the cold coffee.

Pittsburgh by then had gained a semblance of control over her 36,000-ton burden, but only after George had dispatched a team to after-steering to hand-crank the ship's thirty-ton rudder three degrees to starboard, which finally offset the mischief the wind was making. They were now making a grand two knots. He walked out onto the port bridgewing. The ship was under tow with only a tiny bit of electricity available. The fires were out on the flight deck, but there remained an ominous red glow visible in the ruined elevator pits and smoke was still boiling out of one of the hangar bay side doors. Two much-depleted firefighting crews were pointing hoses down into the hangar bay, their fire mains powered by a clutch of gasoline-powered pumps set up out on an undamaged sponson and that other mysterious source of power from back aft, probably the after-diesel. He'd asked his emergency-steering team to confirm that.

Damage Control Central was reporting that they were still trapped in their spaces due to there being no oxygen in the outside passageways. Also, what was left of the repair parties were reporting that the P-250s and the P-500s were running out of gasoline. Great, he thought. He looked out to where the horizon should be. Fortunately, it was darker than that apocryphal well-digger's behind. The ship's one remaining radar showed that there were now four destroyers creeping along with their grievously wounded carrier, keeping station 1,000 yards off her port and starboard sides. There were two more ahead of *Pittsburgh,* close in, to augment her air defenses. Unable to maneuver, both the cruiser and the carrier were essentially defenseless.

The weather was neither better nor worse. The rain squalls had diminished somewhat as darkness fell, but the God-sent overcast remained, with low-flying scud maintaining a ceiling of what looked to be about 1,000 feet. The forward emergency diesel generator had allowed flag plot and the secondary CIC right behind the bridge to light back up, although the air-search radars were still not functioning. This allowed the bridge team to listen in to the task force air defense net, where there were indications of yet another major raid inbound. George got a whiff of stack gas. He looked aft to the top of the island, but the smoke wasn't coming from there. Then he saw a grayish cloud puff out of the top of the island. Then another, bigger one huffed out right at flight deck level. The uptakes had been ruptured, and that boiler was sending stack gas wherever it could.

"XO."

He went back into the pilothouse. It was the chief engineer on the phone.

"Go ahead, Walt."

"Is it possible you can send a repair party to Central and find a way out for us? The passageways are full of smoke, and our normal escape route is all collapsed decks and bulkheads."

"Um," George said. "We no longer have organized repair parties, Walt. It's mostly guys manning portable fire pumps. I'm estimating we have only six hundred or so men left on board, and maybe half that number are effectives."

"Good God," Forrest said.

Then George remembered Lieutenant McCauley, up in the forward emergency diesel compartment. "Lemme see what I can do," George said. "You have OBAs?"

"We do, but not enough. We'll have to share masks. My whole GQ team is in here."

"You have the people you'll need to bring up an engine room?"

"These are the Damage Control Central folks, XO," Forrest said. "My main-hole snipes all had to bail out when the fire and smoke came down the uptake spaces. I have no idea of where they went or if any of them are even on board. People came topside when the main holes filled up with oil smoke. Topside wasn't much of an improvement."

"Got that right, Walt," George said. "They're probably riding around on our destroyers right now. *If* they were lucky. If the boiler room can make steam, can you get an engine up and running?"

"Absolutely, XO, if I have to do it by myself."

"Okay, call me back in twenty minutes."

"Aye, aye, sir," Forrest said.

George contacted the forecastle detail that was monitoring the towing rig. He asked the chief to see if Lieutenant McCauley was still in forward diesel. Two minutes later he got his answer.

"Yes, sir," the chief said. "He's down there. Says he's watching the load. The whole world is calling for power and he said he's gotta make sure they don't drag that generator off the line."

"Get him to this phone circuit. I need to talk to him."

J.R. came up on the circuit three minutes later. George explained what he needed. "You've been loose in the interior," he said. "You know your way around. I need those guys in Central to man up an engine room, especially your boss. If you can lead them out to a sponson, even, they can get below. Number two fireroom has a boiler lit off."

"I'll try, XO," J.R. said. "All the big topside fires have quieted down, but inside—well, we aren't done yet."

"Try your best, Mister McCauley. If you can't get through, then you can't get through. Don't go killing yourself trying."

J.R. made an impolite noise.

"What?" George asked.

"You obviously haven't been belowdecks, XO. Think of it as a beehive—with all the honeycombs burning."

George hesitated. Maybe he shouldn't ask this young officer to go back into whatever hell lay belowdecks.

"Lieutenant?" he asked.

There was no answer. The lieutenant was gone. Well, good, George thought. That boy's gonna go take care of business. Thank God.

"XO?" another talker called.

Oh, shit, George thought. What now.

32

J.R. got himself back up to one of the starboard side catwalks. It was dark, cold, and with that familiar chilly wind blowing across the flight deck, but now that wind was coming from ahead, which meant they were moving at last. He was still in his khakis, with no coat or hat. He could barely make out the front of the island in the darkness, and the only light was a menacing red glow from the midships elevator well. The flight deck itself was totally dark, with only a bunch of gray shapes aft of the island to indicate the scope of the disaster. The ship was still listing to starboard, so he had to be careful to keep to the "uphill" side of the catwalk to keep his feet dry.

Off in the distance he could see the streamers of falling flares as the Jap recon aircraft circled the task force, probably looking for *Franklin*. There was some anti-aircraft fire, but the Japs had learned to stay out of range until they found something worthy of an attack. He thought he could hear some Corsair engines, most likely night-fighters, who'd be out hunting snoopers. The big gray bulk of the island didn't look right, and then he realized the ship's mast and several antennas were draped over its uppermost levels. He jumped when one of the after catwalk guns suddenly went off.

The strangest part was that there was no one about on the flight deck. He thought he could see the dimmed red lights way up on the bridge, but there were no planes or people up on the flight deck itself. He looked over the side. Dozens of monkey-lines were draped along the starboard side, making tiny white wakes as their bitter ends trailed in the dark water below. Up ahead was the dark bulk of that heavy cruiser, pulling the invisible towing rig and a reluctant carrier in the away direction. The ship felt heavy, waterlogged no doubt. He wondered if, perversely, all that water down below was keeping her from capsizing.

Enough rubbernecking, he thought. Time to figure out how the hell I'm going to get down four decks to DC Central. That red glow rising from the elevator well told him that the fires were *not* out belowdecks. He leaned against the cold catwalk sides and tried to visualize the interior layout. Flight deck, gallery deck, hangar deck, second deck, third deck. From what he knew, the flight deck was a shamble of burnt wood, melted airplanes, and big holes. The gallery deck had been crushed up against the bottom of the flight deck when all that gasoline vapor blew up. The hangar deck itself was probably still an oven. The second deck was so filled with smoke that he'd had to go *down* to get those people out.

And yet, we're still afloat. The hangar deck was armored, so even with 500- and 1,000-pound bombs going off right *on* the hangar deck, what lay beneath should have been protected. He was tired, very tired. He desperately wanted to sit down or even lie down, even if that meant doing so in a semiflooded catwalk. The ship was rolling, ever so slowly, causing sooty rainwater to spill over the edge of the flight deck. He opened his mouth to get some fresh water and then started to chase those little waterfalls as he realized how thirsty he was. It was rainwater, with a tinge of badly scorched Douglas fir. It tasted wonderful.

If I'm going to go back down below, I *must* find an OBA, or at least a gas mask. At some point he'd had a gas mask, but it was long gone now. He knew what kind of fires would still be burning down there: insulation, wiring, linoleum tiles in the passageways, cans and boxes in storerooms, hydraulic lines, all of them creating a noxious brew of chemical fumes. The big oil fires might be mostly out, having consumed everything in their path, but these residual fires were just as dangerous *and* they were consuming oxygen. *Gotta* find an OBA and some extra cannisters. And then: What if I do get down to Central? How the hell do I get *them* out of there if the passageways are filled with toxic gases? He knew there was an OBA locker in Central, but were there enough units to get everyone out?

You're the fire marshal—you should know the answer to that, he thought. But he didn't and his brain was sufficiently fogged that he almost didn't care.

He lifted himself up onto the flight deck and started aft, keeping to the seaward side of the island structure, which was relatively undamaged. When he got to the after five-inch mounts he encountered small mounds, which he knew used to be human beings. The upper mount looked intact with its hatched locked back; then he realized the lower mount wasn't there anymore. The smell of charred flesh was everywhere, despite the wind.

That upper gun mount, he thought. They kept some OBAs in the gun mounts. He found a ladder going up to the second mount. Inside, the gun machinery seemed undamaged, except that all the wiring and hydraulic hoses were melted and hanging down from the ceiling of the mount like silver and copper stalactites. The guns' breeches were open. Then he found the DC locker, all the way at the back of the mount. He cranked it open and found a pool of rubber down at the bottom.

No joy here, he thought. He got out of the mount and tried to remember where there were any other DC lockers. Maybe inside the island? He went back down to the flight deck and entered the island from the flight deck level hatch on the seaward side. But as he opened the hatch a great sigh of the most horrible-smelling air pushed out and he quickly slammed the hatch shut. He was *not* going to go in there. Period.

He turned around and went aft along the starboard edge of the flight deck. It was fully dark now and he had to thread his way through all sorts of *things* lying about. He deliberately didn't look to his right where all those planes had been, fully armed and fueled. There were gray shapes out there, too; some of them were rolling around as the ship moved ahead.

He tripped and fell over an arresting wire in the darkness, which let him know he was approaching the round-down, the very back of the flight deck. Flashlight, he thought. Why in God's name didn't I bring my flashlight. The wind freshened suddenly, which told him he was approaching the edge. He got down on his hands and knees and crawled until he could hear waves down below. There should have been a temporary lifeline stretched across the back of the ship, but it was long gone.

He closed his eyes and recalled what it looked like back here. Straight down was the fantail, an open platform over the stern of the ship. A place where sailors congregated in the evening to have a smoke or to dump trash and garbage into the wake. There was no way to get down there from the flight deck and if he slipped and went over, he'd land on a steel deck some thirty feet below.

He was now several hundred feet behind the spot where Central was. Even if he found a way down to the fantail, he'd then have to re-enter the interior of the ship at the very back part of the hangar deck, where the machine shops were. They were well aft of where the major conflagration had been but there was no guarantee that there weren't residual fires down there. So why are you all the way back here? He didn't know, which made him recognize that he was semi out of it. He stepped back from the round-down and tripped over a tangle of broken arresting wires. He sat down hard and then the ship's starboard list started him sliding toward the deck edge. The rough surface of the flight deck slowed him down but not enough and over he went, arms flailing, only to tumble into a catwalk and crack his head.

That woke him up. Central, he thought. You're supposed to be leading men out of Central. What in God's name are you doing back here? Looking for an OBA. Right.

He went forward in the catwalk until he was halfway back to the dark bulk of the island. He was directly downwind of the conflagration area and he began gagging. The whole area smelled like the rendering plants outside of Omaha, where the offal was cooked down into by-products. Then he looked down: the after sponson deck was right below, only there were no monkey-lines back here. He continued forward and tripped over a one-and-a-half-inch fire hose. That'll do, he thought. He pulled the hose back to a point right over the sponson and began dropping it down until he heard the brass nozzle hit the deck below. He tied an awkward knot in the canvas-covered hose to make a loop and passed that over an antenna mount. Then he went over the edge and slid down the hose until he reached the sponson deck. The deck was wet and slippery, especially with the list, but he made his way uphill to the sponson hatch, grabbed it, and held on.

Time to think, he told himself. Where am I, and what's inside this hatch. The hangar deck was the ship's main deck. The next one down was called the second deck, which is where he was. Central was on the third deck. But—this was a way in, and it was below the hangar deck and well aft of where most of the fires had been. So maybe, just maybe, he'd found a route. Even as he thought that, he remembered all the smoke and toxic gases, and he still didn't have an OBA.

So, Mister Fire Marshal: ventilate it. Open the hatch, stand aside, and let all that crap boil out of the interior until it was safe to traverse the fore and aft passageway. Go forward until you find the first companionway ladder going down to the third deck, where there shouldn't be any smoke or fire.

Except, genius: if that were true, the guys in Central would have been out a long time ago.

Dammit. It was really hard to focus.

Do it twice, he thought. Open this hatch, ventilate it, go forward to the companionway hatch, and then ventilate that bastard. Then you'll have a way out.

What could go wrong? he asked himself and then barked out one sharp laugh in the darkness and began undogging the hatch.

33

Gary sat on an overturned trash can watching the boiler-front gauges. The light-off blower was chugging away and the firebox sight glass showed its usual yellow-white glare. The pressure gauge showed 230 pounds, which meant that the stop valves were holding. He started to think ahead. Once they got the boiler up to pressure, they'd then need to find somewhere for all that steam to go to do some good work for Jesus. Main feed booster pumps. Main feed pumps. The big blowers. Cutting in the DA tank to start scrubbing the feedwater. The ultimate objective remained: that all-important ship's service turbo-generator in Main Control. If they could get a crew of machinist mates into the engine room right behind them, they could then cut in the superheater tubes and eventually roll that generator, and, maybe, with any luck, one, even two main engines.

He caught a whiff of stack gas. That made him sit right up.

The big blowers were large steam turbine-driven fans that produced much larger volumes of air to maintain the higher energy combustion in the firebox. The light-off blower had been getting its air from the boiler room; smelling stack gas in the boiler room meant that the light-off blower was creating negative pressure in the fireroom. Worse, it meant that the flow of "outside" air to the boilers was coming from *in*side the ship, instead of down the intake plenums. He called the chief over.

"Once we get this boiler up to set point, we're gonna have to roll the forced-draft blowers to maintain main steam pressure," he said.

The chief nodded, as in, well, yeah.

"I'm smelling stack gas," Gary said. "That means the intake plenums have been compromised, too. We roll the big blowers, I think we're gonna take suction on the entire interior of the ship. What kinda air we gonna get down here?"

The chief closed his eyes for a moment. "We're gonna get whatever fire and smoke that's still left inside," he said. "And *that's* gonna draw fresh air through all the holes in the flight deck. And *that's* gonna reflash fires that're probably dying out right now for lack of oh-two, because they'll be getting brand-new air and a lot of it."

"Shit," Gary said. Except, he thought: the boiler wouldn't care, as long as it got great quantities of air into its firebox.

He was very tired. He tried to think of a reason *not* to light off the big forced-draft blowers once the required steam pressure was available. He closed his eyes for a moment to gather his thoughts. They want me to roll a ship's service generator, and eventually, a main engine. But God help anyone who was trying to move around inside the ship when that big draft of outside air came howling through the smoldering remains of *Franklin's* interior spaces. The chief nudged him, thinking he'd gone to sleep.

"Tell the bridge what the problem is," the chief said. "Tell 'em what might happen. See if they wanna go ahead."

Gary just looked at him for a moment. "Right," he said. "You smell it, too?"

"Smell what?"

"Stack gas, loose in the space."

The chief grinned. "I'm a chief boilertender, Boss," he scoffed. "I *breathe* stack gas, drink fuel oil, eat fireside soot, and fart fire. A little stack gas in a main hole ain't no biggie in the P.I."

Gary rolled his eyes and relayed his concerns to the XO on the bridge.

"Do what you have to do, Lieutenant," the XO told him. "We desperately need more power and a way to go faster than two knots. The whole Jap air force is out looking for us tonight. Our fighters are reporting torpedo bombers. Those evil bastards know we've been hurt bad, but unless they get some torpedoes into us, they know we're gonna get away. I've got Lieutenant McCauley on a mission to get some more snipes down there. Don't let up."

"Aye, aye, sir," Gary said. He glanced at the pressure gauge. Four hundred pounds and rising. This was going to get really interesting. "Bleed aux steam to the big blowers," he ordered. "Warm their steely big asses up."

34

Acting on a hunch, J.R. stepped back away before knocking aside the final dog. That turned out to be a great idea. A small tornado of smoke, hot air, and an ugly whirlwind of soot roared out of the hatch. He had to grip the bulkhead and kneel down to keep from going with it. After a few minutes everything subsided and he was able to step through the hatch and start up the passageway. He thought it was a good sign that all those toxic gases had been under pressure. The whole ship was full of that stuff; getting it out would help everybody. There was still a light haze in the passageway, but the battle lanterns, God bless 'em, were still giving out a little light.

He came to the down hatch he needed about a hundred feet forward from where he'd started. It was a double companionway, locked down tight. He touched the hatch metal with the back of his hand. Warm, but not fire-hot. The hatch had two round scuttles, one for each of the two parallel ladders below. In normal circumstances, a man who needed to go through the hatch would open one scuttle, go down through it, turn around, and then lock it back down again without ever moving the hatch itself, thus restoring watertight integrity. There were noises now, metal against metal and then the sounds of debris rolling across the blistered decks above. But no more explosions, he thought. Be grateful for small favors. He grabbed the round operating handle of the scuttle and began to turn it counterclockwise. Almost immediately he could hear air whistling past the seals.

Under pressure, he thought, just like the last one. Now what: wait for some of that pressure to bleed off? Or go ahead and flip the damned thing open. He recalled the tension in the XO's voice. Jap torpedo bombers probing the defensive perimeters of the task force, all of them looking for one carrier. He lay down on the deck and spun the wheel. Once again, he released a muscular column of air, even noisier than the last one because it was being channeled through a much smaller opening. It helped that he knew what to expect. He put his head down and waited for the steady roar of air to subside and immediately fell asleep. He was awakened by the sudden silence. It took him a full minute to gather his wits and to remember what he was there to do, and falling asleep wasn't it.

He slipped down through the scuttle and scampered down the ladder. There were no battle lanterns still alive in the companionway vestibule, although he saw a dim yellow glow in the passageway going forward. He landed in the passageway only to discover there was two feet of water on the deck.

For a moment he froze. The ship's sinking, he thought. Has to be. There's no way there can be water here. It took everything he had to get ahold of himself. His arms and legs hurt. His feet hurt. The air in the passageway was so humid that he could hardly breathe. He started forward and immediately tripped over something. He went down and hit his head on a bulkhead. Once again, the sudden pain cleared his brain.

Firefighting water. The whole world had been shooting firefighting water into *Franklin*'s roasted innards. Water had to go somewhere. Some of it had gone over the side, but most of it had come down here.

He hurried now, trying to convince himself that the water wasn't rising. Part of his brain knew it wasn't; another part, the survival part, wasn't so damn sure. Here and there some battle lanterns were still barely glowing; most had died. He knew where he was, though, and he'd traveled this route at least a couple of times a day. Still: it was more than a little unnerving. The ship was unusually quiet, with no ventilation, no throngs of sailors moving fore and aft in the passageways, no other machinery running, no lights, and an atmosphere that was an ugly stew of soot particles, high-explosive residue, and the unmistakable stench of violent death. The starboard list was icing on the cake, and when the ship rolled, even just a little, part of his brain waited to make sure it rolled back the other way. Each and every time.

Finally, he reached the passageway that led to Damage Control Central and the Log Room. The doors to the various offices along this passageway were not watertight doors, the theory being that if the sea was loose on this deck, the ship was a goner anyway. There was one operable battle lantern that had come off its bracket and now lay on the deck, covered by three inches of water on the down side of the list. It stared back at him like a baleful, slightly green eye, as if daring him to go past it. He reached for the Log Room door handle and then had an evil thought. He pulled out his pocketknife and rapped sharply on the door. He grinned as he imagined the expressions inside—this passageway had been filled with hot smoke, so what kind of hoodoo was banging on the door? He knocked again and the door finally opened. It was the chief engineer who was staring back at him. Behind him a small sea of wide-eyed faces looked ready to bolt.

J.R. adopted a formal messenger posture and informed the cheng that, in the parlance of the eighteenth-century Royal Navy, the captain sends his compliments and that the chief engineer's presence was required in number one engine room. It looked like the cheng got the joke, although the men behind him still didn't seem to be so sure. The last guy who'd cracked that door had gasped when he saw the conditions, thereby inhaling enough carbon monoxide to actually kill him on the spot.

J.R. stepped in and closed the door behind him. He explained to everyone that he had a relatively clear route for them to get down into Main Control and that Lieutenant McCauley had a boiler lit off and was close to bringing the forced-draft blowers on the line. He decided to forego any talk of Jap torpedo bombers out there in the darkness until one petty officer declared *he* wasn't leaving the space. But before J.R. could explain the need for haste, the chief engineer announced that anyone who didn't want to leave the space could stay, as long as they understood that when the big blowers came on the line, they'd suck all the air out of the ship's interior because the intake plenums had been breached. Any resistance to leaving vanished.

It took J.R. and his trusty parade much less time to get back to the ladder leading down to the engine room. The chief engineer led the way down, leaving J.R. alone at the top of the ladder. The entrance to number two fireroom was fifty feet away, and already he could feel a strong draft of air ruffling his uniform as that boiler began to crave some serious air. He tried to decide where to go: back to the flight deck and forward again? He experienced a sudden blinking fit as the grainy air swept by him. God, he could absolutely murder a cup of coffee.

That's it, then, he thought. They get steam up in number two firehouse? The *first* thing they'll do is make coffee. He trotted over to the hatch leading down into the fireroom and happily dropped down into familiar territory. The sudden smell of steam, hot wet lagging, and fuel oil made him think he was finally home. And coffee. By all the gods, he could smell coffee!

35

George gave a short yelp of joy when he got the word that there were snipes in both a fireroom and an engine room. If they could get and keep that boiler on the line, they'd have serious electrical power, not to mention a way to roll machinery in other spaces. They'd get the big fire pumps going. Lighting in the undamaged passageways. Maybe even guns and radar. And, perhaps most importantly, a way to get this damned list off the ship.

George knew that the list was a much more serious problem than most people appreciated. The Essex-class carriers had gone to sea with slim margins when it came to stability. As everything else had been unfolding, he'd been doing some calculations on what it would take to get the ship back on an even keel. They'd have to counterflood, filling some voids on the port side built into the ship for this very purpose. More water in counterflooding tanks would actually help the stability problem by lowering the ship's center of gravity. The other way to make the ship's stability less precarious was to jettison topside weight, especially on the flight deck. Normally he'd have called the air boss, but the Air Department had been decapitated when PriFly was blown off the side of the island. At that moment Father Joe showed up on the bridge. He'd been out exploring, apparently, looking for stragglers who might have taken shelter in nooks and crannies around the forward flight deck and leading them to safety on the starboard side of the island. He reported he had a "crew" of about two dozen badly frightened sailors.

George seized on the sudden availability of "hands." He explained to Father Joe what he needed. The chaplain seemed a bit confused, but George didn't have time to explain the concept of metacentric height just now.

"Listen to me, Father," George said. "I need every Goddamned thing that can be moved thrown over the side. *Every* Goddamned thing out there. Yellow-gear, cranes, plane wreckage, loose guns, ammo, burnt-out ordnance, bodies—*every* Goddamned thing."

"Um, yessir, XO. But, bodies too? Can't we—"

"Everything, Father. Our metacentric height right now is probably measured in inches."

George could tell from the chaplain's expression that he didn't have any idea of what George was talking about, but being Father Joe, he nodded and left the bridge to get to work. Give me ten officers as good as that Jesuit priest, George thought, and he could send the whole rest of the wardroom home.

"XO." This time, it wasn't a phone-talker.

George looked across the pilothouse. The captain was awake and calling for him. He walked over to the captain's chair, still holding the coffee mug he'd filched earlier. "What time is it?" the captain asked, in a groggy voice. "What's our status?"

George looked at his watch. He'd forgotten to wind it. He looked back across the bridge at the ship's clock. "Almost twenty-three hundred," he said. "We're still afloat. *Pittsburgh*'s got us making three knots. The task force night-fighter CAP has been engaging Bettys who are probably looking for us."

A sudden rain squall lashed the front windows, sending a fine spray through the tattered glass panes. The captain blinked when he felt his face getting wet. His face looked extremely haggard in the red light from the central pelorus.

"This shitty weather is probably saving us right now," George continued. "That and our night-fighters. The good news is that the snipes have re-manned a couple of main spaces and we soon should have both ship's service power and maybe even an engine."

The captain closed his eyes for a long moment. Then he sat up. "How many snipes we still have on board?" he asked.

"The B-division officer, Lieutenant Gary Peck, has one partial fireroom crew manning up number two fireroom," he said. "The chief engineer is headed down into number one engine room with his Log Room and DC Central people if Lieutenant McCauley can find a route."

The captain frowned. "The Log Room?" he said. "Those people aren't main-hole engineers."

"They're about to be," George said. "They've been trapped in the Log Room since the first explosions. I'm guessing they'll be very happy to go make steam. Lieutenant McCauley reported he found a way to de-smoke the third deck main passageways and is working on leading them out."

"God Almighty, XO," the captain said in a low growl. "Two lieutenants, one department head, and what, thirty Log Room yeomen? How many of this crew have deserted?"

George saw some of the enlisted watchstanders around the pilothouse recoil when they heard the captain say that word.

"I'd hardly call it desertion when the choice is to burn to death or jump," George said. "And if they jumped with their helmets and life jackets on, they probably didn't survive the fall. As to your question, until we get an actual face-to-face muster, we won't know what we've got left."

"I don't understand," the captain said. "The entire engineering department is below the armored deck. Where are all those people?"

George realized then that the captain had not fully absorbed the scale of the calamity that had befallen his ship.

"The Jap bomb or bombs ruptured the structure containing the air supply to the main holes, as well as the uptake ducting leading up to the stacks. The main spaces were enveloped in smoke from the hangar deck as well as stack gas from the boilers themselves. The main holes were all abandoned once the air ran out."

"I was never told that," the captain complained.

"Well, actually, the chief engineer requested permission to abandon the main spaces and you gave it to him, Captain. By then the world was ending back aft, so I can well imagine you might not remember it."

"So, where the hell are they now?" the captain snapped, ignoring what George had just told him.

"In the event of a big fire in the main spaces, they train to get out and then muster by watch-section on the hangar deck so they can be put on damage control teams. That wasn't possible, so many of them ended up out on sponson decks or all the way back on the fantail. Those who survived the jump are probably on the *Santa Fe* or one of the destroyers that came in to recover our people. Or hiding out in various shops or even their berthing compartments. They'd have no way of knowing it's safe to come out. Especially since it probably *isn't* safe to come out. There's no breathable air belowdecks."

"You're telling me that a third of my crew made their *own* decision to abandon ship."

"When burning avgas started pouring over the round-down and onto the fantail, I'm guessing that wasn't a hard decision for anybody back there to make," George pointed out.

"XO." A talker, this time.

"What?" George snapped.

"Lieutenant Peck says he's ready to bring number two boiler on the line and send steam to number one engine room."

"XO, aye," George replied. "Tell him the priority is to get a generator on the line as soon as possible."

The talker acknowledged and repeated the message to the boiler room.

"XO?" the captain said, softly.

"Sir?"

"Those are *my* decisions to make from here on out, got it?"

George felt his face flush in the darkness. He'd been handling everything for so long he'd never thought to consult the captain, who'd been sitting right there. "Aye, aye, sir," he said, automatically. "Do you have other orders?"

"Getting power is important," the captain said. "But right now, getting away from the Japs is paramount. I want whatever steam number two fireroom is producing to be dedicated to one ship's service generator and *two* engines. Instruct the chief engineer to limit power distribution until we have *two* boilers on the line. That'll give us fifteen knots and we can then break this tow. Then we'll start distributing power throughout the ship, starting with air-search radar and guns."

"Aye, aye, sir," George said. He wondered if the captain remembered the air-search radar antenna landing on top of the island in the first few minutes of the disaster.

The captain got out of his chair, gave everyone in the pilothouse a stony look, and then headed aft to his sea cabin. George took a seat on the navigator's stool and dialed up number one engine room to tell the cheng the plan. He was still a bit red-faced about his chain of command faux pas. And yet, the captain had seemed to be strangely passive for the worst of the conflagration; George had simply stepped up. Now that the captain was apparently "back," he felt a little bit better. He realized he was more than ready to hand command back to someone else.

Now, he thought: Why am I sitting here? Oh, yeah, number two fireroom: when can we have *two* boilers?

36

"XO."

George opened his eyes. "What?"

"Fresh coffee," the junior officer of the deck said. "And I think the captain's up."

George took the hot ceramic mug and sat back to inhale the fragrant steam. Then he realized the significance of what the JOOD had just told him. Balancing his mug, he slid down out of the unit-commander's chair on the port side of the pilothouse. If an admiral had still been aboard, that would have been *his* chair. George definitely didn't want to have the captain find him occupying the admiral's chair. He stood by the center pelorus with one arm hooked around it. He'd been so tired that he'd finally just had to sleep. Sitting in the captain's chair was an even bigger sin, so he'd opted for the port side. He remembered someone draping a coat over him as he fell asleep. Now he could barely make out the outlines of the flight deck below in the light of false dawn. "Where are we?" he asked.

One of the quartermasters told him the ship was 150 miles from the southernmost home islands of Japan. Well, that's better than fifty miles, he thought.

The officer of the deck joined him at the center pelorus with his own coffee in hand to bring him up to speed.

"We're headed southeast and we're making ten knots, courtesy of two boilers and two engines," he began. "The captain called out from his sea cabin and told us to break the tow, so we've just sent a flashing light message to *Pittsburgh* that we want to disengage."

"How many boilers we have on the line?" George asked. "Two?"

"Two now and a third one lit off and raising main steam. That'll give us fifteen knots."

George nodded. The sun hadn't yet risen. The air was clear but still cold. A sea breeze was blowing lazily over a slate-gray sea. "We have escorts?" he asked.

"Indeed, we do," the OOD replied. "*Enterprise* and *Wasp* are out ahead, about three or four miles. *Santa Fe* and four destroyers are out on defensive stations around us. Admiral Davison formed up a new task group of damaged ships, Task Group 58.1. We're all headed to Ulithi."

"What happened to *Wasp* and the Big E?" George asked.

"Kamikazes," the OOD said. "They're nowhere as bad off as we are, but we're guessing Admiral Spruance decided to get them away from all those airfields on Kyushu and Shikoku. *Hancock* has CAP up because there've been Jap snoopers out all night. They apparently know about Task Group Cripple."

George snorted. The American fleet had come to introduce the Japanese home islands to carrier warfare, he thought. Seemed like the Japs had been more than ready to introduce the Americans to two unsinkable island aircraft carriers named *Kyushu* and *Shikoku*. All that talk of invading Japan soon would need some rethinking if what had happened to *Franklin* was any indication.

He could finally see the other ships as daylight bloomed. *Pittsburgh* was in the process of dropping back to get closer to *Franklin*'s bow. There was a small crowd on her fantail preparing to heave in their towing hawser. Three destroyers cruised along in the light chop nearby, two on one side, one on the other, and probably a fourth astern. He couldn't see *Santa Fe*.

Normally there would have been several hundred men on the flight deck by now, swarming around planes and getting ready for a launch, but this morning there wasn't a single soul. Bloody coils of ship-to-ship lines still dangled into the catwalks over on the starboard side. George registered the sad silence down below while the reality of the catastrophe came flooding back. He was almost afraid to go out on the port bridgewing.

Then the coffee began to take hold. There was *everything* to be seen to. They needed to get a muster to see how many of the crew were still aboard. How much of the air group was still aboard? They needed food and fresh water. They needed to comb through the interior to see how many people were still trapped in the steel honeycomb of compartments below the hangar deck. Hundreds, he hoped. They had to continue the task of clearing the flight deck of debris, including human debris. He wondered how far Father Joe had gotten with his crew of sweepers. There were undoubtedly some small, stubborn fires still lurking along the hangar deck and on the deck immediately below.

Communications, he thought. First and foremost, I need to re-establish internal communications. Rebuild fire-parties. Establish a new sick bay. Get a galley back in operation. Wait a minute, I already—

"XO." The captain was on the bridge.

"Sir," George said. He wanted to say, good morning, sir, but it didn't seem appropriate. It was most definitely *not* going to be a very good morning.

"First thing, XO, after we ditch the tow: a muster. I want to know how many people are left aboard, and how many of those are effectives."

"Yessir," George said. "We need to get the sound-powered phone system back up so we can call around the entire ship. I think that's the fastest way to find out."

"Do what you have to do, XO," the captain said, dismissively. "But quickly, please. Got it?"

"Yessir," George replied automatically.

"Because I am determined to find out who stayed at his post and who deserted his post," the captain said.

What's *that* got to do with getting the ship to come alive again? George wondered, but then he saw the captain's clenched jaw and that baleful glare in his eyes. Great God, he thought. He's serious. He tried not to make eye contact with any of the bridge watch standers.

Once the tow was broken, *Pittsburgh* would speed off to the northwest to rejoin the remainder of Spruance's fleet, which was also withdrawing. As soon as *Franklin* could reliably make fifteen knots, they could gradually get out of range of the Jap suicide bombers. Ulithi Atoll was a thousand miles to the southeast. At fifteen knots it would take them almost three days to get there. He knew that the next twenty-four hours would be crucial—the Japs had long-range bombers and fighters who would pursue this seagoing ambulance train to the limits of their endurance.

Now, for a muster: he realized the telephones would take too long. He called down to the number one engine room and asked the chief engineer if he could reactivate the 1MC. Thirty minutes later, the cheng said it should be back up, except where wiring or speakers had been destroyed. George checked the control box at the back of the bridge. The red light was indeed shining. He told the bosun mate of the watch to pipe "all-hands" on his call over the 1MC. The shrill piping notes seemed unusually loud after being silent for so long. George pressed the all-circuits button and then addressed whomever was left alive in the ship.

"This is the XO speaking. The ship is back under her own power. We're heading for the Ulithi anchorage. We need to find out how many people are still on board because many of our crew had to go into the sea to stay alive. If you're trapped by wreckage, smoke, or fire, try hard to make noise. We're organizing search parties to find everyone still alive after what happened yesterday. The engineers are restoring power and water, but that's going to take a while because we don't have a full crew. We'll get a galley going as soon as we can to feed everybody. We're almost out of range of any more Jap attacks, and we have escorts if they do come. For the next twenty-four hours, we'll be combing the ship for survivors, wounded, or trapped personnel. We are *not* sinking. Anyone still alive even in the most damaged part of the ship *will* be rescued. But the first order of business is to reconstitute the crew, so if you can hear this, it's relatively safe to come out. As soon as we can organize rescue teams, we will search *every* compartment, so if you're hurt and can't help with your own rescue, or there's no air, we *will* find you. All department heads assemble on the bridge. That is all."

He hung up the microphone and looked over at the captain, who was nodding his approval. Then the moment was interrupted by gunfire, as all the destroyers around them opened fire on a two-plane formation of Bettys, the dreaded Jap torpedo bombers, that was coming in low from the starboard side. The captain erupted into a string of curses, jumped out of his chair, and ordered right standard rudder. To George's amazement, the forwardmost five-inch turret swung slowly, agonizingly slowly, out to starboard and began firing. Then the one above it did the same. Between the two of them the sky around the low-flying Bettys turned black with airbursts, until one and then the other were sent cartwheeling into the sea in clouds of flame, pursued all the way down by both *Franklin*'s and the destroyers' gunfire. George knew that the five-inch fire-control directors above the bridge had been damaged by the big radar antenna when it came down, so those gun crews had knocked those two bastards down in local control, meaning the pointer and the trainer had had to muscle their control yokes to get the guns on target. And with no power to the mounts, they had hand-cranked the hydraulic pumps in those turrets. He felt a sudden burst of pride. He looked over at the captain, who was now standing at the center pelorus. Even he was nodding his approval, a rare enough sight in itself.

"XO," a talker called.

George took a deep breath, but this one came with a ray of hope. "XO, aye?"

37

Gary was proud of his guys. They had two boilers going and a third one building pressure back aft. In Main Control, directly behind them, the chief engineer and his crew of admin yeomen had managed to roll both a turbo-generator and—after a few more hours of cleaning, draining oil sumps of any water, checking and rechecking valve lineups—first one and then two main engines. But right now, he had another problem: his boiler room's reserves of pure, uncontaminated feedwater were getting perilously low. They'd had to pump two feed bottoms' worth of water over the side because of contamination. They would have to get the ship's evaporators going soon or they'd run out of makeup feedwater, especially when they began filling other boilers.

The only good thing was that the list was just about gone. The chief engineer had been supervising the gradual filling of the counterflooding tanks over on the port side with seawater. Normally this would have been controlled from DC Central, where the DCA would be sending orders down to the main holes to line up special pumps and send water from the open sea over to the dozen or so voids to bring the ship back into trim. The extra water would also have the effect of improving the ship's stability by adding tons of weight right where it was needed—way down below. The inclinometer in Main Control was now reading three degrees to starboard, which made even the most basic tasks much easier to do than with a thirteen-degree list.

There were two seawater evaporators all the way forward in the chain of main spaces, in what was called "forward auxiliary." That meant they'd have to cross-connect auxiliary steam from number two fireroom, through the still-unexplored number one fireroom, and on into forward auxiliary. He'd already taken the up-and-over route through seared passageways to join the chief engineer in Main Control. He wasn't sure he could even *get* to forward auxiliary because of all the damage to the uptake plenums, and he was really in the dark about conditions in the number one fireroom. To make things even hairier, the cheng now wanted Gary to send all but two of his boilertenders to Main Control, because they needed more people to go aft into the next fireroom.

The lack of qualified engineering personnel was beginning to really squeeze. Gary had sent his pitifully small head count to the bridge after the XO's announcement. Main Control had more people, but only two, the chief engineer and the main propulsion assistant, were fully qualified main engineering snipes. In one sense, Gary's two boilers were stable; as long as things stayed that way, two guys could manage, especially since the ship wasn't maneuvering or ordering up a lot of big bells. But if anything went wrong, about the only thing two BTs could do would be to pull fires and call for help. He'd told the cheng that they also would not be able to get more boilers on the line until he got his full crew back. Cheng told him the captain was yelling for more steam. Gary had had to remind him that, without feedwater, they would shortly have neither.

"You're the boilers officer," Cheng had said. "*You* tell him that."

"You're the department head, *sir*, dealing with screaming captains is way above my miserable pay grade." Gary grinned as he hung up to the sounds of swearing.

The interior of the ship was like a ghost town as he headed forward toward number one fireroom, reminding him again of how many people were gone. There'd been 3,000 men aboard twenty-four hours ago, counting the air group. Surely there'd be pockets of survivors in the hundreds and hundreds of compartments throughout the ship. But then he had to remind himself that the stiff breeze blowing down the passageway meant that the two operating boilers were getting most of their air from *in*side the ship. They'd better find those pockets of survivors pretty quick because, inevitably, those big forced-draft blowers would come seeking air from compartments and not just passageways. The hot draft coming through the locked-back hatch for number two fireroom had almost taken his shirt off.

He knelt down to feel the scuttle on the main hatch to number one fireroom. Just warm. Good. He began to work the scuttle's operating wheel, carefully watching the dogs as they retracted until they were just on the edge of coming off their wedges. The breeze moving through the passageway made it difficult to hear any sounds coming from the hatch or the compartment down below. He got down on the deck and put his ear to the round edge of the scuttle. A tiny whistling sound got his attention. Pressure difference, but which way? He looked around the dim passageway and spotted a six-foot-long fire hose applicator, mounted on the bulkhead. It was basically a one-and-a-half-inch pipe that connected at one end to a fire-hose nozzle and had a spray nozzle on the other end, allowing a firefighter to stand back from the flames while he worked the fire.

He dismounted the applicator and wedged it against the base of the scuttle's operating wheel, and then turned the wheel the final few degrees before jumping back. The scuttle popped up forcefully, opening about an inch before the applicator stopped it. A jet of dense, hot black smoke came boiling out. It would have filled the vestibule instantly if not for the fact that the boilers in number two fireroom were drawing air from this passageway. Even so, Gary had to blink furiously to clear his eyes from the acidic vapors in the smoke and deliberately exhale to get the sudden sting out of his throat. He tentatively pushed down on the scuttle but the pressure from below was too strong. Finally, he just stood on it, which allowed him to spin the operating handle to close it back up and discard the applicator.

Now what? he thought. I've *got* to get into One Firehouse. Then he had an idea. He went in to search for the escape trunk hatch for number one fireroom, which should be behind him. When he found it, he opened it as quickly as he could. That same river of black smoke rose up out of the escape trunk like a chemical cobra, but then began streaming aft toward number two's main hatch. Sorry, guys, he thought. The sudden appearance of that black incubus would scare the hell out of those two guys. Then he trotted back to number one's hatch, spun the wheel to fully open the hatch, and now air in the passageway was being pulled *down* into number one fireroom. All he had to do now was to wait for the airstream to pull all that crap out of the fireroom and replace it with breathable air. He knew the two guys left in number two fireroom would be aghast and were probably cowering in the bilges, but the blowers would quickly suck it into the combustion airstream. He didn't think the boilers would care about some more damned smoke.

He waited for five minutes until he thought all the pressure down below had been equalized and then cautiously went down the ladder into number one fireroom. Once again, a few battle lanterns were still glowing valiantly in the gloom as he landed on the upper-level deck gratings. None of the machinery appeared to have suffered any damage; the space had been abandoned when the power dropped and heavy smoke completely filled the space.

Before leaving number two fireroom, directly behind this space, Gary had opened the cross-connect valve for the 150-psi steam piping that led forward into number one fireroom. All he had to do now was go to the forward bulkhead of this space, open the 150-psi valve that would feed forward auxiliary, and then go forward, find the hatch down into forward auxiliary, hope that it, too, wasn't full of smoke, and get an evap or two on the line.

He suddenly felt the ship begin to turn, and then, to his amazement, he thought he heard gunfire. Five-inch gunfire. He knew that the cheng had managed to get one SSTG on the line, so that might be *Franklin's* guns firing. The gunfire stopped and the ship began turning again with an awkward motion because of the starboard list. He tried not to think of all those burnt cable ends, dangling from blackened and deformed bulkheads, which now might have 440 volts in them, just waiting for some poor unsuspecting soul to brush up against them. He banished the thought and went to complete the valve lineup. He still had to get forward and light off a couple of evaporators. And then figure out how to get the distilled water they produced back into the firerooms for the boilers. Eventually, all eight of them, he realized.

Jeez.

Climbing down into forward auxiliary was a repeat of accessing the number one fireroom, but in reverse. Instead of encountering a pressurized space, he found he couldn't budge the hatch. Either it had deformed and was jammed, or the space was under negative pressure. He undid all the dogs on the hatch and then bent down to listen. Sure enough, he could hear the hiss of air bleeding from the passageway *down* into the auxiliary machinery room, but at this rate it might take an hour for the pressures to equalize. They might never equalize if number three fireroom brought a third boiler fully on the line, thus sucking even more air out of the ship's interior. Then he had an idea. He took the dogging wrench and tried it on the scuttle wheel's hub nut. It fit. He had to use the base of a nearby CO_2 fire extinguisher to start the nut turning. Once it came off, he lifted the wheel off the scuttle mechanism. He then picked up the fire extinguisher and pounded on the threaded operating spindle until he punched it through the gearing under the scuttle.

Immediately he felt his ears pop as a jet of air from the vestibule was sucked down into the space below, making a screeching sound. Two minutes later, once the noise stopped, he was able to pop the hatch as if nothing had happened. Two overhead lights were broken but still on when he got down to the space; he quickly wished that they weren't because down in the bilges, beneath the deck gratings, he saw eight bodies, partially submerged in oily water, and all clustered around a small air vent as if they'd been taking turns getting air. It was pretty clear that they'd all eventually suffocated. He sat down on a short stool and began to weep.

38

It was fully dark by the time J.R. made it up to the bridge and reported in to the XO. The sea around them was as dark as only the sea can be when there's a low overcast and a new moon. J.R. was pretty sure that there were destroyers all around them, but they, like the carrier, were running at total darken-ship and were thus invisible. The XO finished checking the quartermaster's latest fix and then called the captain in his sea cabin to report their progress toward Ulithi. When he was done, he turned to J.R.

"I'm hearing you did some great stuff today, Lieutenant," he said. "Like rescue three hundred people from the messdecks and bring them out of the fires."

J.R. didn't know what to say. He could still see that thrashing school of terrified sailors trying to get over to the *Santa Fe* as massive steel hulls closed in on them. "I'm glad I could help them, XO," was all he could manage. "It's a real mess belowdecks."

"So I'm finding out," the exec said. "I had a ringside seat for what happened on the flight deck, but below . . . ?"

J.R. could only shake his head, recalling the sights—and the smells—from the interior, especially his brief glimpses of the hangar deck, where he watched sailors being turned into blackened, liquid pools by the red-hot steel.

"You okay, son?" the XO asked in a quieter voice. "You need to lie down somewhere?"

"I'm hungry," J.R. said, surprising himself. "Wait. I'm sorry. But I can't—I can't—"

"I know, I know," the XO said. "Everybody who's still here, who's still alive, can't get over what's happened. But—our duty right now is to save this ship, and I think we can, thanks to guys like you. And Lieutenant Peck, who got us some steam. But now we need warm bodies to—"

The exec stopped when he saw the almost stunned look in J.R.'s eyes. *Warm bodies?*

"Oh, God*dammit,*" he blurted. "That's not what I—You know that's not . . ."

Then J.R. closed his eyes and started laughing hysterically; the exec followed. The two of them stood there in one corner of the pilothouse, face-to-face, their eyes closed, each trying to control himself, which did not help one bit. The rest of the bridge crew could only stare at them.

Finally, the both of them caught their breath, sniffed, and wiped their eyes on their sleeves. The XO took a second deep breath and tried again. "What we need most is to recover anyone who might be trapped belowdecks, especially main-hole snipes. I need someone who's been down there to organize a deck-by-deck, compartment-by-compartment search for anyone who survived the fires and the smoke but had to hole up to stay alive. We need people, or we'll never make it to Ulithi."

J.R. by then had regained his composure; he'd never experienced hysteria before and it had scared him. But, of all the words . . .

"Yessir," he said. "I can do that. But I'll need some helpers. Runners, guys who can get to the nearest sound-powered phone and get more helpers to lead guys out to clean air."

"Okay," the exec said. "For right now, take the bridge lookouts and the signalmen. Nobody's gonna start sending flashing light as long as there are torpedo bombers out there."

"Still?" J.R. asked.

"The formation's got three picket destroyers trailing us twenty miles back. They shot down a pair of Bettys just after sundown who'd been hugging the deck to avoid radars. This is still Injun Country, even if we are nearly two hundred miles from Japan."

At that instant everyone on the bridge froze in place. A ponderous metallic groan was rising from the ship's hull, almost but not quite subliminal. It sounded like every large piece of steel throughout the ship was straining and complaining, making a terrifying sound that was felt as much as it was heard. And then, to everyone's absolute horror, *Franklin* began to capsize to port, slowly at first but then gathering speed, sending everything not tied down on the bridge to the deck in a clatter of coffee mugs, binoculars, and navigation instruments, along with every man who hadn't been holding on to something when it started. The ship fell over to port to an almost twenty-degree list, before hanging there while everyone stopped breathing, and then slowly, degree by degree, righting herself to about a ten-degree starboard list, by which time some of the younger sailors were screaming in fright. And then she did it *again,* a gut-grabbing roll to port, where this time she hung there at twenty degrees port, worse than when it had all started, before coming back, but not very much.

J.R. knew immediately what had happened: the engineers had miscalculated what it would take to reduce the list and pumped too much water to the port side, and by so doing they had actually induced a worse situation in the other direction. The XO was yelling at the hysterical sailors to pipe down, so he, too, must know what had just happened. But knowing what was going on and keeping calm about it were two different things, and he had to admit he'd been scared out of his wits for a moment when the ship began that roll. Three phone-talkers were trying to get the XO's attention as stations throughout the ship wanted to know if she was going to capsize.

The captain was standing in the navigation passageway in that big white bathrobe, giving the XO a what-the-hell look, so he knew what was going on, too. J.R. could not imagine the fright belowdecks. They were going to need laundry services much sooner than anyone had anticipated.

An hour later, J.R. mustered his team of two bridge lookouts from the deck division and two signalmen from OI division. They gathered in the chartroom right behind the bridge, which was under red-light conditions to keep their eyes acclimated to the darkness outside. He'd had to talk them down from their stations for twenty minutes after the ship's sudden stability scare. If *Franklin* was going to roll over, they wanted no part of going back inside. It had taken some stern words from the exec himself to budge them.

"Okay, guys," he began. "I'm Lieutenant McCauley from the engineering department. You and I have been detailed by the XO to go through the interior of the ship and find shipmates. Preferably live ones."

The two deck seamen were not amused. They'd been on watch topside ever since the attack began and had seen the entire disaster unfold right in front of their now-terrified eyes. One of them began shaking his head. "Inside?" he said. "We can't go inside. *Nobody* can go inside. It's all fire."

"It certainly was," J.R. said. "And I'm sure there still is stuff smoldering inside. But all the big stuff—the bombs, the planes, the rockets—has been burned away. Here's what I know: We can't go out on the flight deck because of all the holes. We can't go onto the gallery deck because it was crushed. We can't go into the hangar deck because it's still too hot to even walk on it. The entire second deck had to be abandoned because of all the fire and smoke coming down from the hangar deck. So, our first objective is to get down to the *third* deck. I personally don't think there are *any* survivors above the third deck.

"Now, I've been down there. It's scary. There's very little light because the explosions broke most of the light bulbs. The battle lantern batteries have mostly given out. The main-hole snipes are getting boilers back on the line when they're not scaring the shit out of the whole crew. But, the air-supply plenums for the firerooms, which run from the top of the stack all the way down to the main spaces, were torn all to hell. Both ways—air supply for the boiler fires, and the smokestacks for the smoke being produced by the boiler fires. The deeper we go inside, the more you're going to encounter wind in the passageways, which is going to feel really strange. But it's not fire—it's just air being sucked in by the boilers because the stack is busted."

He paused for a moment to let all this soak in. The four young faces staring back at him were clearly still scared to death. He knew that, even after he'd explained what had caused that sudden roll, they were still highly attuned to every move the ship was making. Truth be told, so was he. He knew the counterflooding water should have *helped* the ship's tender center-of-buoyancy problem, but it was hard for stability theory to overcome what that first flop had felt like.

"Normally we wouldn't conduct a search like this without a fully manned repair party," he continued. "Everybody dressed out in face masks, OBAs, big-ass fireproof gauntlets, and everybody carrying forced entry tools, fire hose applicators, fresh battle lanterns, extra OBA cannisters, and other stuff like that. We don't have *any* of that.

"The only way we're gonna be able to do this is *because* of the plenum chamber damage. The passageways would normally be still full of poisonous gases after a fire like we went through. But—the boilers are actually sucking all that shit out of the interior. Here's the problem with that. The ship's supply ventilation is hard-down. That means that any survivors huddled up in compartments belowdecks are gonna start losing their breathing air, because there's nothing coming in from the vent system. Sooner or later, the boilers are gonna take it all. So that means I'm gonna get us down to the third deck, and then we're gonna go fast, checking each compartment for the length of the ship, centerline, port, and starboard sides. We're gonna bang on hatches, open 'em if we can, and let people know it's safe to come out. Understood?"

There were reluctant nods all around.

"Whenever we find a compartment with survivors, one of you will have to lead them back the way we came until they make it to clean air on their own, so pay attention to how we get down there to the third deck. And then we'll need you to come back to escort the next group. Ready?"

They stared at him. J.R. began a slow shake of his head from side to side until one of them grinned. "Right," he admitted. "Neither am I. But right now, we gotta get people out before they all suffocate. We've had enough of that, right? So—follow me."

39

Gary was hungry. Everyone was hungry. They'd been condensing steam from a low-pressure drain to get a little drinking water as the space warmed up. The water had been flat, tasting slightly of metal, but wonderful. Then one of the boots had unearthed the fireroom's coffee supply, and the smell of fresh coffee had made the whole boiler room crew, all three of them, feel much better. Now he was alone in forward auxiliary, babysitting two evaporators and the piteous remains of the space's crew down there in the bilges while the evaps grumbled reluctantly to life. He needed some more of that coffee.

He'd felt that sudden motion of the ship's hull, but it really hadn't registered that much because he was so far down in the ship. He simply thought it was weather or possibly a turn.

The sound-powered phone squealed.

"Cheng here, Gary," the chief engineer said. "A search party just found a berthing compartment where there were about forty main-hole snipes holed up because of the passageway fires and warped hatches. They're not in the best shape but they're coming down to the main spaces to help us get more of the plant up. I need *you* to try to get into number one fireroom and see what we've got. If it's tenable, I'll send a light-off team. Be careful going in there—the last report we got from One Firehouse was that there was *no* oxygen left in that space."

"There is now," Gary said. "I had to go in there to get the aux steam cross-connected to these evaps. Had to vent the whole space, but now it should be tenable."

"Shit," Forrest said. "Of course you did. I must be getting tired."

"Getting?" Gary said. "I'm way ahead of you on that score, Boss."

"Right," the cheng said. "Okay, if that's the case, go back in and get me a kettle going. Where's the evap water heading?"

"I've lined it up to the feed bottoms for Two Firehouse," Gary said.

"Perfect," the cheng said. "See what you can do to get number one back up. I'll send help as soon as they get down here and I see what we've got. They were apparently damn near dead for lack of air."

"Aye, aye, sir," Gary said. He knew all about that lack-of-air business.

He checked the two evaporators one more time, rechecking the valve alignments to make sure the hot distilled water was going to where it was needed first and not being drained off to the ship's potable water tanks. Then he went back up the ladder to the main engineering passageway, which still reeked of burnt gasoline, seared steel, scorched asbestos insulation, and that inescapable scent of burned flesh.

He started down the ladder into number one. He thought he could feel passageway air still coming down the ladder. He wondered where it was all going. There were now no lights on in the fireroom, but as he entered, he saw a glow coming from the space's main switchboard across from the entry hatch on the upper level. The air was warm and smelled of the usual steam, bilge water, and fuel oil. And a new smell that brought him up short: gasoline. He cautiously climbed the ladder from the lower level and followed his flashlight beam over to the switchboard panel.

Two lights indicated that there was power available to the board. He examined the breakers and saw that the evacuating crew had opened every electrical machine's breaker before getting out. Now the question was: if I close a breaker and there's a spark, will this whole space flash into flame? He sniffed the air again. The steam smell came from wet asbestos piping insulation. Lube oil dripped out of some of the larger machines' bearings. Fuel oil, well—that might be a problem, too, because volatized fuel oil could ignite if the newly refreshed supply of oxygen in the space provided a good enough air–oil mixture, but it wasn't likely. It was that stink of gasoline that bothered him.

He swung his flashlight around the space. He was standing on the upper-level deck gratings. The tops of the two boilers were on either side, along with asbestos-clad turbines for auxiliary equipment and the top of the deareating feed tank. Below lay the boiler-fronts and even more pumps and motors.

He hadn't smelled avgas the first time he'd been down here. So, what had changed? You do this wrong, he thought, and the last thing you're gonna see is a big flash of light.

He sniffed the air again. Maybe he was wrong. Maybe it wasn't avgas, but just fuel oil. Oh, goody, he thought. Then there *is* vaporized fuel oil down here.

That's better than vaporized avgas, he thought, but, still. His weary brain tried to decide what to do. His initial efforts at getting all the bad stuff out of the space had worked, or so he thought. So where were these new indications of bad stuff coming from? He stood there, his exhausted brain trying to figure out what to do. The last thing the ship needed was for a fireroom to explode. They'd all be dead meat if that happened. He tried to think his way out of this box but simply couldn't do it. He was too tired and even a little bit weak from lack of food.

Screw it, he thought. That big rush of air the first time he'd come down here *had* to have taken the lion's share of any explosive vapors right out of the space. He scanned the switchboard again by the light of his flashlight. The evacuating electrician had done his job—every service and equipment breaker had been opened. You already know that. The two lights at the top of the board said there was 440 volts available to the switchboard from the ship's service grid. He realized he was thinking in circles here. He took a deep breath and then closed the board's main breaker.

Nothing happened. "That's a good thing," he announced out loud to the empty, stinking space.

Then he scanned the board and found the breaker for main-space lighting. He closed that and the entire fireroom was filled with light. He looked for the ventilation breaker. Here he had to be careful; after his experiences with the ruptured uptake and intake plenums, he needed to be damn sure that supply ventilation wouldn't immediately take a suction on, say, the hangar deck, and bring seriously dangerous gases back into the space. He found the exhaust blower system and activated that, instead. To his relief, the light in the space began to change, from milky white to the familiar white-yellow glow. He found a sound-powered phone panel and called Main Control.

"One Firehouse seems to be intact," he reported. "I've got lights and exhaust vents going. I can see standing water just below the lower-level deck grates. I smell some gasoline, but nothing happened when I closed the breakers. Don't know if the boilers have water in the fireboxes. I need some BTs."

"Here they come, then," the cheng replied. "Good work. Before you light off, make sure the main access hatch is wide open. I still have no idea of where we're getting combustion air from."

Me neither, Gary thought. He waited for a crew to arrive before going down to the lower level of the fireroom. Toxic gases, such as carbon monoxide, tended to lurk in low spaces. He realized he'd been sweating, but now there was a relatively cooling breeze moving through the space. He sat down on the watertender's stool in front of the boiler-water gauge. Oily water sloshed back and forth beneath his boots.

Take five, he thought. Let's make sure this place is all according to Hoyle. Sure, his exhausted brain replied. Just close your eyes for a minute. Maybe two.

40

George finished tallying the muster reports from throughout the ship. They painted a bleak picture. *Franklin* had joined Task Group 58.1 with a total of 3,600 men on board, including the approximately 900 men of the embarked air group. His first attempt at a muster had yielded a total of 516 total personnel left on board, including officers, chiefs, and enlisted. Of that number, he estimated that he had slightly over 300 men who could be considered "effectives" to run a 36,000-ton aircraft carrier. That also meant that he had 200-some men in various states of disrepair to attend to. The ship's sick bay had been destroyed in the original bomb attack. The ship's senior doctor had bravely stayed behind to tend to the wounded and had succumbed to suffocation along with his patients. There were no doctors on board. The air group's doctor had tried his best to remain on board during the height of the cataclysm on the flight deck, but he'd been ordered to evacuate to the *Santa Fe* by the air group's commander, who'd probably been convinced that *Franklin* was about to go down. Hard to fault the man for that, George thought.

The sun was finally up and the skies were painted with the usual spectacular colors of an Asian sunrise. There were light whitecaps lining up in endless ranks as *Franklin* steamed southeast toward the sanctuary of

Ulithi Atoll. The relative wind was from ahead, for which everyone on the bridge was grateful, given the mounds of human debris out on the flight deck. George got on the 1MC again and called for two working parties to muster on the flight deck forward to begin removing wreckage. The supply officer and some of his storekeepers had taken shelter in a storeroom on the third deck to wait out the fires. He called the bridge after the XO's announcement and said he could probably activate one galley. The total loss of power plus the ambient heat belowdecks had spoiled most of the ship's provisions, but since the freezer compartments were kept at zero degrees, there was enough frozen meat to feed the crew steak, of all things, for the next three days. Some of the ship's cooks had taken refuge in the cold stores section; they would be the ones bringing a galley on line. George told him that he'd only be feeding approximately 500 instead of 3,600, at least until they got some of the crew back on board. Which reminded him of the captain's feeling about everyone who'd "jumped" ship, many literally. With a heavy heart, he took the personnel tallies over to the captain.

"That's *it*?" the captain asked, in total disbelief. "We can't sustain this ship with only three hundred men. And another two hundred wounded? Ask our destroyers if any of them have doctors on board, or even a chief hospital corpsman."

"I did that earlier, Captain," George replied. "There are two doctors among the escorts. Each ship will also send a corpsman. I'm going to designate what's left of the forward messdecks as a temporary sick bay. I'll get them alongside as soon as we can rig a highline."

"Yes, good," the captain said. Then a familiar look came over his face. "Now—I believe there are *hundreds* of our people on *Santa Fe*. I want to get them back. Correction: I want *some* of them back."

George was at a loss for words. The captain saw his discomfort.

"Look," he said. "All those guys back on the fantail, running from the fires and the bombs going off? *They* had no choice. Same for anyone who was in the hangar deck. But far too many able-bodied men crawled over to the *Santa Fe* from the forward flight deck when they saw their chance. *Those* are the people I'm going to hold accountable. They're Goddamned deserters."

George shook his head. "Captain," he argued. "Deserters are men who jump ship in port, ditch their uniforms and their ID cards, and go back home to Mommy or to their girlfriends. All that flying ordnance coming up the flight deck was killing people who had nowhere else to go. Besides—if you declare all those people who fled the fires as deserters, we're not going to have a crew."

"Just as well," the captain growled. "As far as I'm concerned, they deserted their posts. Even if those ships somehow *do* get them back to Ulithi, or even Pearl, I won't take them back. And I'm going to court-martial the lot of them."

George was shocked. He still had no idea of how many dead crewmen were still out there on the flight deck waiting for their surviving shipmates to sweep their remains over the side with fire hoses. And then he'd have to send men into the hangar bays and the gallery deck to do the same thing. He'd been given reports that the gallery deck had been smashed up against the bottom of the flight deck. There'd been at least two squadrons' worth of pilots waiting for the call to man their planes in the ready rooms on the gallery deck. And now the captain was saying he'd sail on to Pearl with just the remnants of the crew rather than take back the hundreds of men who'd had to jump into the sea to avoid being burned or blasted to death?

He tried to think of something more to say but just drew a blank. He was also peripherally aware of the reaction of the people on the bridge, who had to have overheard what the captain had just said. He thought about reminding the captain about his saying that all personnel who were not necessary to save the ship could get away from the calamity that was the USS *Franklin*. He was saved by a phone-talker.

"XO?"

"Yes?"

"Father Joe wants to know what to do about all the body parts."

His heart fell. "Tell the chaplain to get on the phone."

"This is Father O'Callahan here, XO."

"Thank you for taking this on, Father. I'm at my wit's end. I think we've lost almost a thousand men."

"We all are, XO," O'Callahan said. "Once an hour I'd think it would have been better if she'd rolled over and ended everyone's misery. But she didn't, so now we have to tend to the dead."

"You're right," George said. "Okay, see if you can organize a working party with fire hoses into a single line abreast, the width of the flight deck. Walk as many firefighting hose streams down the deck as you can and sweep *everything* that will move into the catwalks. Then split the teams to hose out the catwalks. We'll do a memorial ceremony at the appropriate time, but right now, all those bodies are a health hazard. And once the flight deck has been cleaned, they'll have to go down to the hangar deck and do the same thing. Who's in charge of the working parties?"

"I guess that would be me, XO," Father Joe said. "No one else showed up."

George sighed. "Right, Father. Thank you very much. I wish there were another way."

"Their souls won't care, XO. You're correct—this mess out here *is* a health hazard. Are there any gunner's mates left?"

"I'm sure there are a few, Father."

"Send a few up here with shotguns from the armory, assuming it survived."

"Shotguns?"

"For the seagulls, XO. The word is out among the gulls that there's food here."

Jee-zus, George thought. I did *not* need to hear that.

41

Two days later, J.R. found himself on the ship's open forecastle, the scene of the towing operation. It was cooler in the shade of the overhanging flight deck than up on deck. He was a bit spellbound by the sight of 700 warships at anchor as *Franklin* entered the Ulithi Atoll anchorage area, a thousand miles distant from the bloodstained waters off Japan. He normally would have climbed up to vultures' row to get a look at the Navy's largest floating base west of Pearl, but the intense sun and the sight of all the damage on the flight deck had driven him down to the relative sanctuary of the forecastle and the anchor team. Besides, vultures' row was gone.

The anchorage itself was huge—ten miles by fifteen miles—and surrounded by several small, bright green islands. *Franklin* had been there before, most recently after the October kamikaze strike. That time the anchorage had been full of carriers, battleships, cruisers, and destroyers; now it was stuffed with the amphibious shipping getting ready for the impending invasion of Okinawa: troop transports, LSTs, LCIs, the rocket ships, and naval gunfire support destroyers. There were even four of the rocket artillery ships which had been refloated from the wreckage of Pearl

Harbor and put back in service as shore bombardment platforms. J.R. hadn't been aware that there were this many ships in the entire Navy.

There was a stiff evening breeze blowing across the atoll, so three fleet tugs were making up to *Franklin*'s scorched sides to hold her in position while she dropped and then backed down to set her port anchor. A large hospital ship, painted all white, was anchored nearby. There were several small boats circling her stern, apparently waiting to head for the *Franklin* with a fresh complement of doctors and hospital corpsmen.

He was entirely ready for this day to end, and still so shocked by what he had seen that he'd entirely lost his appetite by the time the wardroom reopened to feed the officers. The chief engineer had given him a truly horrible assignment the day before. J.R. was the fire marshal, and, as such, he'd been tasked to make a physical survey of all the fire-damaged parts of the ship. He was given two young Log Room yeomen to accompany him and record his findings, and, with a heavy heart, he'd set off down the flight deck to begin his dismal survey. The efforts of the previous days had swept most of the gore away from both the flight deck and the cat-walks. Teams were now working on wrangling equipment that could lift the 1,000-pound engine carcasses in the hangar and get them overboard. The engines were the only visible remains of the fully armed and fueled aircraft that had been assembled aft in readiness for the morning launch. He and his two white-faced yeomen documented the holes in the flight deck, both from the Jap bomb that had penetrated as well as all the bombs that went off in the fire. They measured the holes left by the elevator assemblies that had been blown out of their wells when the big gasoline vapor explosion hit.

The wooden flight deck was a charred memory aft of the island. The fires had been so intense that the underlying steel structure had sagged down into the remains of the gallery deck, and, in some areas, all the way down to the hangar bays, creating blackened stalactites that in too many cases were still festooned with human remains. His two yeomen had abandoned him once they entered the forwardmost spaces of the gallery deck, that maze of air group offices, ready rooms, berthing compartments, and flight deck support equipment. They'd dropped their clipboards and run for the side to be sick as a man could be. The gallery deck had been subjected to what damage control experts called deck heave. In simplest terms, that meant that the deck of a compartment was hammered up into the ceiling of that compartment, with ghastly results for any occupants. He realized that every now fully compressed compartment would have to be cleaned and disinfected, which was going to be really tough as many of them were only two feet high instead of eight and stuffed with shattered furniture, crumpled bulkheads, tangles of wiring and ventilation ducts, and, worst of all, the reeking remains of a few hundred personnel.

He decided to give up after going halfway back into the wreckage. Between the bombs going off on the flight deck and the prolonged blast furnace that followed down on the hangar deck, there'd be no cleansing operation needed. When he arrived at a patch of sunlight shining through a sixty-foot-square hole in the flight deck, he reversed course and got the hell out of there. He took a breather up on the flight deck, sitting and then lying down on the scorched wooden deck, on his back, staring into the late afternoon sky and wondering if he was man enough to do this job. Two guys had come over and asked if he was okay.

"I've been down on the gallery deck," he'd replied. "And, no, I am not okay. But I'm not hurt, if that's what you're asking."

"I know you," one of them said. "You're the officer who got us out of the messdecks. I've been dying to thank you. A lot of us have."

"*That* was easy," J.R. had said. "This shit—cleaning up, seeing what happened to people, counting—is Goddamned awful."

It was evident that neither of them knew how to respond to that, so they both had saluted half-heartedly and trotted off. J.R. lay back on the deck and began to weep. He discovered that evening was approaching when he woke up. He tried to sit up but his eyes just wouldn't stay open. The next time he woke up it was morning and the 1MC was calling for the special sea and anchor detail for entering port. He'd spent the night sleeping in one of the ten-foot-long dimples in the flight deck. He wondered where his two scribes were.

42

George felt a sense of relief when the words "anchored, shift colors" blared out over the ship's general announcing system. Ordinarily this would have been followed by the colors being hauled down from the mast, the Union Jack being raised forward on the jackstaff, and the national ensign aft on the flagstaff. Both the jackstaff and the flagstaff were missing, so George decided to just leave the stars and stripes up on the remaining stump of the ship's mast.

The ship was eerily quiet in the late afternoon. There were no aircraft on deck or in the hangars. The normal hum of ventilation fans was missing, as only a few ventilation systems were intact. The deck division was busy rigging an accommodation ladder from one of the sponsons on the starboard side to receive the small flotilla of hospital ship boats headed their way. That fifteen-knot breeze was a Godsend. It was warmer down here in the Carolines, and that breeze blowing down the flight deck and especially through the hangar deck doors would make it possible for the recovery crews to keep working into the night without being constantly sick.

The captain had taken his evening meal in his sea cabin behind the bridge; George had been brought a hot steak sandwich and some fresh coffee while he remained on the bridge. Apparently, a great quantity of steak had thawed out during the fires, so everybody was eating steak in some form or other. He finally had a better idea of the human cost of their disaster off Shikoku, and he was dreading the moment when he presented it to the captain. Even more disturbing was the captain's continuing grim determination to accuse all the able-bodied men who'd left the ship of desertion in time of war. The whole idea was unprecedented, if not outright preposterous. Anyone who'd seen what was happening to the *Franklin* that morning would be appalled at the notion that men trying to escape a holocaust on *that* scale would ever be charged with anything at all. He knew that at some point he would have to testify as to what the captain had said at the height of the explosions, and yet that order had been so vague that it was no wonder that men had leaped at the chance to get over to the *Santa Fe* or one of the destroyers. Many of them had probably believed that the order *had* been given to abandon ship.

He stared down at his piece of paper, the results of an hour-long confab with the department heads. Two more musters revealed that there were actually 704 men presently aboard; of those, only 285 were able to fully resume their duties. The remaining 419 were classified as wounded, some superficially, some with work-inhibiting injuries but who could remain aboard, and some who needed hospital attention. That left almost 3,000 men who needed to be accounted for.

There was no way of telling how many had been killed outright or who had died jumping overboard. Reports from *Santa Fe* and the escorting destroyers were incomplete, but it looked like there were about 1,000 men who'd been recovered, which meant that between 800 and 900, maybe more, men had been killed. These numbers didn't include the air group's casualties. A lot of the air group had been on its way to Japan that morning. Those who hadn't launched yet had been either sitting in their planes, warming up, or waiting down on the gallery deck. He knew that none of them could have survived what happened.

He knew the numbers didn't quite square but the reports from other ships were fragmentary. Still these numbers were beyond devastating. Eventually he would have to prepare a preliminary report for the Navy Department, but until the ship got back to Pearl *and* all the recovered men got back to Pearl, they wouldn't be able to construct an accurate picture. If ever, he thought. He'd toured the hangar deck earlier with the captain. The blackened shards of human remains hanging everywhere brought home how hard this was going to be. The captain, once he'd seen what had happened to the gallery deck, had declined to go any further, especially since going up one of the ladders to the gallery deck level meant walking on crusty remains still coating the ladders throughout the hangar. Even worse was how the working parties were dealing with all the bits and pieces. They were working in two-man teams. One was carrying a steel GI can, the other a shovel. While one held the can, the other would scrape the deck and deposit whatever he'd scraped up into the can. When the can got too heavy, they'd carry it out to a sponson and jettison its contents overboard.

He and the captain walked over to the port side where one of the missing hangar bay doors was allowing in fresh air. The captain's face was ashen. George thought his own face was probably ashen, too. "Great God," the captain said softly. George could only nod. And God had certainly been missing in action that day, he thought, bitterly.

He wanted to curse the Japanese, but the American fleet had stuck its haughty face into homeland airspace, a mere sixty miles away. Of *course* they'd attacked. The captain turned around and stared into the blackened cavern that was the hangar deck. "This must have been what it was like for them at Midway," he said softly, echoing something George had thought earlier. Only unlike the Japanese, they had managed to bring *Franklin* back. To what end George could only speculate, but it was something.

"The difference is," he said, "they worship the idea of death in battle. Everyone has to die sometime, but the man who can die in battle garners supreme honor. We revere life; they revere death in service to their emperor."

"Yeah, the divine Hirohito," the captain sighed. "Divine spider is more like it."

George decided to broach the topic of repatriating the *Franklin* personnel from the *Santa Fe* while he had the captain to himself. "Sir, I think we need to get *all* our people back from *Santa Fe*," he began. "They don't have room for that many additional people, and they're not going back to Pearl when we do."

The captain shook his head. "Nope," he said, setting his jaw. "I want all *Franklin* officers and chiefs who are now on *Santa Fe* and the destroyers, and who are fit for service, to return to the ship, where I propose to serve them with a letter outlining what I propose to charge them with. The rest of the crew can go to a transport here in Ulithi to await a trip to Pearl. There's always some ship or other going back to Pearl. They're Goddamned deserters, and I won't have them back aboard fomenting insubordination. Did you see my 'personal-for' message this morning?"

George nodded. The captain had sent a message out directly to the commanding officer of the *Santa Fe,* and a copy to all the ships who'd reported they had *Franklin* crewmen aboard, informing him that the *Franklin* crewmen aboard *Santa Fe* who hadn't come aboard as casualties were to be treated as prisoners awaiting court-martial for desertion in time of war. He'd then said that *Franklin*'s damaged berthing and messing spaces could not accommodate the return of any *other* crewmen who'd been forced to go over the side.

George cringed when he'd read it and then wondered if any of the other commanding officers, including the skipper of *Santa Fe,* would comply. And what about the *Franklin*'s air group personnel who'd gone over to the cruiser? Were they facing charges? He made a mental note to write down that order the captain had issued when he'd said that men not necessary to the survival of the ship could escape. Maybe get it into the ship's log as a late entry. That was going to be the only thing that could save all those people on *Santa Fe.* What a mess.

"I'm serious about this, XO," the captain continued. "By the latest count, there were some seven hundred or so men who stayed aboard to save the ship. I want to honor them as much as I want to punish those who ran."

"Some of those seven hundred didn't get a choice, sir," George protested. "They were trapped in various spaces by fire or damaged compartments."

"And yet some of those who *were* trapped and then rescued by ship's officers stayed to fight the fires. I get your point, XO. No broad brush. I will want to know the circumstances surrounding *each* man who survived the attack to be determined officially, from those who chose to remain and fight to those who took advantage of confusion, fires, explosions—to abandon their duty stations and run away."

George nodded. He'd kind of been expecting this. "That'll take some time, Captain," he said. "And manpower."

"Well, XO," the captain said with a faint sneer. "When we leave here, we face something like a twelve-*thousand*-mile journey back to the Brooklyn Naval Shipyard. That's halfway around the world. At fifteen knots, that gives you thirty-three days. I suggest you form a committee of department heads and get on with it. It's not like we'll have anything else to do, is it."

Except keep cleaning, George thought. While trying not to weep.

43

J.R. found himself almost alone in the one operational wardroom. It was midmorning, and the ship had been at sea since yesterday, on her way to Pearl at last, some 4,000 miles to the east. God, he thought, but the Pacific Ocean was big. There were four destroyers in company to provide an escort. Word was that they'd stop briefly for fuel and reprovisioning, and then proceed on to the Panama Canal. It would take them twelve days just to make the transit to Pearl. Apparently, a fleet oiler had been dispatched to meet *Franklin* mid-ocean to refuel her and, more importantly, the destroyers, since the captain was unwilling to have them come alongside to take fuel from the badly damaged carrier. There'd been a series of engineering problems down in the main plant, with boilers being shut down due to contaminated fuel or feedwater. The ship's electrical grid was hanging together by various scorched threads. The captain didn't want to add a collision to *Franklin's* already mountainous woes.

J.R. was also heartsick. He was halfway through his assignment to detail all the damage, and that had turned into a horrendous task, both in its scope and because of what he and his two reluctant scribes had encountered. He'd asked the cheng if his intrepid two ensigns could replace the two kids from the Log Room. A day later the cheng informed him that

Ensign Sweet had been killed in the first hour of the attack when a wave of burning aviation fuel had overflowed from the flight deck down into his gunnery station in the catwalks. Ensign Sauer was officially reported as missing but, like most of those declared missing, was probably gone.

By now J.R. had become like most of the men in the cleanup brigades, who plodded inch by inch through the various decks and compartments, GI cans and flat-bottomed shovels in hand, their eyes empty and minds far away as they did their gruesome duty. J.R. had seen one team hump their GI can over to the side, take their hats off, say a prayer, and then, and only then, jettison the contents of the can into the sea, where the horde of gulls who'd followed the ship out of Ulithi squalled their approval. Father Joe had done a couple of memorial services, but they'd been miserable affairs. The captain had attended the first one, but apparently didn't like all those accusing stares from the assembled crew. He didn't make the second one.

Up until now, J.R. had been a determined warrior, quietly eager to finish this war with the utter defeat and destruction of these barbarians from Japan, whatever it took. To his sorrow, he now knew that the devastation inflicted on this great ship and its crew was one of the things that it was going to take. He could remember actually looking forward to the final assaults against the so-called home islands, where the US Navy, humiliated at Pearl, would finally exact a terrible retribution. Now, well, now he wanted to just go home and lick his wounds, which he understood were spiritual more than physical. If this is what it was like to "win" a war, he wanted no more of it.

44

Ten days later, George found himself cooling his heels in the outer office of the Pacific Fleet Legal Officer, Captain Leland Gentry, JAG Corps, USN.

He had actually walked from the Ten-Ten dock, where *Franklin* was moored, across the base and up the hill to the Makalapa Crater, where the Pacific Fleet Headquarters sprawled in the benign Hawaiian sunlight across ten guarded and fenced acres. He'd never been to the fleet HQ but he'd heard stories about it being a twenty-four-hour, seven-days-a-week beehive of activity, with literally a few thousand people on the staff. Today things seemed somewhat quieter, probably because Nimitz and his operational and logistics staff were now on Guam, preparing for the final showdown with Japan.

Franklin had come into Pearl yesterday morning to a chorus of ship's whistles greeting the battered carrier as she sailed up the narrow channel. There'd been cheering crowds on the breakwater and even bigger crowds in the shipyard, as all work stopped so everyone would have a chance to see the storied Big Ben in all her wrecked glory. This time the captain had graciously allowed the shipyard pilot to bring her alongside. True to character, he'd immediately complained about the great swaths of rust along her sides once he got onto the pier. Once the fires had removed the paint, the ship's steel quickly rusted over in the unforgiving environment of the open sea. Incongruously, there were some areas along the island where the fires had been so hot that they had changed the chemical composition of the actual metal; these shone like accusing mirrors in the bright Hawaiian sunlight.

There'd been several senior officers on the pier who wanted to see for themselves what they'd only heard about. Once people got close enough to realize the full extent of the damage, the cheering turned to somber stares and quiet exclamations of disbelief. The captain had spent almost the entire day walking various visiting firemen through the burned-out core of the ship.

"Captain Gentry will see you now, Commander," a pretty WAVE said, indicating that he should go through the wooden batwing doors into the inner sanctum. Just about every major office had wooden saloon doors because the headquarters, mainly a collection of so-called tempo-buildings, was not air-conditioned. The vintage wooden doors provided the only cross-ventilation.

Gentry was an honest-to-God long, tall drink of water, George thought as he approached the desk. The captain appeared to be in his late fifties, with a friendly smile and a strong handshake. He'd been a federal appeals court judge when the war broke out, and he definitely looked the part. He invited George to take a seat in one of the armchairs in front of his desk.

"Welcome back, Commander," he began. "If half the stories about *Franklin* are true, you guys have truly been through Hell, itself."

George nodded. He tried to think of something clever to say in response but could only shake his head, but then the enormity of the ship's travail seemed to finally hit him. He felt his chest tighten, his face getting red, and tears starting in his eyes.

"Take a moment, Commander," Gentry said. As George recovered himself, another WAVE slipped into the office with a glass of iced tea, summoned apparently by a button under Gentry's desk. She gave George a sympathetic look and quickly scooted out of the office. George gratefully sipped some tea as he tried to compose himself. He'd thought he was past such moments.

"You're probably wondering why the Fleet JAG has asked you to come up the hill," Gentry said.

George shook his head. He knew full well why. "The court-martials," he said.

Gentry nodded. "Yes," he said. "The court-martials. Apparently, your CO wants to court-martial about a thousand of his crew for desertion in the face of the enemy."

George nodded. There was a lot he wanted to tell the JAG captain, but he wasn't sure what to do. Stay loyal to the captain because he was the XO, or plead for consideration for all those men under the gun. He knew that word had gotten out in the fleet that the captain of the *Franklin,* the purported hero who'd saved his ship in the face of the worst fires and explosions ever experienced by a carrier that survived, now wanted to court-martial a third of his crew. Captain Gentry waited patiently. Finally, George made his decision.

"We lost about eight hundred killed and another four to five hundred grievously injured," he said. "Twelve to thirteen *hundred* casualties. One-*third* of the ship's complement. Another thousand or so had to jump over the sides because of what was happening on the flight deck and in the hangar bays. We spent the transit from Ulithi to Pearl sending men with shovels into the hangar and gallery decks to scrape up what was left of the dead, which in many cases was not much more than grease spots, which they dumped into trash cans so we could get the remains over the side. We had to send other teams with steam-lances to disinfect the entire hangar deck."

He paused to let that horror sink in. He deliberately did not look directly at the captain.

"It took us weeks to figure out what our losses actually were, who had survived, who had not, and who was missing, and therein lies a problem. Some men were blown over the side in the initial explosions as one-thousand-pound bombs went off in their faces, while they, against all expectations, were trying to extract their pilots from their planes. *Inside the* fire. Some took shelter down on the fantail and eventually jumped into the sea because a waterfall of burning avgas came over the round-down on top of them.

"There were rockets that went off inside the flight deck fire and then flew up the flight deck at chest level, killing many who had sought safety all the way forward. There were firefighting crews who *advanced* on the fires and explosions who were cut down when burning bombs rolled out of the flames and exploded in their faces. Each time that happened more men came in, picked up the hoses, and headed aft. In many cases they found the brass hose nozzles melted. The officer who took over the organization of the firefighting efforts on the flight deck was the Catholic chaplain, Father O'Callahan. The regular damage control organization had all been obliterated in the initial explosions. The ship's air boss, mini boss, and their entire crew died when a Tiny Tim rocket came through PriFly. Two squadrons of the air group had been killed when the gallery deck was compressed against the underside of the flight deck by—"

"Okay," Gentry interrupted. "I get it."

"I doubt it," George snapped, and then regretted it. The captain was way ahead of him.

"Okay, okay, now tell me about this 704 Club business."

George blinked. How in the hell did the PacFleet legal officer know about that, he wondered?

"When we took the final 'who's left' muster after leaving Ulithi, there were seven hundred and four men who we could pretty safely say had remained on board. The captain declared that because these men had loyally stayed at their posts, they would become charter members of the Big Ben 704 Club. Everyone else who had been able-bodied but who had left the ship without orders was a deserter."

"'Without orders?'" Gentry said. "Tell me about those orders."

"Well, I think this might be a way out of this mess. Two cruisers were sent to our assistance. The *Pittsburgh* and the *Santa Fe*. *Pittsburgh* was ordered to take us in tow. We were only fifty, sixty miles from Japan, and the Japs were determined to finish us off. *Santa Fe* was sent to assist us in firefighting and getting our wounded off if possible. When the explosions aft on the flight deck began to kill men on the front end of the flight deck, I recommended to the captain that we had to get those men—several hundred by this time—off the flight deck. Belowdecks was fire, everywhere. He then said: I am *not* abandoning ship. But—any man who is not vital to saving the ship has my permission to get over to the *Santa Fe*."

"Where was the *Santa Fe*?" Gentry asked.

"She'd made two approaches alongside to assist with firefighting efforts on the hangar deck. Initially the explosions were so big she had to back away. She came in again and this time her skipper purposefully smashed his ship's port bow up against our starboard side and held it there. This allowed men to escape from our forward flight deck down onto the cruiser. Many others jumped into the water between the two ships and were rescued by *Santa Fe* crewmen, many of whom jumped into the water between the two ships to haul men to safety. *Pittsburgh* was maneuvering in front of us to make the tow. Jap torpedo bombers attacked us then, but the two cruisers shot them down. One of their torpedoes actually hit us, but it was a dud. Otherwise we wouldn't be here."

"So—you're telling me the captain gave an order that anyone not necessary to saving the ship could try to escape."

"Yes, sir."

Captain Gentry thought about that for a moment.

"Who," he asked, "would make the determination that Seaman X was vital to saving the ship, while Seaman Y was not?"

"The individual seamen," George said.

"Of course," Gentry said. "And I know on which side of that decision *I* would have come down, when the world was ending five hundred feet behind me."

"Yes, sir," George said. "And you should also know this: I estimate that a third of the guys who went into the water between a listing, burning aircraft carrier and a light cruiser drowned. Too many jumped with their helmets *and* their life jackets on. They broke their necks when they hit the water. It's a big jump."

"Jesus," Gentry said softly.

"Look, Captain Gentry," George said, his voice rising, despite his attempt at self-control. He unknowingly squeezed his eyes shut. "All these so-called deserters had no choice. The ship's own AA guns were cooking off in the catwalks and sending twenty-millimeter, forty-millimeter, and even fifty-caliber machine-gun bullets everywhere. I saw a Tiny Tim rocket go up the flight deck, chest-high, go over and then explode right in front of the *Pittsburgh*. The men back on the fantail were being bombarded by the explosions on the flight deck *and* from the hangar bay— that's the same level as the fantail. They *had* to go. The guys on the edges of the flight deck *had* to go when burning gasoline started coming over the deck edges. Gunners in the catwalks *had* to go, for the same reason. The hundreds of men way up on the forward flight deck were taking shelter behind dead bodies. They *had* to go. This wasn't desertion. This was all about and *only* about staying alive. This—"

George suddenly found himself being held from behind by Captain Gentry's hands on his shoulders. Gentry was telling him to slow down, breathe, it's okay, you're entirely right, we're gonna take care of this. Please, just breathe. Two WAVES from the outer office had come running in when they heard George's hysterical shouting. They surrounded him and joined Gentry's efforts to calm him down. After a minute, George slumped into his chair and wept uncontrollably. "Wrong," he cried. "This is just so fucking *wrong*."

Captain Gentry pulled up a chair in front of George's chair and waited for him to quiet down. Then he had a request. "I want to see the ship," he said.

"The whole world wants to see the ship," George replied. "Every admiral here in Pearl has been down there."

"I want to see it when there aren't any admirals on board. Or the skipper, if that can be managed. I want *you* to show me everything, no matter how bad it is. That way I'll have some perspective on how to deal with this mass court-martialing business. Agreed?"

George had to think for a moment. He was embarrassed at losing control like that, but, on the other hand, it sounded like the JAG was willing to consider the circumstances rather than just granting a blanket order to proceed with disciplinary proceedings.

"The captain has taken a room at the senior officer BOQ," George said. "Can you come aboard at 2000? All the bystanders ought to be gone by then."

"Perfect," Captain Gentry said. "I'll come in an unmarked staff car. You meet me on the pier at 2000. No quarterdeck bells, no announcements."

"Yessir," George said.

45

George waited as inconspicuously as he could at the foot of officers' brow stand at five minutes to eight. He almost felt angry at
the gorgeous Hawaiian sunset painting the sea across the entire western
horizon. The contrast between all that natural beauty and the scarred,
blackened, rusted, stinking mass of steel rising into the sky above him
seemed unfair. There was only a single conveyor belt working the starboard sponsons as food, medical supplies, and mail were still being loaded
aboard. With only 704 personnel embarked, the usual volume of stores
and provisions was much reduced, but it was still taking a long time. One
of the problems was finding a place to put it all, especially food stores.

Precisely at eight o'clock he saw a black sedan coming down the pier,
threading its way through the idle dock cranes. The cranes' working
lights were on now, shining directly down onto the pier, and the sedan
appeared to be playing hide-and-seek as it disappeared from one cone
of light only to appear in the next one. George had briefed the officer of the deck not to formally recognize the officer he was bringing
aboard, even if he was a four-stripe captain.

"But, XO, sir: the captain left strict instructions—*every*body coming
aboard has to be logged in."

"Not this guy, Lieutenant. That's a direct order. Any trouble? I've got your back. But no record of this visit."

"Aye, aye, sir," the lieutenant replied. He was not an aviator. George didn't recognize him and thought maybe he'd come aboard at Ulithi with the other replacements.

"Put it in the Pass Down the Line Log that the Quarterdeck Log is to be brought to *me* at 0730 in the morning," George ordered. "I will take it to the captain personally."

"Yessir, will do." The lieutenant nodded, looking much relieved. "Will we be getting under way tomorrow?"

"I don't think so," George said. "The Brooklyn Navy Yard has asked that the yard here be given a day to tote up the damage. That way they can prepare for our arrival. Or they may send a team to go with us to the Canal. Resume the watch, please."

He then had gone down the three-tiered brow stand to wait for Captain Gentry. Five minutes later they stepped through the starboard side hangar door and into the hangar itself. The shipyard had brought portable spotlight stands into the hangar, so there was no hiding the scope of the damage.

"Jesus H. *Christ*," Gentry whispered as he beheld the devastation.

The hangar was still warmer than the air outside. The smell of char was everywhere, laced with a much more unpleasant smell. George knew it wasn't likely, but the convoluted steel all around them seemed to him to be still radiating heat. There was only some emergency lighting available in the side rooms along the vast hangar, so George had brought flashlights to ensure they didn't walk into any holes. Two officers approached out of the gloom. George introduced Lieutenant Gary Peck and Lieutenant J.R. McCauley.

"These two officers played a very big part in saving the ship," George said. "I'll let them conduct the tour and I'll chime in whenever I think it necessary."

J.R. offered a small plastic jar of Vicks VapoRub to Captain Gentry. When George saw that Gentry didn't know what to do with it, he explained what it was for.

Gentry blinked, and then said: "Oh." He applied a dab of the pungent paste in front of each nostril. George applied some, as did the other two officers. He nodded at J.R., who began the tour of the damage.

It took two hours, total, after which George accompanied the captain back down to the pier. There he waited while the thoroughly shocked JAG stood next to the sedan, visibly trying to compose himself. Gentry's driver had discreetly backed away when he caught a whiff of his passenger's khaki uniform.

At George's orders, the two lieutenants had shown the JAG everything, including portions of the gallery deck which had not yet been entered because the tangle of burned steel simply could not be penetrated without industrial-scale metal-cutting assistance. The eerie silence inside the hangar and even on the wrecked second deck only added to the enormity of the disaster. No one who'd been aboard a carrier had ever experienced such a silence as was now draped over the gutted *Franklin* like an invisible shroud. Even the omnipresent dockside seagulls were staying away, as if sensing that this was no place for the living.

Gentry finally opened the right-side passenger door. "Words fail me," he said, as he stood unsteadily next to the opened door. "I will take care of this, Commander. I promise you. If I have to go to Nimitz himself, I will take care of this." He paused and took a breath. "I'm sorry," he said, finally. "I can't think of anything else to say just now. Other than that. I *will* take care of this."

"Thank you, Captain," George said. "For what it's worth, none of us who lived through this can speak about it, either."

Gentry grimaced, nodded, got into the car, and said something to the driver. George saw hands rolling down all the windows as the car drove away. He watched as the red taillights dimmed and then vanished at the head of the pier. He turned to his two trusty lieutenants. "Not a word about this," he told them.

"Who was that, XO?"

"I can't tell you, but I will, when the time is right. Anybody asks, just another rubbernecker from the big staff up on the hill."

"He seemed pretty damned disturbed," J.R. observed.

"You and I," George said, "lived through it. We might be a little bit jaded. That's a natural reaction—see what happened to our ship and our shipmates, your brain is more than ready to just wipe all that clean. Don't feel bad about that—your brain is simply trying to protect you. Remember that you're both commissioned officers. You see a white-hat wandering around who looks like he's just seen a ghost? Talk to him. Help him out. We're all gonna have to do that from now on out."

"Even the captain?" Gary asked quietly.

George prepared to rebuke him but then relented. "The captain is the sole owner of *every*thing that happens to his ship, Lieutenant. I'm guessing his brain just might have a lot to process just now."

"Yes, sir," Gary said. "Sorry, sir."

George studied the young officer's face in the light from the overhead cranes. Saw lines in that face that didn't belong there at this young age. "But, what?" he asked.

"Nothing, sir. Sorry, I—"

"Spit it out, Lieutenant," George said, boring in.

Gary just bit his lip and then shook his head, but J.R. did speak up. "The captain is talking about court-martialing everybody who wasn't present for duty when you took that first muster," he said. "Talking about men deserting. Abandoning their duty stations. Taking the coward's way out and jumping down to the *Santa Fe*. Well, lemme say something about that, XO. I didn't see the captain down on the messdecks when the air was giving out. I didn't see the captain when all those guys had to jump from the flight deck down and the catwalks and what happened when the avgas river came. I never saw the captain when guys up on the flight deck were running aft *into* the fire, trying to lay down water so they could get pilots out of their burning planes. I saw an awful lot of Father O'Callahan, but I *never* once saw the captain."

J.R. took a deep breath, as if suddenly realizing what he'd been saying. But then he set his jaw and went on.

"Now we've got this 704 Club bullshit. Seven hundred and four guys answered 'here' when you took that first, second, and third muster. The captain's saying that if you didn't answer 'here' after three calls, you were a deserter. I'm hearing there are eight hundred dead. He gonna call them deserters, too, XO?"

"Okay," George said. "Enough."

"No, it *isn't* enough, XO," J.R. said. "This is Goddamned wrong. Everyone knows *you* were the one really in command during this disaster, while the captain went to his sea cabin and cried like a fucking baby."

George closed his eyes and tried to keep calm. It was hard. The lieutenant was indulging in the height of insubordination. The problem was that the lieutenant was entirely right. He raised his hand. "There are things in motion to correct that situation," he said. "But if you persist in sticking your noses into this mess before those efforts can bear fruit, you will fuck it up for everybody. Is that clear enough? I am more than aware of the injustice. But neither of you guys draw enough water to make it better. *I* do. End of discussion, Goddammit."

J.R. and Gary were visibly taken aback by George's sudden and uncharacteristic vehemence. Then they both saluted, turned on their heels, and went trotting up the brow steps in quick time.

George instantly felt bad. But, if the captain got wind that his exec had been to see the PacFleet Jag, he would have a pretty good excuse to proceed with his absurd claim of desertion in the face of the enemy. See? Even my XO is disloyal.

Franklin loomed alongside, all 36,000 tons of her, scorched, battered, wrecked, and ruined, silently encased in a shroud of human loss and pain. The very air in the nearby harbor stank of the death and destruction she'd been through. He thought he could almost hear the ship asking: why did you not let me die? I could have taken the 800 with me to the bottom of the sea, *miles* down, where there *is* eternal comfort, "strong to save." Cold comfort to be sure, but down there in the icy dark are no more vain and vengeful captains, worried about their precious careers. Only the deep and the darkness and ultimate eternal rest—an appropriate, even a well-deserved fate for both a ship of war and all the men who'd died trying to save her and their shipmates.

He shouldn't have yelled at his two best lieutenants. Apparently, he was more exhausted than he knew. He could just see the front entrance of the BOQ from the pier. He started walking, keeping his mind as empty as he could. At the head of the pier he decided he needed to just sit down for a few minutes. *Franklin's* towering bow overhung the pier, with her huge anchor lowered to the waterline. He plopped down on a bollard and leaned back against one of the ship's mooring lines. Halfway up the heavy lines were rat-guards, circular rounds of steel that reflected the shimmering lights from the yard cranes. Some gulls were fighting over scraps in a nearby dumpster. The flash and scratch of a welding torch punctuated the night as the shipyard worked on the hull of a heavy cruiser moored at the next pier. A 500-man personnel barge had been positioned on the other side of the pier so the *Franklin's* crew could have somewhere to go to get hot showers, food, and clean bunks.

He was worried about telling the OOD not to log Gentry's visit. On the one hand, the captain's orders were the captain's orders. On the other, the fate of several hundred *Franklin* men hung in the balance if the captain pressed ahead with this crazy court-martial business. He knew, as the captain might just not appreciate, that the bulk of the crewmen who'd scrambled down the catwalks to safety were high-school kids, eighteen or nineteen years old. They'd watched the towering cataclysm back aft loose a murderous barrage of ordnance down the length of the flight deck and smack into their huddled ranks while they hugged the wooden flight deck. Of *course* they'd bailed out.

"Commander?" a voice called. George opened his eyes. There were two shore-patrol men standing next to the bollard. "You okay, sir?"

"No, I'm not, gentlemen," George said. "I am officially sick at heart."

"You been drinkin' maybe, Commander?" the older of the SPs asked politely.

"Nope," George said. "I'm the *Franklin's* XO. It's been a bitch of a day. I just needed to take a load off for a moment. I've got eight hundred ghosts on my shoulders."

The two petty officers took a step back. This wasn't the kind of language they'd expected, but then the older of the two understood. "Sir?" he said. "We've got a jeep. Can we take you to the BOQ? I think you need to get some serious sleep. This ain't no place to grab a nap, Commander."

George simply stared out into the night, ten thousand miles away.

"Please, Commander? Just come with us and we'll get you all squared away."

George came back to the present. "Okay, gents," he said. "Okay. You're right. Lead the way."

One of them held the right front door open for him and he hopped in. The other one drove while his helper perched on the back bumper, holding on to his white hat. The older petty officer escorted him into the BOQ lobby, where he explained to the front desk who George was. A chief petty officer took one look at George and said there was room available in the senior officers' wing. He offered to show George the way. Five minutes later George was stretched out on a nice bed, his shoes where he'd kicked them off onto the deck, thinking about putting in a wake-up call. The captain would be back aboard promptly at 0730; it wouldn't do for the exec to still be ashore when Himself arrived.

Put in a wake-up call, a voice reminded him.

Just a minute, he thought. I'll get right on that.

46

S o," the captain said when George finally arrived back on board at two in the afternoon of the next day. He found the captain on the bridge, in his chair, reading messages. The captain looked up and snorted. "The Late Sleeper returns. Tie one on, possibly, XO?"

"I wish I had," George said. "No, I went to the BOQ, lay down for just a minute, and just didn't wake up until 1300."

The captain nodded, sympathetically, for a change. "Well, you didn't miss much," he said. "More gawking brass—the shipyard commander, NavBase commander, Supply Center commander. Apparently, there was some combat cameraman footage—in color, no less—that got back here before we did. Now everybody wants a tour, although I will say nobody seemed to want a *second* tour."

"When can we leave?" George asked, fixing himself a cup of coffee from the chart table. Both his and the captain's inport cabins remained untenable after the interior fires, so the captain had been camping out in his sea cabin and George had taken over the navigator's office.

"Day after tomorrow," the captain said. "The shipyard has sent a clutch of surveyors on board to prepare the Brooklyn Navy Yard for what's coming. According to the shipyard commander, the Navy is going to repair

Franklin and put her back in service, just to poke a finger in the Japs' eye, I suspect. Where are you with drawing up the charges and specs for all those yellowbellies?"

"The ship's office is wrecked," George said. "I've been concentrating on getting an accurate tally of who stayed, who left, who was forced to jump, and who died or just disappeared. That's taking longer than I anticipated."

The captain gave him a suspicious look. "Well, lemme help you along," he said. "Focus on all those men who were waiting for us when we pulled back into Pearl, especially the men coming off the *Santa Fe.* Yes, she did come back with the group after all. Our escorting tin cans picked up mostly men trying to escape what was going on back aft, so they really had no choice. Focus on the *Santa Fe* lists. That'll flush the bad actors out."

"And the charge is desertion in the face of the enemy?"

"Goddamned right," the captain said. "Officers, chiefs, especially, but white-hats as well."

"I'm hearing that all those men you refused to take back aboard are already on their way to new-construction assignments," George said. "Rumor is there's a new carrier coming down the ways every other month."

The captain shrugged. "If a precommissioning CO is willing to accept a man under suspicion of desertion, then let him. At some point, the JAGs will show up and ask for Seaman so-and-so. It may end up being a slow process, but those prosecutors will show up, eventually. And I will *not* let this matter rest, got it?"

"Yessir," George said. "I'll get back on it. I've got the chief engineer honcho-ing the refurbishment of enough berthing and messing spaces for the transit crew."

"You mean the Seven Oh Four?"

"I guess I do, Captain."

"You're one of us, XO. *You* never even thought about going over to the *Santa Fe. You* never suggested that I abandon ship, even if the admiral did. So, *you* are, by God, one of us. The rest of them be damned."

"Aye, aye, sir."

"And don't oversleep again," the captain said. "Talk about setting a bad example. I want a briefing from department heads on readiness for sea by noon tomorrow."

The sound of four bells came over the 1MC, followed by the announcement of yet another command title.

"More tourists," the captain grumbled. "I will say, they're all pretty complimentary. I'll take care of them. You get us ready for the trip back to the Brooklyn Yards."

"Aye, aye, sir," George said, again, with as neutral an expression as he could muster.

"Attaboy," the captain said. "Now: where are my Marines, Goddammit? *Orderlies!*"

47

Gary and J.R. were hanging out up on the open-air forecastle, where the deck paint had been freshly restored to cover up what the anchor chain had done to the normally spotless deck during the tow. The forecastle was, strangely enough, a favorite hangout for main-hole snipes after hours. Fresh air, the shade of the flight deck overhang, rarely any officers, and room to stretch out and enjoy a cigarette.

Gary was a bit bleary-eyed, having been up most of the night flushing the carrier's feedwater system in preparation for the long voyage back to New York City and the Brooklyn Navy Yard. They'd kept one boiler on the line to maintain what the snipes called the Hotel Load, while subsequently dumping the other seven boilers and refilling them with certified feedwater from trucks on the pier. They'd done the same thing with the feed bottoms, the tanks which held all the reserve feedwater. After all the explosions, fires, and electrical transients, the quality of the ship's feedwater had been increasingly questionable. The ship had apparently used up just about all of the base's feedwater supplies.

J.R. was still smarting from the exec's behavior the night before. He'd told the cheng what had happened, but the chief snipe had been less than sympathetic.

"Look," he'd said. "You know and I know the XO doesn't support this court-martial stuff. But—he's second-in-command, not first. He's duty bound to uphold the captain's policies or go look for another job. If I know our XO, he's most likely working back channel to undo that bullshit. So, mind your Ps and Qs and trust in the XO's judgment."

"Good advice," Gary had observed when J.R. went and bitched to him. "When the elephants begin to dance, mousies like us get the hell out of the way. Damn, but I need a drink."

"Wanna hit the O'Club tonight?" J.R. asked. "I think it's within walking distance."

"Can't," Gary said. "We're under way tomorrow morning. Gotta light off three boilers tonight and have 'em on the line by morning. Besides, if I hit the bottle now, they'll never find me."

J.R. grinned. Everything seemed so anticlimactic after the horror of the attack and its aftermath. Surreal, that's the word I'm looking for, he thought. We're all pretending we're ops-normal, and yet almost a thousand guys died and another thousand have been dispersed into the fleet of new construction. The ship's a ghost town; hundreds of feet of empty, scorched passageways, no planes, no aviators, no air group. The flight deck had been roped off to prevent people from falling through to the hangar deck. The main engineering spaces were manned, but everything between the main holes and the flight deck was damned near empty. The captain was up on the bridge at the front of the island, giving orders and criticizing everybody; the snipes were down below making steam and keeping their heads down. In between, the few enlisted people he was encountering were sitting numbly at their workstations with 1,000-yard stares. The graceful palms and the gentle night breezes around the harbor seemed almost to taunt them.

The captain had announced that the remaining crew would spend the transit cleaning the ship. Most of the moveable wreckage had already gone overboard between Ulithi and Pearl; now they were going after the smaller bits. Unfortunately, that often involved prying open small storerooms or workshops down on the second deck and finding something horrible. The captain had also ordered Engineering to rig up steam-lances once they left Pearl to deal with the problem of vestigial human remains on the hangar and gallery decks.

And the XO? He was rumored to be up in his temporary cabin in the island, working up court-martial papers involving men who he was *pretty* sure were still alive—but not certain. Surreal. Yup. That was the word. He looked over at his buddy. Gary was leaning against a set of bitts, sound asleep. He still had ahold of his coffee mug, which was now dangling from his finger, dripping cold coffee on his badly wrinkled khaki trousers. The sound-powered phone station on the after bulkhead squeaked. J.R. got up and answered it.

"Mister Peck up there?" a voice asked. "Tell him we're ready to bring three-able in on main and auxiliary."

"Will do," J.R. said, with a tired sigh.

48

The following morning, George stepped out onto the pier-side bridgewing. There was a lot of last-minute activity down on the pier as some stragglers reported aboard and the last of the stores were being loaded. The weather was gorgeous, as always. George wondered if people who lived here ever got tired of the eternally perfect temperatures. He was a four-seasons man, and he thought being stationed out here would be pretty confining after a while. There were six Corsairs tied down in two ranks on the front end of the flight deck, catching a free ride back to a Stateside rework facility. It was strangely comforting to see aircraft again, even if every one of them was out of commission for one reason or another. Two of them didn't even have propellers. A team of shipyard personnel were sightseeing on the flight deck. They'd been put aboard to begin the tedious process of planning and estimating for Franklin's repairs.

He looked at his watch. They were supposed to get under way in one hour, but the captain was still ashore, having been summoned up to Makalapa for a last-minute call on Deputy CinCPacFleet, Vice Admiral Towers. Otherwise they were ready to go. The main plant had four boilers on the line and the harbor tugs were beginning to nose alongside to take up their stations. Once the captain returned, they'd single up all mooring lines. Ordinarily there'd be hundreds of sailors out on the flight deck or lining the catwalks. Up above them radar antennas would be turning and there'd be the clamor of aircraft-handling machinery coming up from the hangar bays. Not today, he thought; not ever again was probably more like it. He couldn't conceive of the Navy trying to put this ship back together, even if it was just to spite the Japs. She'd have to be rebuilt from the second deck on up. All of the messing and berthing and office spaces on the second deck would have to be rebuilt. The entire hangar deck, including parts of the armored deck, would have to be replaced. The gallery deck. The flight deck. The elevators, the arresting gear, PriFly, the five-inch guns, the secondary guns. How could that be worth the money? Surely it would be cheaper to just scrap her and build a brand-new one instead.

A quartermaster came out and asked him to come join the navigator for a final departure track briefing in the chart house. As he stepped back into the pilothouse, he heard the four bells on the 1MC announcing the captain's return. George told the OOD to set the special sea and anchor detail and make all preparations for getting under way.

Three hours later the ship had rounded Diamond Head and was now pointed fair for the Panama Canal. The captain had sat in his chair during the entire sea detail, leaving oversight of the sea detail to George. He was uncharacteristically quiet, as if preoccupied with something. Once the pilot had disembarked, things on the bridge quieted down and the ship settled into her 5,000-mile voyage across the Eastern Pacific. Three escorting destroyers were spread out in a wide fan ahead, although PacFleet Intel considered the submarine threat to be minimal. George walked over to the captain's chair.

"The ship is secured for sea and the regular underway watch has been set," he announced. "I've set Condition Three modified."

"Very well," the captain answered. "We're almost five thousand miles from Okinawa now and we'll be getting farther away each day. The Canal is what, ten thousand miles from Japan?"

"Yes, sir, about that. I just figured it would be good to keep the troops on a wartime watch rotation."

"Yes, indeed," the captain said. "Absolutely right. You're probably curious about that sudden come-around up at Makalapa."

"Me, curious?" George said. "Why, Heavens, no."

"Hah," the captain said. "He had two things to talk about. One, the Navy Department is going to fully repair *Franklin*. I asked him if he'd been apprised of the scale of the damage. He said yes but that there were some larger issues bearing on the problem. He said the war in Europe was just about over and that senior Nazis were reaching out to Eisenhower to talk about an armistice."

"A cease-fire?!" George exclaimed. "Not again. That's what got us Hitler."

"Not a chance," the captain said. "Ike told them his terms were unconditional surrender. But now there's a new wrinkle—the Soviets. They're advancing on Berlin by leaps and bounds and evidently intend to occupy as much of Germany as possible before the war ends. That's not necessarily in our best interests or those of our European allies. Anyway, the Navy isn't ready to demobilize just yet, especially with the Japs showing no signs of giving up. If the first days of the Okinawa invasion are any indication, we've got a hard slog ahead of us. Well, I guess not us. So—rebuild *Franklin*, and keep producing more carriers."

"And the second item?"

"Well, he directed me, and through me, you, to concentrate on lining up awards for those people who earned them. While everything is still fresh. We need to decide who's going to be recommended for what, and then get the write-ups done by the time we get to the Canal. We've been limited to fifteen knots, so we're looking at a two-week trip. I have my own ideas, and I'm sure you have yours. The surviving department heads know who the heroes were—hell, I'm hearing stories of cooks stopping little fires from becoming really big fires. You personally will need to interview each man recommended for a medal, and then get corroboration if possible. The awards board is a stickler for evidence."

"So I've been told," George said. "But there's an elephant in the room, Captain."

"Yes, of course," the captain said. "Put that business aside for now, but just for now. PacFleet wants priority to go to the awards. The folks back home *want* to hear about heroes. We have all the time in the world to deal with that other issue. Between you and me, I think the brass is worried about the Navy getting a black eye when we least need one, know what I mean?"

George struggled to control his face. "Yes, sir, that makes perfect sense. I'll get right on that. There were some amazing things done out there. It will be a pleasure to recognize each and every one of them."

"Don't be stingy," the captain said. "Go for the big medals where you can. The board will cut some back—they always do. But make *them* do it. And don't forget Father Joe."

"Who could forget Father Joe," George said. "Certainly none of those guys he bent over on the flight deck right in front of the end of the world behind him will ever forget Father Joe."

The captain nodded, then gave him a long, silent look. George read the acknowledgment in that look. There weren't going to be any court-martials and the captain was telling him that he knew that, too. That must have been a really interesting office call, George thought. He wondered if the captain knew about his own office call on the Fleet Jag. If he did, he wasn't letting on.

The captain blinked and looked away. He seemed to have nothing more to say. He settled back in his smoke-stained captain's chair and gazed out over the vast Pacific Ocean. George quietly left him to it. He grabbed some coffee and wandered out onto the starboard bridgewing. Nobody seemed to want to go out onto the port bridgewing anymore. The quartermaster called him to report the ship's position. George asked him how many miles away was the Brooklyn Navy Yard. That took the navigators a few minutes to compute, but then they came back and said 12,650 miles.

Not far enough, George thought. Not hardly far enough.

He stared down at the wake foaming along *Franklin*'s battered starboard side while deliberately not looking aft. He tried not to think about what lay ahead, but that was too hard. Once the ship went into the yards he'd be transferred, as would most of the crew. He tried to think of what he might want to do next. Command? It was possible. It would be a natural next step—from XO to CO, probably of new construction. He could just see it: four stripes, a brand-new ship, bands playing at the commissioning, a brand-new crew, all calling him "captain." But—having had a taste of command at the bloody and fiery opposite end of commissioning-day celebrations, he wondered. He'd seen a number of *Franklin*'s surviving crew walking around with thousand-yard stares. He suspected, no, hell, he *knew* he was one of them. The thought of taking command and then going back west to do it all over again appalled him.

He thought about Karen. Theirs was a typical wartime romance, with most of it conducted by lifesaving letters from halfway around the world. They'd grown close, but now what? He'd get thirty days' leave when they got to New York, and of course he'd go to Portsmouth. And then? He was very fond of her, but at the same time he knew that his picture of her was partially a figment of his own imagination. What would it be like to see her every day? Had she found somebody else? There were countless stories of women back home continuing to write wartime lovers mostly out of sympathy while getting on with their lives with someone else, and who could blame them? What would she think of this somber naval officer who'd aged fifty years since she'd last seen him?

He looked forward all the way to the eastern horizon, where a flat blue line merged with a gray-white, cloudless sky. He took a deep breath. One day at a time, he thought. You're still the XO. Enough with the navel-gazing; it's not like you have nothing to do. As if to reinforce that idea, a bridge messenger called to him from inside the pilothouse.

Turn to, he thought. Recommence ship's work. "XO, aye," he replied.

AUTHOR'S NOTE

When my father, Vice Admiral H. T. Deutermann, USN, retired from active duty in 1965, he sent me two large boxes via the cargo arm of the Greyhound bus company. In those days Greyhound offered the most cost-effective shipping service in the country. I had no idea when I picked them up what was inside. I had just come off my first sea tour in a destroyer and was living in Newport, Rhode Island, while attending Destroyer Department Head school.

The boxes contained two ship's navigational running lights, one with a red lens and one with a green lens. Red for port, green for starboard. They were big, much bigger than the running lights on my destroyer, and they'd obviously seen some wear and tear, with visible welds in their steel sides. Each had a single black, three-wire cable hanging from the bottom; inside, their glass bulbs, each about eight inches high, appeared to be intact. A plate on the bottom announced that the lights were powered by 440 volts, which seemed to me to be extreme for running lights.

At the time, my father was serving as the commander of the Eastern Sea Frontier, headquartered at 90 Church Street in Manhattan. He had two other "hats," as the expression went: head of the UN Military Staff Committee, an organ of the UN Security Council, and also commander of the US Atlantic Reserve Fleet. It was in this latter capacity that he received the running lights. A chief petty officer over in New Jersey, who'd served under my father some time past, called his office with sad news: Big Ben's going to razor blades; would the admiral like to have a souvenir? Dad said yes, which is how I eventually became the owner of the last physical vestige of USS *Franklin,* her emergency running lights. Dad included a note to me, which said simply: There's an incredible story behind these lights. Not so much the lights, but the ship, which had indeed been brought back to the Brooklyn Navy Yard in 1945, completely rebuilt, and then immediately transferred to the mothball (Reserve) fleet. She never went to sea again.

I kept them for the duration of my own naval career, and they eventually landed in my workshop at our farm in Georgia. Heavy, awkward to move around, and more substantially made than just about any Navy equipment I'd seen during my twenty-six years in the Navy, they gathered dust until one day I decided to see if they still worked. I, of course, didn't have 440 volts available in my workshop, so I decided to see if 120 volts would bring them to life. A neighbor watched me set this up and commented that I was certainly brave. Not very smart, mind you, but definitely brave.

Undeterred, I made the connection, and there, in my workshop, those lights shone dimly, red and green, after nearly half a century in the mothball fleet. The last vestige of a famous ship, which had suffered the most awful damage and loss of life during the entire Pacific war, exceeded only by the USS *Arizona,* flickered defiantly to life. By then, of course, I'd read the story. We instinctively took our hats off and just stood there for a moment, trying in our very small way to pay some respect.

I am indebted to the author and historian, Joseph A. Springer, who wrote a book called *Inferno,* the story of the *Franklin's* ordeal off the coasts of Japan in 1945. In a genius move, he tells the story of the ship's immolation through the eyes of men who went through it. The book is eminently readable, accurate, and most of all, heartbreaking.

I also used the official US Navy after-action damage report. Interestingly, the report begins with the words: "This will be a long report." Given the normally antiseptic tone of formal US Navy after-action and

damage reports, that line was quite telling. The findings are nothing short
of appalling. I've tried to faithfully depict the horror of what happened
without the reader needing to put the book down because it's too awful
to contemplate. But I think it's a story well worth telling. I also think
anyone who aspires to be a naval officer should know this story, if only
to absorb a realistic appreciation for what he or she might be getting
themselves into. An Army formation can move forward against an enemy,
encounter overwhelming strength, and, if necessary, retreat. It is the nature
of war at sea that when you do finally come to grips with the enemy, it's
a fight to the finish. The option of tactical retirement in naval warfare is
usually a bloody illusion.

The captain's attempt to court-martial a large percentage of his own
crew is a true, if embarrassing story. The captain was Captain Leslie Gehres, USN. He'd risen from enlisted ranks to command of an aircraft carrier, a first in the Navy's history. He looked and acted as I have described
him; in short, he was a first-class bully. The executive officer, Commander
Joe Taylor, USN, was the officer truly in command throughout the bulk
of the ordeal. My research encountered some serious murk when I tried
to find out who finally calibrated Captain Gehres and quashed the whole
sorry court-martial enterprise. Gehres was ultimately awarded the Navy
Cross for bringing *Franklin* home. He'd been nominated initially for the
Medal of Honor. As the story goes, it was Fleet Admiral Chester Nimitz
himself who said, no, make it the Navy Cross. It's the nation's second
highest military honor, so it was hardly a slap in the face. Still.

The 704-Club business caused no end of distress over the years, as
Springer makes clear. Once the war was over and the crew reunions began, there were always two: one led by Captain Gehres and the 704; the
other held by the bitter outcasts. Given that a big part of ship reunions has
to do with remembering shipmates, this distasteful and wholly unnecessary schism rankled members of both groups.

The characters portrayed by Gary Peck and J.R. McCauley are based
on real junior officers whose repeated acts of heroism resulted in a Medal
of Honor for one and a Navy Cross for the other. It is doubtful that
Franklin could have gotten away from Japanese waters without their
efforts. The Catholic chaplain, Father Joe O'Callahan, was also awarded

a Medal of Honor. He was first recommended for a Navy Cross for his continuing heroics on the flight deck in the first four hours of the fire, but was reluctant to accept the award, as he didn't think chaplains ought to receive military awards for valor. According to Springer, when President Truman got word of that, he bumped the award up to the MOH, which even O'Callahan couldn't decline. Those of you who are students of World War II in the Pacific will remember that amazing picture of a helmeted chaplain kneeling over a downed crewman on the flight deck, administering the last rites, with all those volcanic explosions going off only 300 feet away.

The intelligence estimates regarding how many military aircraft Japan still had were wildly off the mark, based more on wishful thinking than cold hard facts. The intelligence community assumed that, once Japan's carriers were no more, so were their aircraft. The problem was that the Japanese had thoroughly dispersed their warplane manufacturing infrastructure and never stopped making them. Since there were no operational carriers, they just warehoused them throughout the country against the day when the Americans invaded. The official estimates were that they had hundreds left. The truth was that they had *thousands* left.

Making pilots was a whole different problem, unless of course all the pilot had to do was take off on a one-way suicide mission. Following the Kyushu strikes and the subsequent withdrawal of the carriers back to Ulithi, the next two operations firmly and finally removed any Pollyanna notions that the end was going to be swift and soon. Those operations were the invasions of Okinawa and Iwo Jima. For the first time in the long, bloody slog of island-taking, the Navy lost more people killed and wounded than the Army and Marine divisions which landed on those two islands, mostly to kamikaze attacks. The high command was shocked, especially when they began to think about the consequences of invading Japan itself. By definition, an amphibious operation required a concentration of hundreds of ships off the target coast. I think the decision to employ the atomic bombs was driven in part by the realization that the kamikaze was unstoppable. It only took one plane to remove an entire carrier from the board.

In 2011 the Naval Supply School was moved from Athens, Georgia, to Newport, Rhode Island. Due to a lack of space in their new building, the school's World War II museum artifacts were gifted to the Navy's Historical Collection, and are now packed away somewhere in a large warehouse in Suitland, Maryland. I may try to get them back one day.

ACKNOWLEDGMENTS

I am in debt to the author Joseph A. Springer, whose remarkable book, *Inferno,* inspired me to create this novel. He had the genius idea to tell the *Franklin*'s story through the eyes of several air group pilots and aircrewmen, ship's officers, chiefs, and enlisted men, interspersed with a thoroughly researched narrative of what was happening that day off the coasts of Japan. I must also acknowledge the copious and user-friendly resources of the Naval History and Heritage Command in Washington, D.C. And finally, I want to thank my father, Vice Admiral H.T. Deutermann, USN, who first introduced me to USS *Franklin* and her incredible story.